THE GHOST
AND THE WITCHES' COVEN

Haunting Danielle

The Ghost of Marlow House
The Ghost Who Loved Diamonds
The Ghost Who Wasn't
The Ghost Who Wanted Revenge
The Ghost of Halloween Past
The Ghost Who Came for Christmas
The Ghost of Valentine Past
The Ghost from the Sea
The Ghost and the Mystery Writer
The Ghost and the Muse
The Ghost Who Stayed Home
The Ghost and the Leprechaun
The Ghost Who Lied
The Ghost and the Bride
The Ghost and Little Marie
The Ghost and the Doppelganger
The Ghost of Second Chances
The Ghost Who Dream Hopped
The Ghost of Christmas Secrets
The Ghost Who Was Say I Do
The Ghost and the Baby
The Ghost and the Halloween Haunt
The Ghost and the Christmas Spirit

The Ghost and the Silver Scream
The Ghost of a Memory
The Ghost and the Witches' Coven
The Ghost and the Mountain Man

HAUNTING DANIELLE - BOOK 26

THE GHOST
AND THE WITCHES' COVEN

USA TODAY BESTSELLING AUTHOR
BOBBI HOLMES

The Ghost and the Witches' Coven
(Haunting Danielle, Book 26)
A Novel
By Bobbi Holmes
Cover Design: Elizabeth Mackey

Copyright © 2020 Bobbi Holmes
Robeth Publishing, LLC
All Rights Reserved.
robeth.net

ROBETH
PUBLISHING, LLC

This novel is a work of fiction.
Any resemblance to places or actual persons,
living or dead, is entirely coincidental.

ISBN: 9798567791653

ONE

Scotland 1618

Calloused bare feet carried Blair Tolmach across the wet field, away from the lush woodland, with its abundance of oak, downy birch, wych elm, holly, hazel, and other treasures of nature her mother, Gavenia, taught her to respect. Many of which provided valuable ingredients for Gavenia's magical potions.

Having completed her morning chores, the young girl raced home. The hem of her long tattered wool skirt flapped along her ankles, yet she managed to avoid tripping. Overhead, the Scottish mist grayed the afternoon sky. To her right she glimpsed the sheep of her neighbors', lazily grazing. Yet her focus remained on the humble cottage in the distance she shared with her mother. Careful not to drop the basket she carried and risk spilling the herbs she had spent the morning collecting in the woodland, Blair clutched tightly to the basket's handle.

Those in the village called women like her mother a wise woman, a cunning woman, or a witch. Gavenia called herself midwife and healer. While respected among her neighbors, Gavenia had impressed upon her daughter caution in representing her powers or intent. When a local healer ran afoul of her neighbors, they might accuse her of witchcraft. An accusation alone could mean torture and death.

When Blair was old enough to understand the danger her mother faced by helping others, she wished her mother had not been born with her gifts. Yet she also understood those special gifts made Gavenia the woman she was, and Blair dearly loved her mother.

She had also loved her father—Gavenia's late husband—who died from the fever the previous winter. Even his wife's potions could not save him. Blair sorely missed her father. A fisherman, she remembered him as being tall and sturdy as an oak, with flaming red hair. He had loved to sing and carve magical animals from the whalebones he brought home with him from his fishing trips. Her mother wore one around her neck—a hawk, a white hawk—fastened to a thin leather cord. But her father would no longer be carving from whalebones, singing songs, or sharing their cottage.

Just weeks after his death, their landlord, Laird Douglas Blackwood, informed her mother that she no longer needed to pay rent for the cottage. Instead, she could move into Blackwood Hall and work in his kitchen. Gavenia possessed many talents and attributes. Not only was she considered one of the fairest women in the village and a talented healer, she was also known as an exceptional cook.

When Blair asked her mother why she turned down the laird's offer, Gavenia muttered, "'Tis not my cooking he wants, lassie." Whatever the reason for declining the proposal, it relieved Blair. Both the laird and his wife terrified the young girl. Just last spring the wife had accused a local beggar woman of witchcraft, resulting in the woman's death. Blair did not know if the beggar had been a witch or not, but she heard that while they tortured the woman for a confession, she had died before giving one—and before accusing others. According to some local villagers, they believed a witch's spell had killed the beggar woman, placed on her by someone who did not want to face the same accusation.

When Blair reached her cottage a few minutes later, she spied a horse tied up along the front rail. She recognized the animal immediately. It belonged to Laird Blackwood. She had never seen him at her cottage before and wondered why he was here. Glancing from the horse to the open kitchen window, she spied the laird standing inside with her mother. Not wanting to make her presence known, she crept up to the house and crouched below the window, still holding onto the basket. She listened.

"Laird, ah tell ya, ah cannae be accepting yer generous offer," Blair heard her mother say.

"It's nae an offer. It's an order. Ya wull move up tae yer freish quarters by nightfall th'morra. Thare wull be duties expected o' yer daughter, o' course. Ah notice she's grow'n up tae be faire a bonny lassie."

"Mah laird—'n' if ah refuse?" Gavenia's trembling voice asked.

Terrified, Blair continued to listen. The laird expected her mother and her to move up to Blackwood Hall by nightfall tomorrow. He had even promised their cottage to someone else. When her mother asked what would happen if she refused, he called her a willful woman and then pointed out it was a sure sign of one consorting with the devil. Blackwood questioned what evil practices Gavenia had taught Blair.

The frightened child listened as her mother's resolve vanished, and she heard Gavenia agree to move up to Blackwood Hall. Tears slid down Blair's face as she continued to huddle under the window. Although tender in years, Blair understood Blackwood's implied threat against her had ultimately swayed her mother. She knew children were not safe from the accusation of witchcraft and could face torture and execution, as did an adult.

A moment later she heard the slamming of the cottage door, and several minutes later, the sound of hoofs trotted down the road, presumably carrying Laird Blackwood to his next destination. Instead of standing up and going into the cottage, Blair remained frozen to the spot on the damp ground. She expected to hear her mother crying, but instead she heard the slamming of pots and pans, as if someone was tearing apart the kitchen. Hesitantly, she stood up and looked into the cottage. She watched as her mother hurried around in the room, gathering up items and setting them on the kitchen table. Still clutching her basket, Blair turned and headed for the cottage entrance.

"We're gaun awa', lassie," Gavenia said breathlessly the moment Blair walked into the kitchen, basket in hand.

"Ah heard, Mama," Blair whispered. "Ah was ooutdoors by th' windae. Ah heard whit Laird Blackwood said."

Gavenia stopped dashing around the kitchen and studied her daughter a moment. Silently she took the basket from Blair's grasp, set it on the table, and drew the girl into her arms for a comforting hug. "We ur aff tae mah cousin's," Gavenia whispered. "It's a lang journey, bit we wull be safe thare. We'll travel thro' th' woodland. We mist lea noo, tae be far fae 'ere afore he kens we hae gaen."

Blair felt relief knowing they were not moving to Blackwood Hall. But she also understood the dangers of fleeing. Yet she trusted her mother and understood Gavenia felt safer going through the woodland, a vast wilderness she knew well and a place they could easily lose themselves in while surviving off the land as they traveled to her mother's cousin for refuge.

Gavenia told her daughter what they needed to take, knowing it would limit them on what they carried. Since they owned only one horse, they would ride double or take turns riding. Gavenia wanted to get as far away from Lord Blackwood as soon as possible. Riding double and carrying less while traveling such a distance seemed the most reasonable plan.

"It's probaly fur th' best," Gavenia said when Blair expressed sadness at having to leave so much behind. "Shuid Laird Blackwood come by th'morra efter we've gaen 'n' see oor belongings stacked as if we intend tae tak' thaim tae Blackwood loaby th'morra forenicht, he won't suspect we hae gaen."

Gavenia released hold of her daughter, and the two began gathering up what they planned to take, while stacking all they intended to leave by the door. They were almost finished when a young boy name Jamie pounded on the cottage door.

"It's Mama!" Jamie shouted when Gavenia opened the door. She knew immediately why the young boy wanted her. His mother was expecting a baby, yet it wasn't due for several more weeks. "Ye hae tae come!"

Gavenia and Blair exchanged worried glances before Gavenia looked down at the boy and told him to hurry back to his mama and that she would be there shortly. She left him standing on the front porch and closed the door behind her as she turned and faced Blair.

Knowing her mother would never abandon a woman in need, Blair asked what they were going to do now. Gavenia assured her daughter they would leave as soon as she finished with the woman. They would meet at their secret place and be far from Laird Blackwood before he discovered they had gone. She went on to tell Blair what she needed to gather for their escape.

Gavenia started to turn away from her daughter, yet paused a moment and removed the leather cord with the white hawk carving

THE GHOST AND THE WITCHES' COVEN

from her neck. She turned to her daughter and carefully secured the necklace on the young girl.

"Wi' this, ken yer papa is keekin ower ye 'til ah come tae ye," Gavenia whispered to her daughter before kissing her forehead. "Ah love ye, bairn."

Reverently, Blair reached up, her fingertips brushing the delicate carving. She looked back to her mama and whispered, "Hurry, Mama. Ah love ye."

When Gavenia opened the door a few minutes later, it surprised her to find Jamie still lingering on the front porch. Leaving her young daughter behind to prepare for their escape and wait in the nearby woodlands, Gavenia hurriedly followed the boy. They reached his home within twenty minutes. Waiting outside was the boy's anxious father and ten siblings; they ranged from ages two to sixteen. The husband stayed outside with his children while Gavenia rushed in the cottage to her patient. The moment she found the woman in bed burning with a fever, she knew something was drastically wrong.

Within minutes of Gavenia's arrival, the baby came. Yet it was stillborn. Minutes after the delivery, the weary and delirious woman looked up into Gavenia's eyes and moved her lips to say something. Yet, before she uttered any words, her eyes closed, and her spirit drifted away, leaving the children outside motherless.

Moments after Gavenia left the family to grieve, Jamie informed his father what he had overheard outside the Tolmach cottage while waiting for the midwife. After hearing his son's story, the man was convinced Gavenia was a witch and had just murdered his wife and daughter. He immediately went to Laird Blackwood and repeated the tale. He knew Laird Blackwood would do something; hadn't that witch told her daughter she intended to flee from the laird?

The laird's men captured Gavenia before she ever entered the woodland. She might have escaped had she not first stopped along a desolate section of road to weep for the dead woman and her stillborn child.

Blair waited for her mother, and when she didn't come, she began to worry. After nightfall she left her belongings and horse at the secret spot in the woodland and made her way to the village.

Blair escaped the laird, yet primarily because he focused his attention on punishing the woman who intended to run away from him. Had he considered the additional pain he could inflict on

Gavenia by searching for and bringing in the ten-year-old girl with a charge of witchcraft, he would not have done so.

Truth be told, Blackwood was a little in love with the fair Gavenia, and while that might not prevent him from persecuting her for witchcraft, it kept him from charging the daughter.

The details of her mother's incarceration, torture, trial, and eventual execution were for a week or more kept from Blair, although she did witness the ultimate conclusion of her mother's witch trial when they burned her at the stake in front of the entire village.

TWO

Four Hundred Years Later

Late Tuesday evening, the last day of July, Walt pressed send on his computer's email program and marveled that his manuscript would reach his agent's computer within minutes. In his first lifetime, an author or the author's secretary would need to type a copy of the manuscript on paper—copy machines had not yet been invented—and mail it through the postal service, which could take days or weeks to reach its destination.

Celebrations were in order, yet it was too late for champagne. Danielle was already in the shower, getting ready for bed, and when she was done, it was his turn. Walt stood up from his desk, stretched, and went to turn down the bed before taking his shower.

The next morning the couple decided on a low-key celebration for Walt's second submission to his editor. They walked down to Pier Café for breakfast. When they returned home, they each grabbed a book and headed to the back patio to read. Clouds dotted the sky and the afternoon temperatures hovered in the mid-sixties. When they heard the mailman arrive, they both went inside. Walt settled on the sofa with his book while Danielle went to retrieve the day's mail. When she joined Walt in the living room several minutes later, she had already unwrapped a package that had arrived in the mail, and carried it proudly, tilting it from side to side to get Walt's attention.

He looked up from his book and silently watched Danielle break into a lively jig. In her hand she carried a broom. Not a typical broom one might buy at the hardware store, but one that looked homespun. Its handle appeared to have been cut directly from one of a tree's smaller branches and polished before attaching a bundle of twigs to one end.

"What is that?" Walt asked, closing his book and setting it on his lap.

"Isn't it obvious? It's a broom."

"Yes, I see that. But what are you doing with it? Certainly, you don't intend to have Joanne use that thing?"

Danielle laughed. "Of course not, silly." She held the broom out for him to inspect and asked, "What does it make you think of?"

Walt shrugged. "A broom?"

Danielle rolled her eyes. "A witch. It looks like a witch's broom!" She moved the broom to her backside and pretended to sit on it while grinning at Walt.

"You're planning to join that local witches' coven?" Walt teased.

Danielle groaned dramatically and stood up straighter, now holding the broom by her side. "I'm talking about Halloween."

"Halloween? That's three months away. You're already working on your costume?" Walt asked.

Danielle rolled her eyes again. "The broom isn't for me."

"Well, I'm not dressing up like a witch. And stop rolling your eyes."

"It's for the haunted house. I saw it online. It was on sale, and I figured, not too early to plan for the haunted house and collect some new decorations."

"Whoa! Who said anything about doing another haunted house this year? I thought we decided not to do another one?" Walt asked.

Danielle looked down at the broom and shrugged. "I thought we just hadn't made a commitment to do another one again. I don't recall us saying we absolutely wouldn't do a haunted house this Halloween."

"I don't know why you would want to, considering all the trouble we had last year."

Danielle let out a sigh. "There were fun moments." She looked at the broom again. "Doesn't this thing make you think of witches and Halloween?" She looked up to Walt and asked, "Do you know why they say witches flew brooms?"

"Because they couldn't afford a car?"

Ignoring Walt's answer, she held up the broom and said, "From what I read, witches used a broom something like this, but smaller, called a besom. I think they used it to brush away evil spirits or something."

"And what does that have to do with flying?" Walt asked.

"One article I read said they rubbed oil on the broom to make it fly."

"You could always ask Heather. Maybe one of her oils will work." Walt snorted.

"I don't think Heather has those kinds of oils," Danielle said with mock disappointment. "But it's too bad. I'd love to take this thing for a spin."

Walt chuckled. "I think you need to do a little more research on witches and broom flying. The oil they rubbed on the broom had nothing to do with making a broom actually fly. Reportedly, whatever they rubbed on the brooms were hallucinogens."

Danielle frowned. "Heather definitely doesn't have those types of oils. Are you telling me they were tripping out and just thought they were flying?"

Walt shrugged. "So some believe. The purpose of the broom, applying the oils."

Danielle wrinkled her nose. "I need to google this again."

"Well, if you really want to fly on that thing, I know one way you can do it, and it won't require taking any drugs."

Danielle perked up. "Really?"

"Sure. Want to take a little spin around the living room?"

She answered with a grin. Wearing denims, Danielle easily straddled the broom, holding onto the stick as a witch might actually do when flying through the night sky.

"Get ready," Walt called out. The next minute the broom took flight, with Danielle on board, holding on for her life. Of course, had she thought about it, she would have realized Walt's telekinesis moved both her and the broom through the air, and even if she had not been holding on, she would not have fallen to the floor, not unless Walt lost concentration.

Danielle laughed in delight as she circled the living room overhead and looked down at Walt, who sat on the sofa looking up at her. Movement from the door caught her attention, and she spied her cat, Max, strolling into the room.

"Hey, Max!" Danielle called out.

Max looked up toward the ceiling and froze when he saw Danielle flying overhead. He sat down, let out a meow, and continued to watch, his black tail twitching back and forth.

OFFICER BRIAN HENDERSON had not seen his cousin Kitty for over five years. And that had been at the funeral of her husband, Tim. Brian had always liked Tim. Unfortunately, Kitty couldn't say the same about Brian's last two wives.

As children, he and Kitty had been especially close. She was his favorite cousin—and he was hers. In those days she was a tomboy and hadn't been afraid to give him a punch if she felt he needed it. After they had grown into adults, she had given him one of those punches when he had announced his engagement to his first wife. He should have paid more attention to that punch.

She had liked his second wife more than his first. That was until she left him six months after their twenty-fifth wedding anniversary. Kitty had been supportive during that time, calling frequently and inviting him to visit her and Tim. But then Tim had died, and Kitty had her own life and sorrow to handle. Unlike Brian, she had adult children and grandchildren that help fill the void. She eventually began traveling with one of her daughters, and she and Brian kept in touch with infrequent phone calls and frequent post cards. But Kitty was finally coming for a visit, and he had taken off some time to spend with her.

Brian left work early on Wednesday. He planned to run some errands before his cousin arrived later that evening. On his way out of the police station, the chief stopped him and asked if he would mind stopping by Marlow House to give Danielle and Walt a message. He would do it himself, but he had a meeting in a few minutes, and he thought this message should be delivered in person. Brian agreed.

After parking in front of Marlow House, Brian got out of his car and slammed the door closed behind him. He headed up the front walk. Just as he started through the front gate, motion from the living room window caught his eyes. He looked that way and froze.

THE GHOST AND THE WITCHES' COVEN

He couldn't be seeing what he was seeing, Brian told himself. It looked like Danielle, and she was flying around the living room—on a broomstick. He stood and stared in the window, his right hand resting on the front gate, preparing to open it so he could continue to the front door.

Brian had to admit, she looked like she was having one hell of a good time. Was it a jet pack? It had to be a jet pack, he told himself. People didn't really fly around on broomsticks. Maybe witches did, if there really were witches. But there was no such thing as witches, right? Just like there were no such things as ghosts.

A moment later Danielle's flight ended and the broom, with her on it, drifted to the floor. It was then he noticed Walt, who had been sitting on the sofa but now stood. Brian watched as Danielle tossed the broom aside and then ran to her husband, throwing herself into his open arms for a hug.

Brian shook his head in disbelief and muttered, "Just another day at Marlow House."

"BRIAN, HELLO!" Danielle greeted in surprise when she opened the front door five minutes later.

"Hello, Danielle. The chief wanted me to stop and tell you and Walt something, but first, I need to ask. Was it some sort of jet pack?"

Holding the door open, Danielle stared at Brian for a moment and then laughed nervously and said, "Oh, the flying broom? You saw that. Um…that's just a little magic trick Walt was working on."

"Walt is still interested in magic?" Brian asked.

"Yeah, he likes to dabble."

"I'd sure like to see how he did that one," Brian said.

Danielle opened the door wider. "Come on in. No reason to keep you standing on the porch. You can wait in the parlor, and I'll go get Walt. You said you had something to tell both of us, right?"

A FEW MINUTES LATER, after situating Brian in the parlor, Danielle rushed to get Walt from the living room.

"That was Brian Henderson at the door," Danielle said in a low voice when she reached the living room sofa, where Walt had returned to his book. "He wants to talk to us about something."

"Why didn't you bring him in here?" Walt asked.

"Because I needed to give you a heads-up. He saw my spin around the room. And if he asks about it, tell him it's one of your magic tricks. And if he asks how you did it, you need to tell him you can't give away your secrets."

"Or I could tell him how I really did it. I'm sure he'd believe that." Walt snorted.

"Why didn't we close the blinds first?" Danielle groaned.

Walt closed his book, tossed it on the coffee table, and stood up. "Don't worry, love. I don't think Brian can arrest you for flying around your own living room without a license."

Danielle gave Walt's arm a playful swat and said, "Oh, shut up." She then paused a moment and cocked her head as if considering something.

"What is it?" Walt asked.

"You know what is kind of weird? He didn't seem too freaked out about it. When Pearl saw Connor flying around the living room, she fainted in our bushes."

"I'm rather glad Brian didn't faint on the front walk. He could have hit his head and gotten a concussion."

"Walt, take this seriously."

"I am. A concussion is a serious thing."

Danielle smiled. "What am I going to do with you?"

Walt grinned. "I have a couple of ideas, but first we need to see what Brian wants, and get him out of here."

Danielle shook her head at Walt, reached up and gave him a quick kiss, and then started with him to the door. Just before they stepped out into the hallway, Danielle turned abruptly and ran back into the living room. She grabbed the broom and shoved it under the sofa cushions.

"What did you do that for?" Walt asked.

"I don't want Brian to come in here and start looking too closely at that thing."

"Why? It's just a broom."

"Exactly. And Brian saw me flying around on it."

THREE

Brian stood at the parlor window, gazing outside, his fingertips tucked lightly in the back pockets of his denim jeans. His thoughts weren't on the sights before him, but what he had seen just minutes earlier. He heard Walt and Danielle enter the room. It wasn't until Walt greeted him that he turned around and faced the couple.

The memory of his first visit to Marlow House flashed in his mind. Back then, some four years earlier, he had been investigating the disappearance of Danielle's cousin and the Missing Thorndike. He had believed Danielle was involved in the disappearance. His opinion of her improved several months later, after she helped clear him of Darlene Gusarov's murder. Yet he still did not understand much of what had happened that day. Or in many of the days that followed at Marlow House.

"Danielle said you have a message from the chief," Walt said, breaking the silence, while gesturing to a chair for Brian to sit on.

Brian's attention turned to Walt Marlow. He was truly an enigma, Brian thought. There were so many unanswered questions. Questions that his boss, Police Chief MacDonald, did not want to discuss.

Marlow could have been the twin to his distant cousin, the original Walt Marlow, whose grandfather had founded Fredericksport and built Marlow House. Since first meeting Danielle, Brian had believed she had an unhealthy fixation on the original Walt Marlow, a man who had been murdered on the premises over ninety years earlier. Brian always suspected that had played a role in her eventual marriage to the distant cousin.

When Clint Marlow had arrived on the scene several years earlier and then was in an accident that claimed his fiancée along with his memory, he had stayed at Marlow House to recuperate after waking from his coma. From all accounts, and from what Brian had seen back then, Clint hadn't been a very pleasant man.

But then he changed his name to Walt—okay, maybe Walter Clint was his proper name, and he had been going by his middle name—but it all seemed so weird to Brian. What was stranger still was not just that Danielle had fallen in love with Walt, but those closest to her accepted the relationship. Even Chris Glandon, aka Chris Johnson, who had once dated Danielle, seemed supportive of the couple and had been Walt's best man at their wedding.

Had Brian made any predictions back then, he would have thought the unlikely relationship doomed, but he had to admit, they seemed to be happy and in love. Sometimes he wondered if the spirit of the original Walt Marlow had taken over Clint's body. But that was an insane notion.

"Won't you sit down?" Walt said after Brian failed to take his silent invitation to sit.

"How did you do it?" Brian asked. "The flying broom."

Walt grinned. "The wires. Are you saying you really didn't see them?"

"Wires?" Brian frowned.

"I was afraid people might see them. It would ruin the entire illusion," Walt said.

"But how—" Brian began.

"A magician never gives away his secrets," Walt interrupted in a conspiratorial whisper.

Brian frowned but did not respond. Instead, he took a seat on the offered chair and watched as Walt and Danielle sat on the sofa, facing him.

"So what is this message from the chief?" Danielle asked.

"He wanted to let you know the DA dropped all the charges against Brad and Kathy Stewart."

"Why?" Danielle asked. The thirty-something, unmarried Stewart siblings had broken into Marlow House and had held

Danielle at gunpoint while forcing her to open the safe. They had taken some old letters Walt had written in his first lifetime. Since they had been wearing ski masks, Danielle could not identify them. Later, Brad had helped his father kidnap both Walt and Danielle.

"The only evidence they had against them was the testimony of their father," Brian told her.

"Wait a minute, what about my testimony?" Danielle asked. "I saw Brad Stewart in the barn with his father after they chained us up and practically killed Walt."

"According to his lawyers, he wasn't there during your attack. And as you've said, you never saw who hit you. You were alone in the barn when you came to," Brian reminded her.

"Yes, but after I regained consciousness, Beau came into the barn, and so did his son," Danielle said.

"The lawyers are insisting Brad thought you tried to break in, and his father was holding you for the police. They say Brad had no reason not to believe his father."

"That is ridiculous!" Danielle blurted.

"There is another thing the chief wanted me to tell you. Beau Stewart's attorney has made a plea deal. They have committed him to a mental institution."

"Mental institution?" Danielle repeated.

"The state's own doctors agree; Beau Stewart is not fit to stand trial. He has totally taken a trip to crazy land," Brian said.

"Crazy land? Is that some official place?" Walt asked with a chuckle.

Brian shrugged. "It should be. All I know, since his arrest, he's gotten progressively worse each day."

"Maybe he's faking it?" Danielle suggested.

Brian shook his head. "They don't think so. They've had him under constant observation for the last few weeks. From what I understand, hidden cameras in the room. Watching him while he's alone."

"What does he do?" Danielle asked.

"For one thing, he's obsessed with witches." Brian paused a moment and looked toward the direction of the living room, where he had seen Danielle flying around on a broom. He then looked back to the couple and said, "I imagine your little magic act would send him over the edge if he hadn't already gone there."

"Obsessed by witches, how?" Danielle asked.

"Not just any witch. Heather Donovan," Brian said.

Both Walt and Danielle could not contain a smirk.

Brian arched his brows at the pair. "This is serious. The poor man has totally lost his mind."

"Excuse me for not being more sympathetic," Danielle said, the humor gone from her voice. "But he almost killed Walt, tried to smother me, and planned to burn us alive."

"If he planned to smother you first, then you really can't say he planned to burn you alive," Brian joked.

Danielle's glare at Brian earned her his chuckle. He then said, "Okay, I get it. I understand why you aren't especially sympathetic toward the man's current state. But I wonder, what exactly did Heather do to him? When she asked to see him, it surprised me he agreed. What in the world did she really say to him?"

Danielle shrugged. "I guess you'll have to ask Heather that."

"We have, but I suspect she hasn't told us the entire story."

"Why are the doctors convinced he isn't faking it?" Walt asked.

Brian looked to Walt. "Like I said, he has been under constant observation. They don't believe it's an act."

"What did Stewart say Heather did? Surely, he said something," Walt asked.

"From what I understand, he insists Heather used her witchy powers to make him fly around the barn, and then in the holding room." Brian paused a moment and then added, "He didn't mention anything about a broom—or wires."

"Are you suggesting they don't believe he's capable to stand trial because he feels Heather made him fly? That's it? Perhaps there is a valid reason for Stewart to believe that, and it has nothing to do with losing his mind," Walt said.

"I don't think there were wires in the barn or in lockup," Brian said.

"Some believe that a hallucinogenic experience convinced some people—those who professed to be witches—that they could fly. Stewart was on the old Barr property digging up—well, you know what he was digging up. It's entirely possible he came in contact with organic material, maybe some mushroom or some fungi that's a hallucinogen," Walt suggested.

"From what I understand, they did a complete blood panel on him. There was nothing in his system. Of course, I suppose it's possible he had been exposed to something, and it was gone by the time they took the blood tests. He's also fixated on food and water," Brian said.

"Fixated how?" Danielle asked.

"He breaks out into giddy laughter whenever he finishes eating or drinking. Apparently, it has something to do with the curse Heather supposedly put on him."

"Curse?" Danielle already knew all about the curse.

"Stewart told the chief, and then the doctors, that Heather put a curse on him, and she told him he wouldn't be able to eat or drink anything until he confessed everything." Brian paused a moment and thought, *I can't believe you don't already know that, since the chief seems to tell you everything.* He then said, "According to Stewart, after Heather left him, he wasn't able to eat or drink, just like she warned him. I wondered if maybe Heather did some hypnotic-suggestion thing. But according to Heather, when she was asked about it, she swore she knows nothing about hypnotism, and claimed she only urged Stewart to tell the truth. Told him it was bad karma if he didn't."

Walt and Danielle exchanged quick glances. Heather had already told them about the conversation with the police and her karma retort. Fact of the matter, Heather had pretended to be a witch, told Stewart she had cursed him, and to prove the fact, had Marie Nichols send him flying. It would have been an impossible task for Marie when alive, but a fairly easy accomplishment for her ghost.

"What happens now?" Danielle asked.

"I honestly don't know what's going to happen to Stewart. But like I said, unless we can find some evidence on his kids, aside from the rantings of a mentally unstable man, I'm afraid they won't be charged."

"What about the estate?" Walt asked. "Is that still being challenged by the Jenkins family?"

"From what I heard, it probably won't go to court. The Stewarts' attorneys have made an offer to the family, and I suspect they may take it," Brian said.

"So the Stewarts aren't ending up penniless?" Danielle asked begrudgingly.

Brian flashed Danielle a grin. "You don't sound too happy about that."

Danielle shrugged. "I just don't think a family with a history of murder and deceit should end up profiting."

"If it makes you feel any better, I don't believe money is buying happiness. From what I understand, Beau's wife has taken control of the family empire and has already put Kathy and Brad on a strict budget. They've lost their token jobs with the family business. From what I heard, they're not happy," Brian said.

They discussed the Stewarts a few minutes more, and then Brian stood up and said, "I really need to get going."

"Back to work?" Danielle asked.

"No. My cousin is coming for a visit, and I want to go to the store and pick up a few things before she arrives tonight. I'm taking the rest of the week off," Brian explained.

They chatted a few more minutes about the upcoming visit by the cousin, and then Walt and Danielle followed Brian out of the parlor, intending to walk him to the front door. But once in the entry, Brian took a quick left and walked to the doorway leading into the living room. He looked inside and glanced around. Saying nothing, he turned again, headed for the front door, and said goodbye.

"That was close. I'm glad I thought to hide the broom," Danielle said after Brian left the house.

"You think that's what he was looking for?" Walt asked.

"I'm sure he was. He wanted to get a closer look at it. I know I would want one, if it were me."

BRIAN SAT ALONE in his parked car, the ignition key in his hand, making no attempt to start the engine. He glanced back to Marlow House. Once again, he considered what he had just seen when looking into Marlow House's living room. And what had he seen? Nothing. Absolutely nothing.

If Walt Marlow had used wires to lift Danielle and the broom off the floor in flight, what had he attached them to? There was nothing on the ceiling. How had they so quickly disassembled whatever contraption they had used after he arrived?

FOUR

Packed boxes filled the back of her brother's pickup truck. Kathy Stewart stood by the vehicle and reluctantly handed her condominium's key to her mother's real estate agent. Although, technically speaking, the key and the condo had never been legally hers. If she had owned it, she wouldn't be giving up the key right now and moving out.

"I think it will sell much faster empty," the real estate agent said, snatching the key from Kathy's grasp.

"I really don't give a crap," Kathy said dryly.

The agent startled at the retort but said nothing.

Without saying goodbye, Kathy pivoted abruptly to the truck and climbed into the passenger side, slamming the door closed behind her. The agent, now standing alone in the condominium parking lot, looked uncertain, but quickly scurried away.

"You were a little rough on the agent, weren't you?" Kathy's brother, Brad, asked. He sat in the driver's seat, his hands resting on the steering wheel, the engine off.

Kathy shrugged, leaned back in the seat and groaned. "I suppose. But why did Mom have to do it? What is she trying to prove? Selling both of our condos and telling us we're fired and have to find another job. I don't want to find another job. I liked the one Dad gave me."

"Yeah. That sucks. I miss Dad," Brad agreed. "I know he could be a pain too, but at least he never cut us off like this."

"And it isn't like Mom didn't know what was going on. I don't believe that for a minute."

"At least we have a place to stay, and it might be cool to live at the beach. And we have a little money, so no reason to look for a job right away," Brad said.

"Yeah, the money from me selling my car. You got to keep your truck," Kathy grumbled.

"Hey, we both agreed between the two vehicles, the truck would be the smartest one to keep. We sure couldn't haul all our crap to Frederickport in your little car," he reminded her. "And thank God Dad put the vehicles in our names after he gave them to us. If he hadn't, Mom would probably have repossessed them too."

"I guess," Kathy said with a sigh. "I suppose if we want to look at the bright side, at least we didn't have to dig up the rest of the dead bodies."

They both laughed.

"No kidding," Brad said. "Wonder what the place looks like now. Suppose they removed all the crime tape?"

Kathy shrugged. "I guess we'll find out."

Brad removed one hand from the steering wheel and used it to turn the key in the ignition. The engine turned on and a minute later he pulled out of the parking lot.

They drove in silence for about twenty minutes before Kathy said, "As pissed as I am at Mom, at least she hired excellent attorneys. They got us out on bail pretty quick."

"I'm just glad the charges were dropped. I figured they wouldn't be able to make the ones against you stick, but I wasn't sure about the ones against me. I was facing serious time for the kidnap charges alone," Brad said. "I still can't believe Dad ratted us out."

"He's not in his right mind," she reminded him.

"No kidding."

They drove the rest of the way in silence. When they finally reached Frederickport, they went directly to the old Barr place, which their father had purchased months before. While it had been the catalyst for their family's downfall, it was also the only place they could live rent-free. As their mother had pointed out, it would be a while before anyone would pay a decent price for the run-down real estate, not after the discovery of human remains on the property.

Brad pulled his truck down the long drive and parked by the weather-beaten house. The pair climbed out of the vehicle and glanced around, absorbing the atmosphere.

"It feels different," Kathy whispered. She looked over to the barn and spied the remnants of police crime tape, one end flapping in the breeze while the other attached itself to the prickly branches of overgrown shrubbery.

Hands on hips, Brad glanced around and frowned. "You're right. There is something different, but I don't know what."

"You think knowing they removed the dead bodies makes it feel different?"

Brad shrugged. "I wouldn't call those dried-up old bones dead bodies. Anyway, I don't know why that would make a difference. They never bothered me, did they you?"

"Not particularly."

"I so wanted to keep the skulls. How sick would that have been?" Brad said.

Kathy laughed. "They looked wonderfully gruesome."

"Dad just wanted them gone. Stupid Marlows, poking around here. Dad should have let me shoot them."

"The lame thing, it turns out it was all for nothing. Considering the deal the lawyers are working out with the Jenkins family; it was stupid to attempt a cover-up," Kathy said.

"We know that now. But we didn't then."

"Yes, and look where we are. We don't have the money to tear this place down and fix it up. And I'm not looking forward to living in this dump," Kathy grumbled.

"Me either, but for the moment we don't have any other options. Not unless you want to get an actual job and rent something."

"No way!"

"Okay, let's unpack and then get something to eat." Brad walked to the bed of the truck and pulled out a box.

After they finished unloading the truck twenty minutes later, Brad stood outside and brushed the palms of his hands off on the sides of his jeans. "You know, it really feels different here now."

"I know. I'm trying to figure out what it is," Kathy said.

"Before, I always got the feeling someone was ready to jump out from around the corner."

"Exactly!" Kathy turned to face her brother. "You don't think their ghosts were haunting this place or something, do you? And that's why it felt like someone was about to jump out?"

"What, and now that we found their bodies, their spirits can rest?" Brad laughed at the idea and then added, "Almost as lame as thinking Heather Donovan really cast a spell on Dad."

Kathy put her hand out and said, "Give me the truck keys."

"Why?"

"Because you said you wanted to get something to eat after we unpacked, and I want to drive."

"I can drive," Brad argued.

"I want to drive. And you did say the truck was both of ours now."

Brad let out a groan, dug one hand into a pants pocket, and pulled out his truck keys. He handed them to his sister.

Kathy gave the keys a little toss in the air, caught them, and then climbed in the truck's driver's side.

Five minutes later as they drove down Beach Drive past the pier, Brad said, "Where are we going? I thought we were getting something to eat at Pier Café. You just drove past it."

"I want to look at something," she said. A moment later she parked across the street, two doors down from Marlow House.

"What are we doing here?" Brad asked.

Kathy nodded across the street. "That's where Heather Donovan lives."

"So?"

When Kathy did not respond, Brad let out a groan and said, "Come on, you're not on that witch thing again, are you?"

"Something happened to our father. Something changed him," Kathy insisted.

"And you think that something is Heather Donovan? That's just lame, Kathy."

"I know you think that. You've said it enough already. But Brad, how is it that Dad was perfectly fine one day, and the next he's convinced Heather bewitched him. Dad, of all people. When I told him about the witches' coven I heard about in Fredrickport, he said that was lame too."

"I don't think Dad used the word lame," Brad said.

"You're right. I believe he called it silly. Same thing. He sure doesn't call witches silly now, does he?"

THE GHOST AND THE WITCHES' COVEN

Brad turned in his seat and looked at his sister. "You're serious, aren't you?"

"I am. I've been giving this a lot of thought," Kathy said. "I've been doing some research."

"What kind of research?"

"Let me show you something." Kathy drove the truck from the curb. As she did, a car came down the street and parked in front of Heather Donovan's house.

"Where are we going now?" Brad asked.

"Hold on, you'll see."

Several minutes later Kathy turned down Frederickport's business district's main street. She passed the museum and then pulled over and parked. After turning off the engine, she nodded to a shop. There was a new sign out front that read "Pagan Oils and More," with a black silhouette of a witch riding a broomstick painted on the front window.

She turned to face her brother. "I told you I've been doing some research. I started when I first heard about the witches' coven, just out of curiosity. But then this thing happened with Dad, and I dug in more seriously. You know what I found out?"

"What?"

"There are two witches' covens in Frederickport. At least two that I know about."

"What does it have to do with that shop?" Brad asked.

"It's owned by one of the covens."

Brad laughed.

"Shut up, Brad. Think of Dad."

Brad continued to laugh, but then Kathy gave his shoulder a hard punch and he quieted.

"I still don't get it," he grumbled while rubbing his injured shoulder with one hand.

"The witches who opened that store, they have a YouTube channel all about witchcraft. They claim some stuff they sell has magic powers."

"I'm sure they do," Brad said with a snort.

"I am serious."

Brad groaned. "Do you want to get locked up with Dad? Seriously, Kath, you are sounding crazy."

"You know, witchcraft has been around for thousands of years.

Many of the people burned at the stake for witchcraft were actually witches."

"So, tell me, if they were real witches, then how come they didn't just cast a spell on the people who wanted to kill them?"

"It doesn't work like that."

"I guess not," he muttered under his breath. He then pointed down the street to Lucy's Diner and said, "Can we go eat there, and then you can tell me all about this witch thing. I'm starved."

FIFTEEN MINUTES LATER, Brad and Kathy sat at a booth in Lucy's Diner, each with a menu in hand.

"So what were you telling me about this witch thing?" Brad asked.

"Let's order first. I don't want the server to overhear our conversation."

Ten minutes later they sat alone at the booth, menus closed and put away, and orders taken.

"I've been listening to the YouTube channel," Kathy began.

"I assume you're talking about the witchcraft one by the owners of that store."

"Yes. And did you know, you can't destroy a witch by burning them at the stake like they thought?"

"No, I did not know that," Brad said, resisting the urge to roll his eyes because he was afraid his sister might give him a kick under the table if he did.

"A witch's power over someone ends when she dies. And the only thing that will truly kill a witch is a spell cast by another witch."

"Tell that to all those actual witches burned at the stake."

"Burned, but not destroyed. Those witches took on other forms."

"Is there a point to all this?"

"I believe Heather Donovan really is a witch, and she's cast a spell on our father. The only way to break whatever hold she has on him—we need to destroy her. But we need to get another witch to do it."

FIVE

After leaving Marlow House, Brian Henderson stopped first at Old Salts Bakery, where he picked up four cinnamon rolls, a loaf of freshly baked bread, and three dozen chocolate chip cookies. The next stop was the liquor store. As he recalled, his cousin Kitty was a gin martini drinker, and he didn't keep gin in the house. He had already picked up the stuffed olives the day before, when grocery shopping for the week. The last stop was the meat market, to buy steaks. He could have picked those up at the grocery store, but he wanted to splurge for his cousin, and the local meat market had the best steaks in town. Tomorrow night he would take Kitty to Pearl Cove for dinner, but he didn't imagine she would feel like going out after driving in from the Portland airport. He had offered to pick her up, but she had insisted on driving herself, and she wanted to rent a car. Brian knew Kitty's independent streak, so he didn't bother trying to change her mind.

When Brian arrived home, Joanne Johnson was still there, finishing up. He had hired her to give the house a good cleaning before his guest arrived. He found her in the kitchen, wiping down the counter with a sponge.

Turning to Brian and abandoning the sponge on the counter, Joanne said, "There are clean sheets on the bed in the guest room, and I put clean sheets on yours."

"You didn't have to do that, but thanks," Brian said after placing his recent purchases on the counter.

"No problem. I fixed the salad for tonight. It's in the refrigerator. And I have the cheese bread on the cookie sheet, ready to go into the oven. Put it under the broiler until the bread gets light brown. But remember to keep a close eye on it. It can burn before you know it."

"I appreciate this, Joanne. How much do I owe you?"

"I appreciate the extra work. You know, if you need me to come in regularly, once a week or once a month, I can fit you in. I have a lot more free time now since the B and B closed." She then told him how much he owed.

"I hadn't considered how the bed-and-breakfast closing meant fewer hours for you."

"I can't complain. Danielle has always been generous, and frankly, for what I do over there, she pays me far too much."

"Yeah, one thing I've learned about Danielle over the last couple of years, she's a soft touch."

"So is Walt," Joanne added.

Brian studied Joanne for a minute and then asked, "You like him, don't you?"

Joanne nodded. "I really do. Now, had you asked me that question a couple of years ago, I would have given a different answer."

"I remember. What changed your mind?"

Joanne considered the question a moment and then said, "Walt changed. When I first met him, well, frankly, he was an unpleasant man. Tried to get me fired."

"Why is he different now?"

"I suppose it was the memory loss. He still can't recall anything that happened before the accident."

"A person has to remember he was a jerk to be one?" Brian asked.

Joanne laughed and said, "I guess. At least, it feels that way with Walt. But I'll tell you something, you might think I'm a little crazy for saying it…"

"What's that?" Brian asked.

"Every once in a while, when I walk into the library at Marlow House and see that portrait, the one of the original Walt Marlow, well, in my mind, that is Walt. Danielle's Walt, the one she's married to. The one living in Marlow House now. I know it's an insane notion, but sometimes, I do feel as if that's who Walt really is."

Brian didn't respond immediately, but finally said, "No. That's not as insane a thought as you might think."

BRIAN DIDN'T THINK his cousin Kitty had aged a bit since the last time he had seen her. Although, he suspected she dyed her short brown hair to conceal the gray. Tall, slender and physically fit, she still played tennis once a week with her friends. While it had been rough on her after Tim's death, she had moved on and kept active.

Kitty arrived shortly before six that evening. After taking her luggage to the guest room, the cousins enjoyed cocktails on the patio, and then Brian grilled the steaks. When dinner was over, Kitty helped Brian clean up the dishes. They eventually settled in the living room and had another round of drinks.

"Brian, I am impressed. You've finally grown up," Kitty teased.

"What does that mean?" Brian asked with mock indignation.

Kitty waved her drink from side to side, motioning to the surrounding room. "Your home. The last time I visited, it looked like a college boy lived here. But now, it's so clean I almost suspect you have a wife you haven't told me about."

"Isn't that a little sexist?" he teased.

"Maybe." She gave him a brief salute with her glass and then took a sip of her cocktail.

"Well, I'll confess. I hired someone to clean the house today."

Kitty grinned. "I'm flattered. For me?"

He shrugged. "Yeah, I didn't want you going back home and telling the rest of the family what a slob I am."

Kitty laughed. "Oh, I would never do that. I haven't forgotten that blood pact we made when we were ten."

Brian glanced at his wrist. "Yeah, I still have the scar. We weren't very bright, were we?"

Kitty laughed again. "We did some stupid stuff. But we sure had fun."

It was Brian's turn to salute Kitty with his drink. "We did."

"So, tell me, this housekeeper of yours. Did you break down and hire someone who comes in regularly, or was it just because I was coming?"

"It was for your visit, but I am tempted to have her come in regularly."

"You should. I do now. I so don't miss cleaning my house. Where did you find her? A local service?"

"She worked full time for Marlow House. It used to be a bed-and-breakfast. But they closed the business, and Joanne—that's the housekeeper—they cut her hours. So she's taking on new jobs."

"Marlow House? Isn't that the place owned by the crazy woman you told me about?" Kitty asked.

Brian frowned. "Crazy woman?"

"Yeah, the one who inherited the house, and you thought she had something to do with her cousin's murder."

"Well, yeah, I did at the time."

"Didn't you think she killed that other guy too? I remember reading something about it after you told me."

"I guess my view on Danielle has changed since we last talked about her. I consider her a friend now."

"Really?" She arched her brows. "More than a friend? From what I recall, she was single."

"No. Nothing along those lines. In fact, she has since married." Brian then went on to tell his cousin the condensed version of Danielle and Walt in Frederickport, leaving out his unexplained encounters with the pair. While doing so, he had another drink and began feeling less inhibited than normal.

When he finished, she asked, "And he never got his memory back?"

"No. Can I tell you something, Kitty?" Brian asked, his tone serious.

"Of course, anything."

"There is something strange about Marlow House."

"You've told me that before."

He shook his head. "No, not like that. I mean strange in a different way."

"How so?"

"Ever since Danielle moved to Frederickport and Marlow House was again open to the public, there seems to be one strange thing after another happening over there."

"Strange how?"

His gaze met Kitty's. "Like Marlow House is haunted."

Brian's comment surprised his cousin, who then choked on her drink and ended up spitting out a bit. She quickly grabbed a tissue, dabbed her mouth, and regained her composure. "Haunted? What do you mean?"

"Let's see if I can remember all the strange things that have happened over there." Brian leaned back in his chair, drink in hand, and crossed one leg over its opposing knee. "The first unexplained incident I can recall is when we tried to arrest Danielle for Stoddard Gusarov's murder. Lily, that's her best friend, was living with her back then. Danielle wasn't home. Lily was walking away from me and I grabbed her arm—I know I shouldn't have touched her—but then the next thing I know, I'm flying across the room like someone just sucker punched me."

"This Lily, she slugged you?"

Brian shook his head. "No. Lily didn't hit me. The punch came out of thin air. I fell on my ass. The next time something strange happened was when the gun went flying."

"Gun?" Kitty asked.

"The people responsible for Stoddard's death had Danielle at gunpoint. And that gun flew out of his hand—like some invisible hand grabbed it. It landed on the roof. But it wasn't the first or last time something like that happened at Marlow House. There always seems to be an unseen force that protects Danielle and her friends."

"There has to be an explanation," she insisted.

"There are just so many things that have happened over the last few years. Each time I convince myself there is a logical explanation. But then the fingerprints…"

"Fingerprints?"

"Danielle's husband, Walt, used to be a real estate agent in California. But when we checked his fingerprints against the prints the California real estate department had on him, they didn't match."

"Obviously some error on the side of the real estate department's records department."

"But they matched Walt Marlow's prints."

Kitty frowned. "Yes, so? He is Walt Marlow."

"No. I'm talking about the original Walt Marlow, his distant cousin. The one murdered in that house almost a hundred years ago. The one who looks just like the Walt Marlow living there now. Not only do they share the same face, the same name, they also share the same fingerprints."

"That is impossible. There has to be a logical explanation."

"And his signature. The two men have the same signature, the same handwriting. I've found samples of the original Walt Marlow's handwriting. It's identical to Danielle's husband's."

"Someone is gaslighting you, Brian. Can't you see that?"

"And then today."

"What about today?"

Brian told her what he had witnessed in the living room at Marlow House.

"Did you ask them about it?" Kitty asked.

"Yes. They claimed it was a magic trick involving wires. But when I left the house, I looked in the living room, and there was nothing attached to the ceiling. Nothing in the room that could have lifted Danielle and that broom off the floor. Minutes after I saw Danielle flying around that room, I was in the parlor with both of them. How could they have removed whatever they were using that quickly?"

Kitty considered the question for a minute. Finally, she said, "How long were you with them both before you checked the living room?"

"I don't know. Twenty, thirty minutes maybe."

"How do you know there was not someone else in the house with you, someone who removed all evidence of the trick while you were talking to them?"

Brian frowned. "I hadn't considered that."

"Can you think of anyone who might have helped them with the trick?"

"Yeah. Lily and Ian live across the street. Lily is her best friend. And Heather lives a couple of doors down, and Chris, he lives down the street. They're all close."

"See. You have your answer. I seriously doubt Marlow House is haunted. And what, do you think Danielle's husband is really a ghost?"

"No. I don't think that."

"Then what?"

Brian shrugged. "I don't know. There's just something about that place."

SIX

Only the eldest daughter of a blood witch could cast the spell. According to the book, the ideal time was during the waning gibbous phase of the moon, preferably five days after the last full moon. Bridget Parker hadn't told her sisters what she intended to do. Even if the spell worked and they found another blood witch to sacrifice, it might prove unnecessary. Yet, if Bridget missed this opportunity, she would have to wait another month before trying.

Her sisters had already taken their showers and now sat in the living room, watching a movie. Still dressed in the blood-red kaftan she had put on that morning; Bridget had no intention of taking her shower yet. She had a spell to cast. Slipping down the hallway, she peeked into the living room, wanting to make sure her sisters remained occupied. She was in no mood for their questions.

Confident the movie had her sisters' full attention; Bridget made her way to the den. She shut the door after entering the room and walked to the wall safe. Several minutes later she had the safe open. Bridget reverently removed the worn leather-bound book from inside. She took the book with her to the desk and sat down, placing it before her.

Lovingly, she ran her hand over its front cover, letting her fingertips trace the engraving of a pentacle—a five-pointed star within a circle. Slowly moving her fingertips over each point of the star, she thought of the element each one represented: spirit, water, fire, earth and air.

After a moment she gently patted the cover with her right palm and then opened the book, turning to the spell she intended to use after her sisters went to bed. She wanted to read it one more time to make sure she remembered everything.

"The Spell of Attraction," she read aloud and then chuckled. When she had first read the spell's name months earlier, she had falsely assumed it was a love spell—something used to get an unrequited love to take notice. Yet it was nothing like that. According to its description, it could bring something into a blood witch's immediate world, but once there, it didn't mean the person—or thing—you conjured would behave how you wanted. It only afforded you access to whatever you conjured.

This evening Bridget intended to use the spell to bring an object and another blood witch to her. The object, a high-quality ruby, three carats or larger, which she needed for a future spell. She needed the blood witch to try the spell out on before using the spell again on the intended target.

According to the instructions, she had to do this herself—alone—under the moon, preferably the fifth night after a full moon, over saltwater. That meant on a boat on the ocean—or a pier. They didn't have a boat, but Frederickport Pier was just a short walk down the street.

Not anyone could perform this spell. It had to be the first daughter of a blood witch. Her mother had been a blood witch, as had all the women in her family, for over four centuries.

She couldn't take the book with her to the pier, it was far too heavy, and if one of her sisters saw her leaving the house with it, they would force her to answer their questions. Opening a desk drawer, she removed a pen and piece of paper and began jotting down the words she would need to recite when casting the spell.

Several hours later, her sisters came into the den and found Bridget reading a book. Not the spell book; she had returned that to the safe. Bridget told them goodnight and said she planned to read some more before going to bed. They didn't question her words and said goodnight.

An hour later Bridget slipped a jacket on over her kaftan. She wanted the jacket as much for its large pockets as for its warmth. The last time she looked, the evening temperature had dipped below sixty. She had already collected what she needed: candles, matches, a baggie of soil, and a slip of paper with the spell written on it, and her cellphone. After shoving all the items in her jacket pockets, she quietly left her house and began walking alone to the pier.

Overhead, the moon lit her way. When she arrived at the pier fifteen minutes later, no one was around, not even anyone fishing along the pier's edge. The ice cream shop had been closed for hours, but Pier Café remained open.

Standing by the entrance to Pier Café, she looked down the lonely pier and smiled. There, at the far end, a beam of moonlight illuminated a portion of the pier walkway. Determined, she headed for that spot. When she arrived, she sat down cross-legged, paying little concern to the nearby fish guts and other disgusting bits attached to the worn wooden planked walkway. Removing the items from her pockets, she arranged them around her.

ADAM NICHOLS HAD a sudden craving for apple pie. There was only one place in Frederickport where he could get a slice at this time of night, and that was at Pier Café. It was late when he arrived at the pier, yet he expected to see a few fishermen. After all, it was still summer. As he approached the restaurant, he looked down the pier and didn't see a single angler, yet there was someone on the pier.

When he arrived at the door to Pier Café, instead of entering he stood there a moment and looked out at the person sitting alone in the moonlight. It was a woman, with long red hair, and she sat cross-legged on the pier, with her arms outstretched to the night sky, while she looked up to the moon and began shouting.

"What in the world?" Adam muttered, still watching the odd sight. The woman stopped baying at the moon and then picked up what looked like a small baggie. She pulled something from the bag and began tossing it in the air while resuming her baying. What she tossed, he had no idea.

Shaking his head in disbelief, Adam walked into the diner.

"Evening, Adam," Carla the server greeted him immediately. The first thing Adam noticed, Carla's hair was still purple, as it had been last week. The second thing he noticed, there was only one occupied booth; it looked like a couple of fishermen who were packing it up for the night.

"Evening, Carla. Wow, you're dead tonight. Hope you have apple pie," Adam said.

"You should have been here earlier. We got slammed."

Adam groaned. "Don't tell me that means you ran out of apple pie?"

Carla grinned. "I'm pretty sure there are a couple of pieces left."

Adam nodded to the door he had just entered and then asked, "Any idea who the weirdo is sitting out on the pier?"

Carla brushed by Adam, opened the door, and looked outside. It took her just a moment to find the subject of Adam's inquiry. "Aww, that's one of the Parker sisters. Don't know which one. Can't really tell them apart."

"Any idea why she's sitting on the pier, yelling at the moon?" Adam asked.

"I imagine she's casting a spell," Carla explained. "Or hexing someone."

"What?"

"Hey, you want the pie with ice cream?" Carla asked.

"Is there any other way?"

"Then go sit down and let me get it. Then I'll fill you in on the Parker sisters," Carla said.

WHEN CARLA ARRIVED at Adam's booth, she brought along a piece of pie and ice cream for herself, and one for Adam, along with a pot of coffee.

"I shouldn't drink coffee this late," Adam said after Carla set the plates on the table and began filling one cup that she had just flipped right side up.

"It's decaf," she told him before filling a second cup for herself.

"Good…I guess." Adam hated decaf. "So what's this about casting a spell?" Adam asked after Carla sat across from him at the booth.

"Like I said, she's one of the Parker sisters, claims to be a witch. Surprised you don't recognize her. Their store is down the street from your office."

"Pagan Oils and More?" Adam asked.

"So you do know her?" Carla asked before taking a bite of her pie.

"No. I've seen the shop, but never the owners. I know there was an article about the business in the paper the other day. Mel told me about it. You think she's casting some spell?"

"Looks like it to me," Carla said with a shrug.

"More like a PR stunt. For her store," Adam said.

"You're probably right, but why pick a night when no one is around?" Carla asked.

"Have you seen her do this stuff before?" he asked.

"Yeah. One night she and her two sisters were sitting on the beach under the pier, with a dozen or more lit candles around them in a circle while chanting and holding hands. Real weird. Someone said they were casting a spell or something. When they came in later, I almost asked them about it, but figured I didn't want to piss them off. Not saying they're really witches or anything, or can cast spells, but why chance it?"

Adam chuckled. "You want to know what's bizarre?"

"Something more bizarre than a witch casting a spell on the pier outside my work? What?"

"I rent a house to some sisters who claim they're witches too."

"That is crazy," Carla said. "I don't remember anyone in Frederickport ever claiming to be a witch before. There was that vampire a few years back, but no witches."

Adam frowned. "Vampire?"

"Yeah, the guy who went bonkers over *Twilight* and got those fake fangs put in by that flaky dentist," Carla reminded him.

Adam laughed. "Yeah, I forgot about him. But I seem to recall it wasn't so much him wanting to be a vampire as trying to get the attention of all the girls into *Twilight*. I don't think he ever drank blood or anything. I wonder what happened to him."

"Someone told me they ran into him in Vancouver about a year ago. He'd had the fangs removed, and I think he was selling insurance," Carla said.

"I suppose the current wave of witches will eventually go the way of the vampire."

SEVEN

"At least I can have some wine this weekend," Danielle grumbled to herself on Thursday morning. She stood at the mirror in the master bathroom while brushing her teeth. Just minutes earlier, after using the bathroom for the first time that morning, she discovered she was not pregnant. Not that she had expected to get pregnant right away. It had only been a couple of weeks since she went off birth control. But once a woman enters her thirties, she isn't as confident in her fertility. In Danielle's twenties, she had believed one unprotected encounter would lead to pregnancy.

She rinsed off her toothbrush and put it in the drawer. Wiping her mouth with a washcloth, she picked up her hairbrush and looked back into the mirror. Pausing a moment, she grabbed hold of one lock of hair and stretched it out a bit. Over two years had gone by since she'd woven her hair into a fishtail braid. It had been her trademark hairstyle back then until she had cut her hair into a short, perky style. But it had since grown out some, and while not as long as it had been when she had worn the braid, she thought it might be long enough to wear one again. It was August, and she always preferred wearing her hair up or in a braid during the summer. Releasing hold of the lock of hair, she opened one of the bathroom drawers and fished around for a hair tie.

"THAT'S the girl I first met," Walt told Danielle when she walked into the kitchen twenty minutes later. He handed her a cup of coffee.

Holding the offered cup in one hand, Danielle used her other hand to give the back of her braid a short tug while saying, "Not exactly. It's barely long enough to braid properly."

"Are you going to let it grow out again?"

Danielle shrugged. "I don't know." She walked with her coffee to the table and sat down. Walt joined her.

"I'm not pregnant," Danielle blurted.

Walt grinned. "I didn't think you were."

"You know what I mean."

"I do. I just want you to know, I am more than willing to keep trying—again and again." Walt's grin broadened.

Danielle rolled her eyes and said, "So nice to know you're willing to sacrifice so much to start a family."

Walt chuckled.

Danielle took a sip of her coffee and then said, "I just realized, when I get pregnant, I have to give up coffee. Lily gave it up."

"Now that is genuine sacrifice."

"Let's walk to town today. That new candy store is having its grand opening this week, and I heard they're giving away free samples."

"Being not pregnant and all, you sure you're up to walking to town?" Walt asked.

"Didn't you hear what I said? Chocolate, Walt. They are giving away chocolate."

DANIELLE DECIDED WALT WAS RIGHT; she wasn't up to walking. When they left for town a few hours later, they drove. Walt took the Packard instead of Danielle's car. When Walt pulled onto the main street, he saw there were no empty spots by the candy shop, so he had to park farther down the street, near Lucy's Diner. He had just parked the Packard when Heather pulled her car into the space next to them.

"You coming to get free chocolate too?" Danielle greeted Heather as they each got out of their vehicles.

Dressed for work, Heather wore a long dark skirt, sweater

blouse, and black boots, with her ebony-colored hair straight and pulled into a low ponytail and straight-cut bangs covering her eyebrows. Instead of red lipstick, she wore dark purple, with matching nail polish. "No. I'm picking up burgers at Lucy's and taking them back to the office," Heather explained as she shut her car door.

Instead of making their way to their respective destinations, the three gathered between the two vehicles for a brief chat.

"Hey, guess who I saw parked across the street from our houses yesterday," Heather said.

"Who?" Danielle asked.

"Kathy and Brad Stewart. I was wondering if maybe we should tell the chief about it. Isn't that stalking or something?" Heather said.

"What were they doing?" Walt asked.

"Just sitting there is all I saw. I had to run home to pick up something, and when I turned down Beach Drive, I noticed a truck parked across the street. I didn't think too much about it, but as the truck pulled away, I saw who it was."

"Are you sure it was them?" Danielle asked.

"Yes. I recognized the truck. Saw Brad in it before. And then I saw both of them as they drove by. If a person is out on bail, is that legal for them to park across the street from the person they attacked?"

"They're no longer out on bail," Danielle explained. She then repeated what Brian had told them the previous day.

"That sucks," Heather grumbled.

"I agree. But there's nothing we can do about it. Yet, I'll tell the chief what you saw," Danielle said.

Heather glanced at her watch and then looked back up to Walt and Danielle. "I'd better pick up those burgers. If I take too long, you know how Chris gets."

They all laughed, knowing Chris rarely got angry.

Danielle nodded up the street. "We're going to check out the new candy store."

Heather looked to Walt and said, "Considering your sweet tooth, is that such a good idea?"

"I'm only here because Danielle needs chocolate," Walt insisted.

"Yeah, right." Heather snorted. She glanced around and added,

THE GHOST AND THE WITCHES' COVEN

"Several new stores have opened up. I need to stop in at Pagan Oils. Curious to see what they have."

"I read in the paper it's owned by genuine witches," Walt said with a mischievous grin.

"Yeah, I read that article too in last Sunday's paper. I thought at first they were Wicca, but whoever they interviewed claimed they are from a long line of witches, not Wicca."

"I thought being Wicca was the same thing as being a witch," Danielle said.

"Danielle didn't read the article," Walt told Heather.

"Wicca's a religion based on witchcraft. It wasn't even a thing during Walt's first life," Heather explained. "A guy in the fifties started it. I think he got the idea from some woman who was messing around in ancient pagan rituals. The women who own Pagan Oils insist in the article they can trace their witchcraft lineage over four hundred years."

"Good marketing gimmick," Danielle said.

Heather laughed. "Yeah, I figured you'd appreciate it."

"We'd better let you pick up your lunch," Danielle said, glancing over at Lucy's Diner. The candy store was up the street, past the diner and a few doors down from Frederickport Vacation Properties.

Three young women walked their way, chatting amongst themselves. Walt, Danielle, and Heather waited patiently on the pavement between the cars for them to pass before they stepped onto the sidewalk. Once they did, they started up toward the diner and then spied another woman coming down the sidewalk in their direction. If asked to describe her, hippy would be the first word that came to Danielle's mind.

When the woman was about five feet from them, Danielle flashed her a smile and said, "Good afternoon."

The woman halted and stared at Danielle, who came to a stop, along with Walt and Heather. The woman then pointed to the sidewalk between them.

They all looked down. Something lay on the concrete. Danielle knelt down and picked it up—a thin leather cord with a delicate carving attached. Now holding it in her hand, identifying it as a necklace, Danielle stood up and looked at the woman.

"I saw one of them drop it," the woman explained, pointing up the street. They looked in the direction she pointed and saw the same three women who had passed them minutes earlier, and who were now walking into Frederickport Vacation Properties.

"If you're going that way, maybe you can return it to her," the woman suggested. "The one who dropped it is the woman wearing the blue blouse."

Now clutching the necklace in her hand, Danielle flashed the woman a smile and said, "No problem."

"Thank you," the woman said.

Just as the woman hurried away in the opposite direction, Danielle noticed something around her neck. Frowning, she looked from it and down to what she held.

"That's odd," Danielle muttered, looking down at the small carving hooked to the leather cord.

"What?" Walt asked.

"That woman, she was wearing the same necklace."

Heather glanced down at the necklace in Danielle's hand and rubbed her fingertips over the carving. "They probably bought it at the same gift shop. It looks like a hawk. I wonder what it's made from."

Walt reached over to Danielle's hand and took the necklace from her. He studied it a moment, running his thumb over the carving, and then said, "My bet, whalebone." He handed the necklace back to Danielle.

Danielle studied it again. "I kind of like it. I'd like something like this, but a whale or dolphin instead of a hawk. And I like the leather strap too."

Heather laughed.

Danielle glanced up at her. "What's so funny?"

"You own a necklace worth a bazillion dollars that you keep in the bank, and you're looking at that like it's diamonds and emeralds."

Danielle grinned at Heather. "But like you said, I already have diamonds and emeralds."

"I guess this means we're stopping in Adam's office before we go to the candy store," Walt said before the three continued up the street.

THE GHOST AND THE WITCHES' COVEN

AILEANA PARKER STOOD by the large picture window inside Pagan Oils, looking out at the front sidewalk. "They didn't even look this way," she called out to her two sisters, Bridget and Davina, who stood together behind the counter. Their mother, when she was alive, had called them stairsteps, with Bridget now twenty-six, Davina twenty-five, and Aileana twenty-four. Often mistaken for twins—or more accurately triplets—the three redheads wore their curly hair long, falling to their waists. With green eyes, pale skin and an abundance of freckles, they had once been called gingers by a snarky neighbor, a term they found derogatory. It was on this neighbor they tried their first spell. She never mocked the sisters again.

While similar in appearance, they each had a unique gift not shared by the other two sisters. Bridget, the eldest, could hear any piece of music and then sit down at the piano and play it beautifully. Davina, the middle sister, had a photographic memory, which proved more useful than Bridget's talent when casting spells. Aileana had learned to read lips, a skill she perfected being the youngest sister and determined to know whatever Bridget and Davina were saying when she was out of earshot.

Turning from the window, Aileana walked toward the counter.

"Was it all of them?" Bridget asked.

"All three sisters, Finola, Ina and Kenzy."

"They would make everything so much easier if they would just walk in here," Bridget said with a sigh.

"I'm surprised they haven't yet. I would have thought with Sunday's article, natural curiosity would lure at least one of them in the store," Davina said.

"Finola is the one we need. She has the Leabar," Aileana said.

"We assume she has it. It's entirely possible one of the others keeps it. Or at least, can get a hold of it," Davina said.

"No. Finola is the oldest. She would be the keeper of the Leabar. And if we can just determine if she is the White Hawk or not, we'll know how to proceed," Aileana said.

"I don't see how she could be the White Hawk," Bridget said. "The Leabar rightfully belongs to me."

"To us," Aileana corrected.

"I am the oldest," Bridget reminded her.

"Bridget is the rightful keeper of the Leabar; no one can own it," Davina said.

Aileana wandered to a display on the counter and picked up a necklace from the rack—one with a whalebone hawk carving attached to a thin leather cord. "Maybe we need to move this display to the window if we want to attract the right type of customers."

EIGHT

Just as Walt, Danielle and Heather approached Lucy's Diner, a departing customer opened its door and walked outside. With them came the enticing aroma of grilled meat; it filled the front walkway. Walt and Danielle paused a moment to say goodbye to Heather.

Walt took a deep breath and said, "I think I'm hungry."

"You're always hungry," Danielle and Heather chorused.

"It is almost lunchtime," Walt reminded them.

"And I'd better go pick up mine before I get in trouble with the boss," Heather said.

The three said a last goodbye, and then Heather went into the diner while Walt and Danielle continued up the street.

"You want to stop somewhere for lunch after we return this necklace?" Danielle asked.

"Those burgers smelled good," Walt said.

"You want to eat at Lucy's?" Danielle asked.

"If you wouldn't mind. They do have the best burgers in town," Walt said.

"Okay. We should wait to go to the candy store after we eat," Danielle suggested.

A few minutes later they reached the offices of Frederickport Vacation Properties, owned by Adam Nichols. Just as Walt reached for the door handle, Adam's grandmother, Marie Nichols, appeared.

Adam wasn't expecting a visit from his grandmother. Marie had been murdered several years earlier, and Adam couldn't see ghosts.

"Are you here to visit Adam?" Marie asked.

Danielle held out the necklace for Marie to see. "We're just stopping by to return this. A woman dropped it on the sidewalk a few minutes ago, and we saw her walk in here."

Marie glanced briefly at the necklace and then said, "If you don't mind, I think I'll join you. I haven't seen Adam for a few days."

A moment later Walt opened the door to the office. When Danielle, Marie and Walt stepped inside the building, they spied Adam sitting at Leslie's desk, talking to the three women, who stood near him.

Danielle estimated the women were in their twenties, and she guessed they were sisters, considering their striking resemblance to each other. She wouldn't call them brunettes exactly, because their hair wasn't dark brown, it was black like Heather's. It was also straight like Heather's. They had delicate features and dark brown eyes, like their hair, almost black. They were around the same height, a few inches taller than Danielle. What varied between the three was hair length and bodyweight.

Adam looked up at Walt and Danielle. He smiled and said, "Hey, Danielle, Walt. I'll be right with you. Let me finish here first."

"Leslie's at lunch," Marie explained to Walt and Danielle. Leslie, who was Adam's assistant, normally sat at the front desk, while Adam's office was down the hall. "I stopped in Lucy's first, thinking Adam might be at lunch. But I saw Leslie there with one of her girlfriends."

"That's okay, Adam. We're actually here to speak to one of these women," Danielle explained, flashing a smile at the woman wearing the blue blouse.

The woman frowned in Danielle's direction, as did the two women with her.

"What do you want?" the woman with the blue blouse asked. "I've never seen you before, and I don't think my sisters have either."

Adam stood up. "Maybe I should introduce everyone. This is Walt and Danielle Marlow," Adam began, gesturing toward the couple.

"I don't really care who they are," she snapped.

THE GHOST AND THE WITCHES' COVEN

"That's rude," Marie observed.

Startled by the hostile response, Danielle held out the necklace and said in a calm, emotionless voice, "I found this on the sidewalk. A woman said you dropped it. I was just trying to return it to its rightful owner."

"Finola, the white hawk!" one woman blurted.

The woman named Finola let out a gasp, and by reflex touched her neck to see if the necklace was truly gone. "I didn't even notice I'd lost it." The hostile expressions worn by the three women transformed into sheepish embarrassment.

"I apologize. I imagine I sounded rather rude," Finola said, taking the necklace from Danielle. "I'm afraid we've been a little overwhelmed this week with strangers wanting to talk to us."

Not understanding what the woman meant, Danielle said, "We just wanted to return it."

"Thank you. I still can't believe I didn't notice it came off." Finola studied the clasp for a moment and then said, "Looks like I'll have to get this repaired." She slipped the necklace in her purse.

Hesitantly, Danielle said, "If you don't mind if I ask, where did you buy the necklace?"

"Buy it? I didn't buy it. It's been in our family for generations. It's one of a kind," Finola said.

"We need to get going," the thinnest of the women announced.

"Yes, we must." Finola looked back at Adam and asked, "Is there anything else?"

"No, that's fine," Adam said.

Finola gave him a nod, looked at Danielle, thanked her again, and then marched out of the office with the other two women in tow.

After the door shut, Danielle looked at Adam and asked, "Who were they?"

"Some of my odder clients," Adam said.

"And ruder," Marie added.

Leslie walked into the office. She said a quick hello to Walt and Danielle and then looked at Adam and asked, "Did the Baird sisters pay their rent? I just passed them out front."

"They did. I left the receipt on your desk," Adam said. He then looked to Walt and Danielle and invited them into his private office. While Danielle had intended to just stop in to return the necklace, she was curious to learn more about the women.

A few minutes later, after going into the private office, the door shut and Adam at his desk and Walt and Danielle sitting in two chairs facing him, and Marie hovering nearby on an invisible chair, Danielle asked, "Who were they?"

"The Baird sisters. The one who lost the necklace is Finola, and the other two are Ina and Kenzy. Kenzy was the skinny one. They rent a house from us. Not vacation rental, but full time. A couple of blocks from you."

"Are they always so snotty?" Danielle asked.

With a shrug, Adam leaned back in his desk chair. "Not really. I think they're just a little overwhelmed from the unwanted attention this past week, since that article came out about that new shop down the street, Pagan Oils. They were telling me about it before you walked in."

"They own that store?" Danielle asked. "They do sort of look like witches."

Adam laughed. "Actually, you're half right. They don't own Pagan Oils, but they are witches—or so they claim."

"Why is Frederickport experiencing a sudden influx of witches?" Walt asked, only half teasing.

"And it isn't even Halloween," Danielle added.

"I don't know. I thought they were a little spacey when I first rented to them. I figured weird, but harmless. They told me the reason they didn't come in yesterday to pay the rent; because when they went out, people kept stopping to ask them questions. You know, small town. They didn't want to leave their house."

"What kind of questions?" Walt asked.

"That article about Pagan Oils, about the witches," Adam explained.

"I thought you said they don't own Pagan Oils," Danielle said.

"They don't. But they've never hidden the fact they call themselves witches. Leslie calls them a witches' coven. Imagine they dance around naked under the moonlight or something," Adam said with a snicker.

"Don't tell me you haven't checked it out yet?" Danielle teased.

"Danielle!" Marie scolded.

Walt chuckled.

"Not them. But those witches who own Pagan Oils, I saw one of them on the pier last night, chanting like she was casting a spell. But she had clothes on," Adam said.

"Seriously?" Danielle asked.

"Yeah. Carla told me who she was," Adam explained.

"So what's this about your tenants getting asked questions?" Danielle asked.

"The Pagan Oils article spiked people's curiosity about witches, especially some claims made about magic and spells, and I guess those curious people started pestering the Baird sisters, assuming they were part of that group. I mean, really, what is the chance Frederickport has two witches' covens?"

"Exactly how many witches are in these covens?" Walt asked.

Adam shrugged and said, "I've never heard about any other witches aside from the Baird sisters and Parker sisters. So, I assume, only three each."

"That's hardly a respectable coven size," Walt said with a snort. "I've always heard it takes a dozen witches to make a coven."

"I have no idea. But obviously the Bairds aren't actively soliciting new members, considering their reaction to people asking them questions," Adam said.

"So that's why they were so cranky?" Danielle asked.

"I assume. They were bitching about it when they came in to pay their rent."

"Are they Wicca witches?" Danielle asked. "Or do you know?"

"Oh god no!" Adam groaned. "And if you run into them again, whatever you do, don't ask them that. They don't have a great love for those who call themselves Wicca. I believe Ina called them wannabes."

"Which sounds a little like what the others said in that interview," Walt said.

"I didn't read the article, but Mel did. She told me about it. Asked me if they were 'my' witches." Adam smirked.

"All I know, they're witches with an attitude," Danielle said.

WHEN WALT and Danielle finally left Adam's office, Marie tagged along with them.

"I thought you'd stick around with Adam for a while," Danielle said when they were outside.

"I enjoy seeing Adam, but frankly, it's rather boring just staring at him. It's not like we can chat. If someone was in there with him, I could at least eavesdrop on a conversation," Marie explained.

"We're going to Lucy's for lunch," Walt said. "You're welcome to join us."

"Thank you, Walt. I'll meet you there. But first, I'm going to stop by Pagan Oils. I'm curious to see the other witches. I don't think I've ever seen actual witches before today," Marie said.

"You do know there really are no such things as witches, don't you?" Danielle teased.

Marie stopped and looked at Danielle. "You think so?"

Danielle shrugged. "Well, sure, I guess people can call themselves witches, like with the Wicca religion. But not witches with spells and magic or flying around on brooms."

"Oh, Danielle," Marie said, letting out a sigh. "There is so much you don't understand. To be fair, I didn't understand until I became a ghost." Marie vanished.

Danielle frowned at the abrupt departure. "Well, that was kinda rude."

"Let's go to lunch," Walt said, reaching out and taking Danielle's hand.

Danielle looked at Walt and asked, "What Marie said about witches and what she now understands since becoming a ghost… when you were…you know…did you learn anything about witches you haven't told me?"

Walt smiled. "Danielle, I spent close to a hundred years in Marlow House. I didn't get out much. And if there really are witches, none ever came to visit me."

NINE

After the Baird sisters left Adam's office, they started back down the street to their car, again passing Pagan Oils. The youngest sister, Kenzy, wanted to look in the window.

"We're not going in there," Finola called after Kenzy. No longer walking, she and Ina watched their younger sister head up to the store window.

"It won't hurt to just look," Ina said.

"I'm not sure about that, considering who owns the store. And did you watch their YouTube video I told you about? I can't believe the nonsense they came up with," Finola grumbled.

Ina chuckled at her sister's annoyance yet didn't let that keep her from joining Kenzy. She hurried to the window while Finola waited on the sidewalk, hands on hips, impatiently watching them.

Several minutes later Ina called out, "Finola, come here. See this!"

"I don't want to," Finola shouted back.

Ina turned to Finola. "Fi, come here."

Finola grumbled and dropped her hands to the sides of her body, her purse hanging from one shoulder. She reluctantly made her way to her two sisters.

"What is so important that I need to see?" Finola sounded bored.

"You will not believe this, but look." Ina pointed inside the store to a display pushed up against the window. Finola looked inside. What had caught her sisters' attention was a necklace display. Leather strap necklaces, each with a small whalebone carving.

What the sisters found uncanny was the necklace closest to the window, a carving of a hawk. One would assume whoever had carved that charm had also carved the one hanging from Finola's necklace. The other charms in the necklace display were of other animals: a bear, a fish, a deer, a dolphin, a horse, and a whale. As far as they could see, there was only one hawk.

"That is impossible," Finola muttered, getting closer to the window.

"It looks just like the White Hawk," Kenzy whispered.

Finola stared in disbelief at the small hawk carving in the window.

After a moment she lifted her gaze, looking farther into the store. She spied a woman standing behind the counter. The woman's gaze met Finola's, and the two stared at each other, trancelike.

Finally, Finola stepped back abruptly and said, "Let's get out of here. Now."

DAVINA CURSED when Finola turned and walked away from the store to the sidewalk, taking her sisters with her.

"They saw the necklace," Aileana said. "She was looking right at it. I thought for sure that would bring her in here."

"I wish they didn't need to come to us, that we could just approach them. It would make things easier," Davina said. "I thought for certain that when we opened the store, they would come in. And when that didn't happen, I was certain the article would bring them here. And now this. They look at the hawk and just leave!"

"Maybe it's all working; we just need to be patient. We've never been good at waiting," Bridget said.

"What do you mean? We've been waiting our entire lives," Aileana said.

"Which means I've been waiting longer than both of you, since I'm older. And they came to our doorstep. I suppose that is some progress. We just need to get them to step inside. Let them think about the white hawk, and they'll be back," Bridget said.

"And if they don't come back?" Ina asked.

Bridget let out a deep breath and looked at her sisters. "Actually, I have been giving that a great deal of thought, so I came up with a contingency plan. In fact, I've already put it in motion."

Davina frowned. "What in all the heavens are you talking about?"

"Remember the other option, using the spell to vanquish the coven standing in our way?" Bridget asked.

"Um, yes, but I seem to recall something about getting our hands on a high-quality ruby a little out of our price range. Unless you're considering a jewel heist?" Davina asked.

"No. but I took another look at the attraction spell. And I thought, why not?" Bridget said.

"What, you honestly think a high-quality three-carat ruby is going to drop out of the sky?" Davina asked.

"And you no longer have faith in spells?" Bridget asked.

"No, it's not that. But how I read that spell, all that would happen, it would put whatever you're looking for in close proximity. Like reading tomorrow about a sale on a three-carat ruby at a nearby jewelry store. We still have to buy it."

"Maybe not," Bridget said. "We can at least try."

"Let's say a ruby drops out of the sky and lands in our hands. How do we know the vanquishing spell will work? At least with the other one, no one will be the wiser if it doesn't work. With the vanquishing spell, we could have serious consequences if it back-fires," Davina reminded them.

"Not if we try it out first on another witch, get the kinks out, so to speak," Bridget said. "Of course, it has to be a blood witch."

"Are you suggesting we kill an innocent witch?" Davina asked.

"Isn't that a bit of an oxymoron," Bridget countered. The three sisters laughed.

When they finally stopped laughing, Aileana said, "While that all sounds promising, this means we have to find not only a blood witch—but a ruby large enough for the spell to work."

Bridget grinned. "You will be happy to learn last night while you two were sleeping, I went down to the pier and cast the attraction spell, asking for the ruby and for a sacrificial blood witch. One way or another, the Leabar will return to its rightful place—with us."

Before her sisters responded, the door opened, and several new customers walked into the shop. Following them was the spirit of Marie Nichols.

NO ONE COULD SEE or hear Marie Nichols as she wandered around the odd little shop, checking out the merchandise. She resisted the temptation to pick up any of the items to get a closer look, not wanting to freak anyone out. Yet, once she thought about it, she figured it might actually help the little business. Once word got out about merchandise literally floating off shelves or racks, it might bring in new customers. Marie chuckled to herself at the thought.

The people she had followed into the store now stood at the counter, asking one question after another of the three women who were already in the store when they had arrived moments earlier. Marie wandered to one wall and looked at the shelves lined with tiny glass bottles. They reminded her of the essential oils Heather kept and frequently used.

Marie stepped closer to the shelves so she could get a better look. While she no longer needed glasses to see clearly, it didn't mean she could read a label from across the room. "Angelica root, bergamot, birch sweet, cajeput, clove bud, lemon grass," Marie muttered as she read some labels. Pivoting from the wall, she spied books on the other side of the store, along with a barrel filled with small straw brooms. Moving closer to the barrel, she didn't imagine a proper witch could fly on one of those things—too small. Next to the barrel the sign read "besom" along with a price.

Marie then noticed a display of necklaces by the window. She went to have a closer look.

THE SERVER SET the plate with a cheeseburger and fries on the table in front of Walt, and the one with a turkey sandwich and coleslaw on the table in front of Danielle.

"Will there be anything else?" the server asked.

Danielle looked over her plate and then glanced up to the server and smiled. "No, I don't think so."

Walt had already picked up his burger. The server flashed them both a smile and then walked away.

"That looks yummy," Marie announced when she appeared the next minute, sitting next to Danielle and across from Walt.

"How was Pagan Oils?" Danielle asked, picking up half her sandwich.

"I know why they call it Pagan Oils; they have an entire wall with those oils Heather uses."

"Essential oils?" Danielle asked.

"Yes. I read the labels, and some of them I never heard of before," Marie said.

"Eye of newt oil?" Walt snickered before taking another bite.

"I didn't see that, but they had some interesting witch paraphernalia."

"Witch paraphernalia?" Danielle chuckled.

Marie shrugged. "Not sure what else to call it. Do you know they have a YouTube channel? I saw a brochure on it, thought you might be interested. I was going to bring you one, but I didn't think that would be a terrific idea. Oh, I also know where that snotty Finola woman got that necklace."

"Pagan Oils?" Danielle asked with a frown.

Marie nodded. "Yes, they have a rack of them, all different little animals. Including one that looked just like that woman's. Although, the leather cord was a little different, so I suppose she might have bought it somewhere else."

"I don't know what the point of her lying about the necklace being some family heirloom was all about." Danielle then asked, "Any whales or dolphins?"

"Yes," Marie said. "If you go to the store, the display with the necklaces is by the window."

Walt set down his burger and looked at Danielle. "You want to see what they have?"

"Yeah."

Marie glanced at the wall clock. "I need to get going. See you two later." She vanished.

"Darn, I wanted to ask her about the witches," Danielle grumbled. "Why does she keep disappearing like that?"

BRIAN HENDERSON OPENED the door to Lucy's Diner, letting his cousin enter first. He followed her inside while looking for an empty booth or table. When doing so, he spied Walt and Danielle Marlow. A moment later, he stopped by their booth with Kitty by his side.

"Afternoon, Walt, Danielle," Brian greeted them.

Danielle smiled up at the pair and then looked at the woman at Brian's side and said, "Is this your cousin?"

"Kitty, this is Walt and Danielle Marlow. I believe I mentioned them," Brian introduced.

Walt stood briefly to greet Kitty while Danielle laughed and said, "I bet you did."

They exchanged a few more words before Brian and Kitty excused themselves to sit at a booth on the other side of the restaurant.

"So that was the infamous Walt and Danielle Marlow?" Kitty asked after she sat down.

"In the flesh," Brian said, picking up a menu and handing it to his cousin.

"He seemed rather—I don't know—old fashioned," Kitty said with a smile as she opened her menu.

"Old-fashioned, how?" he asked.

"I don't know. Something about his manner, his way of dress. And I can tell he's an author. Not that I've ever met one before, but he looks like I would expect one to look like. I'm almost surprised he wasn't smoking a pipe."

"It irritates Joe, how Walt dresses."

"Heavens, why?"

"His girlfriend has been trying to dress him up like Walt. I guess she likes it."

"There is something about a man in tailored clothes. But they are an attractive couple. I can't believe you arrested her for murder."

TEN

Brad Stewart stretched lazily on the worn sofa, his feet propped on the battered coffee table, while using the remote to channel hop. When his father had purchased the property from his cousin, the house came with some furniture. They had intended to toss it out before demolishing the building, but none of that was happening now.

"Where are the truck keys?" Kathy asked.

Brad looked up at his sister, who stood over him with her hand out. She wore a baggy pair of jeans and a blue sweatshirt.

"Where are you going? Slumming it? Mom would love that outfit."

"Yeah, well, Mom is not my favorite person right now, and these clothes are comfortable. Keys."

"I was planning to go get some beer."

"Then you take me, drop me off at Pagan Oils, and buy your beer. You can pick me up when I'm done."

Brad turned the television off and tossed the remote on the coffee table. "Why are you going there?"

Kathy shoved a hand into her jeans pocket and pulled something out and showed her brother.

Seeing what Kathy held, Brad sat up abruptly, putting his feet on the floor. "What the hell are you doing with that?"

"I took it from Mom's jewelry box." Kathy shoved it back in her pocket. She sat down on the sofa next to her brother.

"I figured that. You aren't planning to hock that thing, are you? Mom will skin you alive if she finds out."

"No. I'm not planning to hock it."

Brad let out a sigh of relief. "Good. You had me worried there."

"I'm giving it away."

"What? Are you nuts?"

Kathy looked at her brother. "I know you think this whole witch thing is crazy. But we need Dad back to get Mom under control. I don't plan to keep slumming it. Not when our family is still rich. Even after the settlement to the Jenkins family, we still have plenty of money. And we're entitled to it. We were the ones over here getting rid of all the dead bodies, not Mom. What has Mom done beside spend Dad's money?"

"What does Mom's ring have to do with any of that?"

"The website I told you about. It talked about a spell to destroy a witch. It didn't say what the spell was exactly. That's too dangerous for them to post online."

"Yeah, right," Brad muttered.

"Only another witch can do the spell, and it requires a ruby—one at least three carats in size. And it has to be excellent quality. Mom's is three and a half carats, and we both know what Dad paid for this sucker."

"So you plan to get the witches to off Donovan? Don't tell me, hit-men witches?"

Kathy let out a huff in annoyance. "It's not like an actual hit. It's safer."

"Safer how?"

"They make her not just disappear, but all memory of her disappears too. So it's not like someone is going to arrest you for murder or anything."

"And why would these witches do this for you?"

"Because I'll let them keep the ruby. According to the website, whenever a witch uses a ruby in a spell, the ruby absorbs power witches can use later. They'll be happy to do it for me."

"How do you know they'll be thrilled knocking off one of their own kind?"

"They are witches, Brad."

"Okay, so let's say this works—which frankly sounds real out there. Dad will still be locked up."

"I know. But he'll be in his right mind again. And we need Dad in his right mind so he can get Mom under control.

AFTER THEY FINISHED their lunch on Thursday afternoon, Walt and Danielle walked up to the new candy store. Danielle got her free samples and ended up spending over forty dollars on gourmet dark chocolate. On the way back to where they had parked the Packard, they walked up to Pagan Oils and peeked in the front window to check out the necklace display.

"The dolphin is adorable," Danielle said.

"You want to go inside and get it?" Walt asked.

Danielle glanced down at the sack in her hand and then looked up to Walt. "We can come back later. It's warm out here, and this free chocolate was kinda expensive. I don't want it to melt."

KATHY STEWART STOOD across the street, looking toward Pagan Oils. She had noticed the Packard immediately, which was why she remained on the opposite side of the street after Brad dropped her off. She stood within the branches of a massive pine tree. Looking toward the store, she spied two people at its front window. It was not until they turned around did she recognize them: Walt and Danielle Marlow. She stepped back in the branches and waited. The Marlows walked to the Packard. Walt opened the door for Danielle and held it as she got into the car.

"Oh, what a gentleman," Kathy snarked under her breath. She watched as Walt closed the door and then walked to the driver's side and got in. After a few minutes, the Packard pulled out into the street and drove away.

When the car was no longer in sight, Kathy walked to the street, paused a moment, and looked both ways for oncoming traffic. When there was none, she hurried across to the other side. Once there, she paused on the sidewalk in front of Pagan Oils for a moment and dug one hand into her pants pocket and pulled out the ring. Its large ruby glittered in the afternoon sun.

"Oh, Mother, you never wore this thing anyway. Let's see if this can help slay a witch," Kathy muttered, shoving the ring back into her pocket. She headed up the walkway to the store's front entrance. Just as she was about to reach for the door handle, the door opened, and a couple of customers walked out. They both greeted Kathy, and one held the door open for her as she entered the building.

Once inside, Kathy glanced around, taking in the shop's unique inventory. There was only one other person in the store, a redhead standing behind the counter. Kathy recognized her immediately. She was one of the women she had seen in the YouTube videos on witchcraft. There were three of them—sisters. Kathy remembered their names from watching the videos: Bridget, Davina, and Aileana Parker. But she didn't know which sister stood behind the counter; they looked so much alike.

As in the videos Kathy had seen, this one wore a kaftan, which seemed to be the sisters' preferred style of dress. In the videos she noticed the fabrics were nature themed, such as the dress this one wore today, a black background with crescent moons and cartoonish sun images.

BRIDGET WONDERED if the new customer was just a curious lookie-loo. She doubted she was a blood witch conjured up by last night's spell. It would be convenient, but unlikely. It wasn't that she didn't think the spell would work, but she didn't expect it to work overnight.

"May I help you find something?" Bridget called out.

The woman walked to the counter and asked, "You're one of the owners of Pagan Oils, one of the Parker sisters, correct?"

Bridget grinned and said, "Yes. I'm Bridget Parker. You saw the article in last Sunday's paper?"

"Actually, I'm a fan of your YouTube channel. My name is Kathy Stewart."

"Nice to meet you, Kathy. Oh, tell me, are you a sister witch?" Bridget asked in a whisper while thinking, *I would not be that lucky—an unsuspecting blood witch walking in my door.*

"The way you ask, might there be some reason I wouldn't want to acknowledge the fact out loud?"

"Well, they did use to burn us at the stake. So the answer is yes?"

Kathy shook her head. "No. Just someone curious about—your way of life."

"If you've watched our videos, you'll know it's more than our way of life. It's who we are. Who we've been since before our birth," Bridget said.

"You've really always known you were a witch?"

"Yes. We are blood witches, meaning we come from a long line of witches. They are the only true witches."

"I watched the one video where you talked about Wicca. I'm sort of surprised you were so—blunt. I would think those people would be your—well—customer base."

Bridget laughed. "Yes, many are our customers. But if I am to help them—or anyone who seeks what we offer—that requires complete honesty."

"And what do you offer, exactly?" Kathy asked.

"First, you need to understand there are two types of witches, the blood witch, which I mentioned, and then the self-taught witch. A self-taught witch can learn how to use spells, but her powers never come from within, always from external sources."

"You have a power that doesn't come from an outside source?" Kathy asked.

"Yes," Bridget said with a nod.

"Would it be possible for a self-taught witch to make something fly, or would that be something only a blood witch could do?"

Bridget smiled. "A self-taught witch could never make something fly. And frankly, only the most powerful of blood witches can make anything fly."

"Do you know many blood witches?" Kathy asked.

"I know of other blood witches. But the only ones I know personally are my two sisters."

"I know a blood witch," Kathy whispered.

Bridget felt her heart race—*a blood witch?* Was it possible the spell had worked so quickly? "Please, tell me about this blood witch. I am…very interested."

"Her name is Heather Donovan; do you know her?" Kathy asked.

"No. I'm not familiar with that name. Is she from around here?" After asking, Bridget thought, *Oh, please say she is!*

"She lives on Beach Drive, near the pier."

"And how do you know she's a blood witch?"

"She told my father she's a witch," Kathy explained.

Bridget let out a disappointed sigh. She knew it was too good to be true. Many people claimed to be witches who were not blood witches.

"She cast a spell on my father. She made him fly around the room. So she must be a blood witch," Kathy said. "She has destroyed my family, and I want her vanquished." Kathy then pulled the ruby ring from her pocket and set it on the counter before Bridget.

Bridget's eyes widened as she stared down at the ring.

"It's three and a half carats," Kathy explained. "You can have it. All I ask is that you vanquish Heather Donovan."

ELEVEN

"I can't believe you wanted to come here for dinner," Aileana said after the hostess showed them to a booth overlooking the ocean at Pearl Cove. She sat next to Davina, while Bridget sat across from them.

"You've both been wanting to come here, and I thought tonight it would be the ideal place to celebrate," Bridget said primly as she picked up the cloth napkin and shook it out before setting it on her lap.

The server took their drink orders and then left them alone at the booth.

"What are we celebrating? It's not the store's first-month anniversary yet," Davina said.

"It is much better than that," Bridget told her.

"Oh, I know. You got your hands on the Leabar, and we can get on with our lives," Aileana suggested.

"Not exactly, but you're getting warmer." Bridget picked up her purse off the seat next to her and pulled out a small box. She removed its lid and handed it across the table to Davina and said, "Look, but do not remove it from the box. I don't want any curious eyes in here to see it."

Davina took the box and held it between her and Aileana. They looked inside and gasped. By reflex, Aileana reached in the box, but

Bridget quickly reprimanded her, and the younger sister withdrew her hand.

"As you can see, the spell worked," Bridget said proudly.

They handed the box back to Bridget and then listened while she explained how she had obtained the ruby. When she finished, Davina said, "If you think about it, there's no reason to try the spell on the other blood witch. Heather Donovan, that's her name, right?"

"Why do you say that?" Bridget asked.

"Wasn't the point in sacrificing a blood witch just to make certain the spell works? Obviously, it does. The proof is sitting in your purse," Davina reminded her.

"The only reason Bridget got the ruby in the first place was by agreeing to vanquish Donovan," Aileana reminded her.

Davina laughed. "I don't think this Stewart person is going to try getting her ruby back. What exactly will she tell the police?"

"Trying the spell on Heather Donovan has nothing to do with honoring our side of the bargain. Although, even if we decided not to do it, we would still keep the ruby. As Davina pointed out, why would we give it back?"

"Why keep the ruby?" Aileana asked.

"Are you forgetting, each time it vanquishes a blood witch, her power goes into the ruby. Why would we walk away from that? And the sacrifice witch is obviously powerful if she could make a man fly," Bridget said.

"And very dangerous," Aileana reminded her.

"Which means we have to be very careful," Bridget said.

"Do you have something specific in mind?" Davina asked.

"We need to find this Heather Donovan and learn as much about her as possible. We need to assess her powers and determine how best to get her into a cooperative state before casting our spell," Bridget explained.

"TO WALT, on success with his second book," Ian said, lifting his champagne glass in toast. Next to him, his wife, Lily, lifted her glass. It was the first time in weeks she had left Connor with a sitter, but tonight was for the adults. To Lily's right was the man of the hour,

Walt Marlow, and her best friend and Walt's wife, Danielle. Next to them sat Chris Johnson and Heather Donovan. They all joined Ian in toasting Walt.

"Will this one be another *New York Times* bestseller?" Chris asked after taking a sip of his champagne.

"I don't think lightning will strike twice," Walt said humbly.

"Don't listen to him," Ian told the others. "I talked to our agent today, and he told me Walt's manuscript arrived in his email late Tuesday evening, and he only intended to have a look at it before going to bed, and once again, he ended up reading the entire thing. He didn't go to sleep until the next morning!"

"Was he mad at Walt for keeping him up all night?" Heather teased.

"Hardly. That's what agents dream about; books readers can't put down. He was rather excited about it," Ian said.

Danielle grinned at Walt. "I'm very proud of him."

"Yeah, well, it seems unfair. He does have the advantage over other authors in the same genre," Chris teased.

"How so?" Danielle asked.

"Think of all the research he can skip on life in the twenties. He lived them," Chris said.

"Not to mention he used to be a moonshiner in his other life," Lily teased. They all laughed.

A few minutes later, the direction of the conversation shifted when Heather spied Brian Henderson being seated across the restaurant from them with a woman.

"Hey, look who's here," Heather said. "Brian Henderson, and he's with a woman. I wonder who she is."

Danielle glanced toward Brian's table and said, "It's his cousin."

Believing Danielle was just trying to be funny, Heather said, "No, I'm serious, who do you think she is?"

"I was being serious. It's his cousin. Her name is Kitty. She's staying with him this week. Walt and I met her this afternoon," Danielle said.

"Ahh, that's too bad. I sort of hoped old Brian was finally getting out there. His luck sucks with women," Heather said sympathetically.

"Why? Just because the last two women he's gotten involved with—that we know about—were killers?" Walt asked.

"Maybe it would be better for ol' Brian if he stuck to his cousin," Heather said with a snort. "Although I'm surprised he's not seeing anyone. He's kind of good looking."

Lily glanced over to Brian and then back to Heather. "I suppose. He's got nice hair."

"It's gray," Ian said.

"Yeah, but men look good in gray hair," Heather said.

Lily let out a sigh. "True. But I confess, it's hard for me to look at Brian and find him attractive, considering how much grief he gave us."

"Oh, I have to tell you guys what Brian saw at our house the other day," Danielle said. She then told her friends about Walt flying her around the living room on a broom and Brian witnessing it all.

"And he believed it was a trick?" Lily asked.

"What else could he believe, that Danielle can really fly a broom?" Ian asked.

"You know what they say," Heather said.

"People believe what they want to believe," they all chorused.

"That flying-broom thing is hilarious," Heather said. "I think Walt should fly me over the old Barr place and scare the crap out of Beau's kids since they're staying there."

"They are?" Lily asked.

"Yeah. Heather saw them parked on our street, watching our houses. We told the chief about it, and he said they're staying at the old Barr house. I guess their mother cut them off," Danielle explained.

Danielle then looked at Heather and said, "And having Walt fly you over the Barr place is a bad idea."

"Why? I'm sure their dad told them how I'm a witch. I guess he's been telling everyone. Would be hilarious. Maybe they would get locked up with dear old dad."

"The problem, I know the son has a gun. He just might try shooting you out of the sky. Target practice," Danielle said.

"Walt could protect me," Heather insisted.

"Sorry, Heather. Danielle is right. I could fly you over the Barr property, but it would require complete concentration. If I had to take my focus off you and use it to stop the bullet—"

"You would fall out of the sky," Chris finished for Walt. "A very undignified ending for the witchy woman. And I would probably have to look for a new assistant."

THE GHOST AND THE WITCHES' COVEN

Heather gave Chris's arm a playful swat, and they all laughed.

"THE ONE IN the blue shirt is Ian Bartley, but you probably know him as Jon Altar," Brian told his cousin as they sipped their cocktails and glanced over to the table with the Beach Drive residents. Brian had noticed them when the server had brought Kitty and him their drinks.

"You told me he lived here. And the redhead next to him, I assume that is his wife?"

"Yes. Lily. She's the one who used to live with Danielle at Marlow House, when they first moved to town."

"Ahh, she's the one who sucker punched you," Kitty teased.

"No. It was not Lily."

"Who is that cutie sitting next to the vampire?" Kitty asked.

Brian laughed. "I assume you're talking about Chris Johnson. Who, by the way, is really Chris Glandon."

"That is Chris Glandon? Wow, billions and he looks like that? You would think he could have any woman he wants. But he goes for goth? Is goth even in now?"

"That's Heather Donovan, and for the record, I don't think they're dating. She works for him. She's also not a vampire," Brian said.

"I am relieved to hear that," Kitty said with a chuckle.

"But rumor has it, she is a witch." Brian took a swig of his drink.

Kitty arched her brows. "Witch? As in one of those Wicca people?"

Brian shook his head. "I don't think so. She's more the cast-the-evil-spell, make-things-fly-across-the-room type of witch."

"Oh, Brian, is this about the weird stuff that happens at Marlow House? The broom flying around the living room?"

Brian chuckled. "No. Actually, it's not. It's what Beau Stewart claimed." He then told his cousin about the arrest of Beau Stewart and his outrageous claims regarding Heather Donovan.

"AILEANA, I ASKED YOU A QUESTION," Bridget said impatiently, annoyed that her baby sister seemed to be ignoring her.

Aileana quickly put up one hand and shushed her sister while she stared across the dining room. "I am listening, and it is very interesting."

Bridget and Davina immediately understood their sister was not listening per se, but reading the lips of someone in the restaurant. They glanced to where Aileana had fixed her gaze.

"Isn't that a cop? I've seen him around town," Davina said.

Aileana nodded. "Yes, and you want to see what Heather Donovan looks like?"

"That's not the woman he's with, is it?" Bridget asked. She had not expected the blood witch to look like a boring middle-aged woman.

Aileana waved her hand again to silence them. Bridget and Davina sat quietly, their eyes shifting from Aileana to the police officer and his dinner companion. Finally, Aileana let out a deep breath and looked back to her sisters and said, "Okay, they're talking about boring stuff now. But that was interesting."

"What did you mean when you asked if we wanted to see what Heather Donovan looks like?" Bridget asked.

Aileana nodded to another table and said, "The round table, with six people. The girl with the long black hair, that is Heather Donovan."

"Are you sure?" Davina asked.

"Yes. I could only pick up a little of what they were saying at that table. But the cop, they were talking about the people at Donovan's table. And guess what?"

"What?" Davina and Bridget asked at the same time.

"According to the cop, someone named Beau Stewart claims Donovan is a witch," Aileana said.

"The woman who gave me the ruby. Her name is Kathy Stewart. Beau Stewart must be her father."

"That's all interesting, but you know, the man making the claim could be a mental case," Davina pointed out.

"I might agree with you if the spell hadn't worked," Bridget reminded her. "If I hadn't cast that spell, and that woman walked in and claimed she knew a blood witch, I would not give her stories of the witch making people fly much credence. We all know it takes special powers to make something fly. But I used the spell to bring a ruby and a blood witch to us. It brought the ruby, and I have to believe Heather Donovan really is a blood witch."

"We still have to learn all we can about her so we don't make any mistakes. Now we know what she looks like. And I also learned she works for the one sitting next to her. While she's at work, I think we plant a camera in her house and learn as much about her as we can before we make our move," Aileana suggested.

TWELVE

Hunny the brindle pit bull sat in the passenger seat, looking out the car window, her tongue sloppily hanging from her mouth in a happy pant. Next to her, in the driver's seat, Chris Johnson, aka Chris Glandon, turned down the alleyway and drove past the rear of Marlow House and then passed Pearl Huckabee's before stopping. Leaving the engine running, he parked behind Heather's house and rolled down the passenger window, letting Hunny stick her snout out to drink up some fresh air. Several moments later, he saw Heather walking toward the car, her calico cat, Bella, scooped up in one arm, while her purse hung from the opposing shoulder.

Today Heather wore her ebony-colored hair pulled up on the top of her head, in a haphazard knot. She wore her high-heeled black boots with leggings, and a bulky lightweight pullover sweater, its hemline falling mid-thigh.

"Morning," Heather called out as she approached the car.

"In the back seat, Hunny," Chris called out. The next moment the pit bull jumped in the back seat while Heather opened the passenger car door and got in. She tossed the cat in the back with the dog.

Hunny, over eight times larger than Bella, cowered in one corner, looking uneasily at the cat, while the petite feline pranced back and forth, taking her time deciding exactly where she wanted to sit.

"Behave yourself, Bella," Heather called out as she shut the car door behind her. "Thanks again for picking me up. They promise my car will be ready this afternoon."

"No problem," Chris said, pulling away from her back drive.

They hadn't gone far down the alleyway when they spied a young redhead walking in their direction. She smiled at them when they drove by.

"I haven't seen her before," Chris noted.

"And I would expect you to notice all the hot young ladies in the neighborhood," Heather teased.

"Does she live around here?" Chris asked, glancing briefly in the rearview mirror. The redhead was no longer walking, but standing in the same place, watching Chris's car drive away.

"Probably a summer visitor. I don't recognize her," Heather said with a shrug.

They turned down another street and a few moments later stopped at the corner. While waiting for the car in the opposing traffic to pass, they both looked to their right at the well-worn two-story house in desperate need of care. Two women—both redheads—stood by a van parked in the driveway, looking as if they were preparing to leave.

"Oh, my gawd," Heather said with a laugh. "The invasion of the redheads."

"That was weird," Chris said, now steering his car across the intersection. "Triplets?"

"The one we saw walking in the alley looked just like those two. Even their dresses were similar, just different colors. You think I should tell Lily her people are looking for her?" Heather joked.

BRIDGET STOOD with Davina by the car, holding her cellphone to her ear as she watched the vehicle carrying Heather Donovan drive away.

"They just went by," Bridget said into the phone, talking to Aileana, who was on the other side of the call.

The previous evening, while having dinner at Pearl Cove, they had asked their server who the woman with the black hair was, saying she looked familiar, and they were trying to place her.

The server told them the woman was Heather Donovan, and

she worked for the Glandon Foundation, as did the man sitting next to her, who was Heather's boss. Bridget thought it useful how people in a small town seemed to know so much about their neighbors and regular customers. Some were even willing to share that information.

According to the server, Heather was single, lived alone, had no dogs, just a cat, was into essential oils, liked to jog, and had a peculiar reputation for finding corpses on the beach. Hearing that, Bridget suspected Heather was not what one would call a good witch. That meant they needed to take special care in the handling of her vanquishing.

When the Parker sisters had returned home the previous night from Pearl Cove, they went online to learn as much as they could about the Glandon Foundation and where its offices were located. They learned Heather Donovan would likely pass their house when going to work the next morning. And she did.

THAT MORNING, Bridget had driven Aileana partway to Heather's house, dropping her off at the entrance to the alleyway so she could walk in to avoid being seen. Since Heather's garage door had been closed, Aileana had assumed that was where Heather parked her car and expected the opening of a garage door to serve as a warning Heather was leaving for the morning, giving her time to hide in a nearby bush. She hadn't expected Chris Johnson to come driving down the alley to pick up Heather. While they had both gotten a good look at her, she didn't feel that reason enough to cancel the plan. Anyway, when this was all over, Chris Johnson wouldn't remember that Heather Donovan ever existed.

After ending the call with Bridget, Aileana shoved the cellphone in her hoodie's pocket and pulled the hood up to cover her bright red hair. If someone saw her entering Donovan's house, she didn't want them to mention her hair color, which could help in identifying her, especially since Heather and Chris had looked right at her when driving off minutes earlier.

Everything she needed was in her backpack. Of the three sisters, she was the techie one, the one who already owned an assortment of computer gadgets and cameras, and the one best suited to install cameras. She had just entered the back of Heather's property when she heard a door opening and closing at the house to the north. Aileana peeked through two bushes into the neighbor's yard and spied an older woman picking up something from a patio table and then returning to the house. She heard the door open and close again. Confident the woman had gone inside, Aileana continued up to Heather's back door.

The cameras Aileana planned to install required Wi-Fi for them to transfer the data to her computer at home. She came up with a plan A and a plan B to deal with providing Wi-Fi. If Donovan had Wi-Fi and had written the password somewhere easy to find, perhaps on the router or on a piece of paper in her desk, then she would use Donovan's own Wi-Fi. That was plan A. But, if she couldn't find the password, she would go to plan B, which required she leave her cellphone hidden outside as a hotspot for the cameras.

It didn't take Aileana long to discover plan A would work, and there was no reason to leave her cellphone behind. Heather had conveniently written her password on her router. Just in case someone found the cameras before they eliminated Donovan, Aileana took extra effort not to leave fingerprints behind.

FOCUSED on reading the incoming emails, Heather didn't immediately notice the snowflakes falling from the ceiling, landing on her desk and disappearing. When she finally noticed, she glanced up, watched the snowflakes for a moment and said, "Good morning, Eva. But it doesn't snow in August."

A moment later the spirit appeared, and all traces of snow vanished. Although she bore an uncanny likeness to Charles Dana Gibson's famous Gibson Girl, she was in truth the ghost of silent screen star Eva Thorndike.

"What are you doing here?" Eva asked once she fully materialized, now standing by Heather's desk.

"I do work here. This is my office, you know," Heather said dryly.

"It's just that I didn't see your car out front," Eva explained as she took a seat on a nearby chair.

Heather swiveled around in her desk chair and faced Eva. "My car is in the shop. Chris gave me a lift today."

Eva glanced around. "Where is he?"

"I heard him go into the bathroom a minute ago. You'll probably find him there."

"It seems people don't appreciate when I show up in the bathroom with them. I think I'll wait here."

Heather chuckled. "Yeah. Probably a good idea."

Heather turned to her desk and then thought of something she wanted to ask Eva, so she turned back to the ghost. "I have a question. I was going to ask Walt about it, but you might know."

"Know what?" Eva asked.

"It's about a house I pass every day going to work. It's a cool-looking old house. I'm sure they built it before you died. It's been boarded up since I moved to Frederickport, but some people moved in about a month or so ago, and I saw them this morning. At least I assume they live there. I was curious about the history of that place and wonder if you might know anything about it." Heather then gave Eva the location of the house she and Chris had seen the two redheads at earlier that morning.

"Yes, of course! That is dear Wallace's place." Eva smiled.

"Dear Wallace?" Heather asked.

"He was a friend of mine, came from family money."

"Like you?" Heather smirked.

Eva shrugged. "It wasn't my fault Mommy and Daddy were so rich."

"I would've liked to have had that problem," Heather grumbled under her breath.

"But like me, Wallace had his own dreams," Eva said.

"Was he an actor too?" Heather asked.

"Wallace? Oh, no. He was a playwright. I'm afraid not a very good one, but he did so try. His enthusiasm was inspiring, yet also distracting."

"How so?" Heather asked.

Eva pondered the question a moment as the tip of her right index finger momentarily tapped the side of her chin. Finally, she said, "He was very…tactile."

Heather frowned. "Tactical?"

"No, no. Tactile. In that he connected to the sensory. But I suppose tactical might also apply. He did carefully plan."

Heather frowned. "I don't understand."

"For example, one of his plays was about a struggling artist. So Wallace spent one summer painting—immersing himself into the life of an artist. He bought an easel, oil paints, brushes, and even started wearing a beret. Those objects, just holding them, touching them, fed his creativity. It also distracted him from actually writing."

"That sounds more like something an actor would do, not a writer."

"Perhaps." Eva shrugged.

"Was he a good painter?" Heather asked.

"Dreadful. Almost as bad as the plays he wrote. But he was a darling, and he kept trying."

"Did he ever achieve success as a playwright?" Heather asked.

"No. But I do believe he enjoyed his life, something you can't say about everyone. He would come up with a new idea for a play, set himself on an adventure, and then try writing about it. I honestly believe the plays were just a front. It gave him an excuse to try new things, walk in someone else's shoes."

"What happened to him?" Heather asked.

"I would look in on him occasionally after I died. Of course, he couldn't see or hear me. He continued to explore and write until the very end. He was working on a play about witches when he had a heart attack and died. I saw him one last time before he moved over to the other side."

"What happened to his play on witches?" Heather asked.

Eva shrugged. "Like all his other plays, nothing."

"Did he have a family? Who inherited his house?" Heather asked.

"He didn't have a wife or children. He wasn't particularly interested in women or children. I imagine the house went to some relative. I recall people living there after he moved on. But a number of years ago, someone boarded up the windows. I'm glad to hear the house is being used again."

"It needs a lot of work." Heather said. "I can't believe the people living there now are renting it. Who would rent a house in that condition? And if it recently sold, I never saw a for sale sign on the house. But I suppose that means nothing."

"I should pop over there sometime and check out the new occupants. Maybe they are distant relatives of dear Wallace."

"Let me know what you find out," Heather said.

"Or you could just stop over there and introduce yourself," Eva suggested.

"Why would I do that?" Heather frowned.

"It is considered good form to welcome new neighbors," Eva said.

"They aren't my neighbors," Heather said.

"They are fellow Frederickport neighbors," Eva insisted.

Heather shrugged and swiveled her chair back to face the desk. "I don't think so."

THIRTEEN

Chris dropped Heather and Bella off at the auto repair shop before five p.m. on Friday so she could get her car. After picking up the vehicle, Heather headed straight for home. She was no longer dating the guy she had been seeing for the last few months, so she didn't have any plans for Friday night. But she knew what she was having for dinner, and she had been thinking of it since Bella had pilfered her tuna fish sandwich when Heather had left it unsupervised while going to the bathroom to wash her hands before lunch.

Friday dinner plans included leftovers from Pearl Cove. Heather had gotten into the habit of requesting a to-go carton when dining at restaurants serving large amounts of food. That way she could put half of the dinner in the carton to save for the next day. Pearl Cove served generous portions, and this way she didn't leave the restaurant feeling stuffed.

"You are not getting my dinner too," Heather told Bella as she used one foot to nudge the cat from the refrigerator. The cat meowed and began weaving around Heather's ankles.

Ignoring the animal, Heather opened the refrigerator door and retrieved the container of leftovers. She had ordered the seafood platter the night before. That meant dinner tonight was rice pilaf, half a portion of salmon, and three shrimp prawns—one fried in tempura and the other two scampi. The only item she would warm in the microwave was the rice. Heather didn't mind cold fish. Bella would love cold fish. But she wasn't getting any tonight, Heather told herself as she prepared her plate and warmed the rice.

Before taking her dinner to the living room to eat in front of the television, Heather gave Bella a can of cat food. Offended by the offering, Bella put her nose up and wandered off to the hallway.

"IS SHE HOME YET?" Davina asked Aileana, who sat in front of the computer in the den.

"Yes. But if this doesn't get more interesting, I'm going to record it and watch it later on high speed."

"But won't that make it difficult to hear what is being said?" Davina asked, taking a seat next to her sister at the desk. She looked over Aileana's shoulder at the computer monitor.

"I don't have sound hooked up."

"Why not?" Davina asked.

"Because the cameras' microphones don't work," Aileana said.

"Couldn't you get some with mics that work?"

"You guys wanted me to set the cameras up this morning. I doubt I could find what we need in Frederickport. I used what I already had," Aileana said impatiently.

"What is she doing?" Bridget asked when walking into the room the next moment.

Aileana glanced up at her sister and said, "She just got home. She's now sitting in the living room, eating dinner. This is boring."

HEATHER HEARD A KNOCK, and then someone called out, "You-hooo!"

With a smile, Heather looked up from her food and said, "It's okay, Marie, you can show yourself."

The next moment Marie appeared in the living room. "I am trying to do better and not just barge in. You're not getting any younger. I might give you a heart attack one of these days if I just pop in suddenly."

Heather frowned at Marie. "Thank you…I think?"

THE GHOST AND THE WITCHES' COVEN

"What's for dinner?" Marie asked, sneaking a peek at Heather's now empty plate before taking a seat on one of the nearby chairs.

"Leftovers from Pearl Cove. It was tasty." Heather set the empty plate on the coffee table and leaned back. "So what's up?"

Bella, who wandered in the living room after hearing Marie, jumped up on the coffee table and started sniffing the empty plate, looking for any tasty crumbs she might salvage. Heather ignored Bella, instead paying attention to Marie.

"I wanted to tell you I stopped into that new store over by Adam's office."

"The gourmet candy store?" Heather asked.

"No. Pagan Oils and More."

"I was thinking of checking that place out. Anything interesting?" Heather asked.

"They have a wide selection of those oils you like."

"Hmmm. Gee, maybe I really am a witch." Heather chuckled.

"Why do you say that?"

"I swear by essential oils, and you're telling me a witch store is selling them," Heather teased. "I have to admit they sometimes act like magic. I like frankincense. I think that's my favorite."

"Ahh, one gift the wise men brought Jesus," Marie noted. "What exactly do you do with it? I have to admit, I never really paid much attention to what frankincense was."

"I am surprised, Marie. Well, my favorite use for it, getting rid of those annoying little skin tags and wannabee moles. I swear by it. Works like magic." Heather paused and then said, "See, I am a witch, working on magic spells with my frankincense oil."

"WHO IS SHE TALKING TO?" Davina asked. The three sisters now hovered around the computer monitor, watching Heather.

"The cat, I guess," Aileana said with a shrug. They watched as the cat stood on the coffee table, sniffing and licking the plate Heather had just set there.

"What is she saying to the cat?" Bridget asked.

"Your guess is as good as mine," Aileana said.

"Why don't you read her lips?" Davina asked.

Aileana scowled at her sister. "Seriously? I might read lips, but I

77

don't have super-vision. You can see her lips; do you honestly believe I can make out what they're saying?"

Davina looked again and shrugged. "I guess it is kind of blurry."

"It's too bad we don't have better cameras with sound," Bridget said.

"I think we were darn lucky I had these on hand," Aileana snapped.

HEATHER AND MARIE'S talk of witchcraft drifted to Danielle's flight around Marlow House's living room on a broom.

"It's too bad I didn't think to bring a broom with me when we went to see Beau in lockup. That would have been a grand exit, me flying off on a broomstick," Heather said with a laugh.

"I admit, that would have lent a certain dramatic flair, but I'm not sure how we could have carried that one off without an officer seeing you."

"I suppose." Heather shrugged. "But Brian saw Danielle flying around."

"True."

Heather considered the thought a moment and then asked, "But if you think about it, why does someone like Brian seem to deal with these things without going nutso, while someone like Beau ends up in the funny farm?"

"Do you feel guilty about that? What we did to him? We did push him over the edge."

"I don't feel guilty, but I do feel a little bad, but only because his insanity helped him avoid going to prison. I think he got off easy. He should do some hard time after trying to kill Walt and Danielle."

"I agree with that."

"But I would have loved to fly around on a broom like that. What a trip." Heather sighed.

"You still can," Marie said with a giggle. A moment later Heather's kitchen broom floated into the living room.

When Heather noticed it, she laughed. "Are you serious?"

"Sure. Let's give it a try," Marie suggested.

Heather narrowed her eyes at Marie. "You won't drop me, will you?"

"I certainly will try not to," Marie said primly.

Heather stood up from the sofa and put her hand out. The broom handle floated into her grasp.

"HOLY CRAP!" Aileana called out, standing up from the desk, her eyes riveted on the computer monitor. Her sisters had minutes earlier wandered off to the nearby sofa, where Bridget had picked up a magazine to read, and Davina had just begun to surf on her cellphone. Getting bored watching, Aileana intended to record Heather and was just getting ready to do that when she spied something floating across the room. It wasn't until Heather took hold of it did she realize what it was: a broom.

She didn't cry out, "Holy crap!" until a few moments later, after Heather had climbed onto the back of the broomstick before taking flight. She was now flying around the living room, laughing her head off like a deranged madwoman. While Aileana couldn't hear the laughter, that was what Heather appeared to be doing, at least each time she flew within the range of the camera before disappearing again.

Hearing her sister call out, Bridget tossed the magazine on the floor and went to the desk, with Davina right behind her. They both looked at the monitor but saw nothing.

"Where did she go?" Davina asked.

"What happened?" Bridget asked at the same time.

Before Aileana told them to just wait a minute, Heather and her broom flew within camera range as she continued her flight around the living room.

THE THREE PARKER sisters stood around their small kitchen table late Friday evening, forming a circle while they held hands. All the house lights had been turned off, and the only illumination came from the candles flickering in the center of the table, their holder a pentacle made from black and gold fired ceramic. Behind each sister was a chair, as if they were getting ready to sit down. On the back of each chair was a white robe.

Had someone peeked into the window, it would be an eerie sight, the illumination of the sisters' pale faces by candlelight, while their voluminous long crimson hair encircled the three like a fiery circle. If someone had been peering through the window and the sight had not scared them off and they looked closer, they would have noticed something else. The three sisters stood nude, yet the sight was not provocative—just weird. And a little creepy. Each with eyes closed, together they recited words that to an outsider would sound like gibberish.

When the chanting stopped, the sisters released hands, opened their eyes, and each picked up a robe. After slipping on their robes, they each sat down, pulling their chairs closer to the table.

Bridget folded her hands on the tabletop and said, "We have truly found our sacrifice blood witch."

"And a powerful one," Aileana said. "We have to be very careful. She is dangerous."

"But can you imagine that power of hers? Soon it will be ours!" Bridget said excitedly.

"With that power, we should have no problem securing the Leabar," Davina said.

"I have great faith in the *Book of Spells*," Bridget said. "No reason to doubt it. It has brought us the ruby and the sacrifice blood witch, and it will guide us on vanquishing the blood witch."

"How do we proceed?" Aileana asked.

"According to the book, we must drug her. But whatever we give her, she must take it willingly, and it must not be a lethal dose. Just something to make her unconscious so we can perform the ritual."

"Like what?" Aileana asked.

Bridget leaned toward the candles and blew each one out. When they were in total darkness, she said, "I need to do some more research. But we are close. So very close."

They each got up from the table, but Davina stubbed her toe in the darkness. "Darn, Bridget," she yelped. "Why did you blow out the candles before you turned on the darn light? You're going to make me break my neck one of these days."

The next minute the kitchen light turned on.

FOURTEEN

Late Saturday afternoon Aileana worked behind the counter of Pagan Oils and More. She glanced up at the wall clock. Closing was less than thirty minutes away, but she hadn't had a customer in the last hour. Davina had left their store to run errands, while Bridget had stayed home to pore through the spell book. Aileana picked up her cellphone to do a little surfing to pass the time, when the shop door opened and in walked Bridget carrying a decorative container the size of a shoebox.

"Where's Davina?" Bridget asked as she hurried toward the counter.

"She went to the store to pick up a few things. She's coming back in a little while to help close up."

Bridget set the covered container on the counter.

"What's that?" Aileana asked at the same time Bridget removed its lid. Curious, Aileana looked inside to find it filled with what appeared to be scrumptious plump chocolate chip cookies. The scent of chocolate drifted up to her.

"Oh, I'm starved. Those look amazing," Aileana said as she reached in the box to snatch a cookie.

Bridget immediately slapped her hand away and said, "You don't want to eat one. Not unless you're okay with sleeping for the next few hours."

Withdrawing her hand, Aileana's eyes widened as she looked up into Bridget's eyes.

Pleased with herself, Bridget smiled. "Now we just have to figure out some way to get these in front of Miss Donovan."

"It would sure be easier if she would just walk through that door," Aileana said.

Bridget let out a sigh. "Unfortunately, we weren't very successful with the Baird sisters. The best we could do was get them to look in the window."

The next minute the door to the shop opened, and both Parker sisters looked to see who had entered, while Bridget quickly covered the box. But when they saw who had just walked in, it was not only the last person they expected to see walk through the door—it was the person they most wanted to see, Heather Donovan.

"Hello," Heather greeted them, walking up to the counter. "I think I've seen you around town. There are three of you, aren't there?"

"Yes, three sisters. My name is Bridget Parker, and this is my sister Aileana. This is our store. Welcome. Our other sister isn't here right now."

"Triplets?" Heather asked.

Bridget shook her head and then removed the cover from the container of cookies. "No. just close in age."

"How can we help you?" Aileana asked.

"I heard you carried essential oils," Heather said, glancing around the shop.

"Yes, over here," Aileana said, leading Heather to the oils and away from the cookies.

Bridget frowned at her sister when she returned to the counter, leaving Heather by the oils, her back to them.

"Go lock the door and close the blinds, and do it quietly!" Bridget silently mouthed to Aileana.

Aileana quickly complied after reading Bridget's lips. A few minutes later, Heather returned to the counter, carrying two bottles of oil, while the sisters stood by the counter, the box of cookies wide open on full display.

Heather glanced to the front window, noticing the curtain was now closed. She then looked up at the clock and back to the sisters. "Are you getting ready to close?"

"Not for a few minutes. Please take your time," Bridget insisted.

THE GHOST AND THE WITCHES' COVEN

"Oh, and would you try one of our cookies? We're considering selling them and would love your opinion."

WALT PULLED into the parking space at the museum and recognized the car next to him. It belonged to Heather Donovan. He assumed she was in the museum, yet that wasn't his destination. Summer parking in downtown Frederickport meant extra walking these days, Walt thought. The last time he and Danielle had come downtown, it had been to visit the new gourmet candy store. They'd ended up parking by Pagan Oils. Today he wanted to go to Pagan Oils, but there were no free parking spaces in front of the store.

A few minutes later, after Walt started up the walkway leading to his destination, he heard a voice say, "Afternoon, Walt."

Turning toward the voice, Walt spied Brian Henderson coming his way.

"Hello, Brian," Walt greeted him.

Brian nodded toward Pagan Oils. "Don't tell me that's where you're going?"

Walt smiled. "They have a necklace Danielle really likes. I thought I'd surprise her with it. Where's your cousin? Isn't she with you?"

"She's at home with a headache. That's why I'm here." Brian nodded toward the shop again.

"Don't tell me you're going to see if they have a magic potion to stop a headache?" Walt teased as the two men started up the walkway.

"Something like that. Apparently, they're the only place in town that sells essential oils, and Kitty insists it's what she always uses for a headache, and she forgot to bring hers."

"Heather is into those essential oils," Walt said.

"A bunch of silly hocus-pocus," Brian grumbled. "But if it makes Kitty feel better."

When they reached the door to the shop, it said open, but when Walt went to open the door, it was locked. Both men glanced to the window, noting the closed shade.

Brian looked at his watch. "They're supposed to be open for another ten minutes."

"They must have closed early, forgot to turn their sign," Walt said as both men turned from the door. When they did, they found a young redhead rushing up the walkway in their direction.

"Did you want to go in?" she asked, slightly out of breath when she reached them.

"Yes. But it seems to be closed," Brian said.

"It's not closed. Sometimes the door sticks." She pushed by them and tried the door. When she found it locked, she frowned. "A customer must have locked it when they left, by mistake."

Brian and Walt watched as the woman pulled a key from her purse and unlocked the door. "Come on in," she urged. "We're open."

BRIDGET SILENTLY PRAISED the perfectly aligned stars as she watched Heather happily consume a cookie and accept a second one. The powerful witch would pass out soon. At least, Bridget believed the stars were perfectly aligned, until her bungling sister came charging through the door with two men by her side. To make matters worse, one was a police officer.

"The door was locked," Davina said cheerfully as she barreled into the store but then halted when she spied Heather Donovan standing at the counter, eating cookies, while her two sisters glared in her direction.

"Hey, Walt, Brian. You guys are an unlikely pair," Heather said cheerfully as she took another bite of cookie.

The next moment a smile replaced Bridget's glare as she picked up the container of cookies and showed them to the two men. "Please try one. We're asking our customers to help test these out."

Not waiting to be told, Aileana slipped quietly and quickly to the door and relocked it, while Davina looked confused.

"Walt will never turn down sweets," Heather said. "You guys should try these." She picked up a cookie and shoved it at Walt. After he took it, she handed one to Brian. Bridget and Aileana silently watched as the three ate the cookies, each giving praise to the baker.

Abruptly Heather grabbed hold of the counter, swaying a bit. "Dang, I think I have vertigo."

Walt started to say something but then grabbed his head. The next moment Heather fell unconscious to the floor, followed by

Walt, and then Brian, the three littering the front of the counter with their bodies.

"What is going on?" Davina blurted, looking down at the three. "Are they dead?"

"No, they are not dead, you idiot!" Bridget shouted.

"Why am I an idiot?" Davina asked.

"Because you unlocked the door and let them in!" Bridget countered.

"Calm down, guys. We need to think," Aileana said.

"I assume those cookies are what you have been working on all day?" Davina asked. "The ones to knock out our sacrifice?"

"Obviously," Bridget snapped.

"Why in the world did you feed them to Walt Marlow and a cop!" Davina asked.

"What else was I going to do after you let them in here?" Bridget asked. "She was getting ready to drop any minute. And if she had done that before they had any of the cookies, they would be calling 911 about now, and we would probably be arrested after they tested those cookies."

"So what now? Do we just leave them somewhere?" Aileana asked. "If you think about it, once we finish with Heather, they won't remember her anyway, and they'll just be a little confused."

"Are you serious?" Bridget asked. "Maybe they won't remember anything about Heather Donovan, but they will remember coming in here, being offered cookies, and then waking up somewhere with one hell of a headache. We have no idea what they might say."

"Then what?" Aileana asked.

Bridget let out a deep breath. "There is only one thing we can do. Consider them collateral damage. We'll take them up to the sacrifice spot with Heather. There's a spell in the book I can use to get rid of them. Unlike Heather, people will notice they're missing. That other spell only works on blood witches. But without their bodies, no one will ever know what happened to them."

"Are you sure it will work?" Davina asked.

"The other spell worked, didn't it? It brought us the ruby and the blood witch," Bridget said.

"But what if someone knew they were coming here?" Aileana asked.

"We will say they never arrived," Bridget said.

"What if someone saw them come in the store?" Aileana asked.

"There was no one outside," Davina said. "I don't think anyone saw them come in."

"What about their cars?" Aileana asked.

"I saw them walking up the street," Davina said. "They aren't parked by the store."

Bridget looked at Davina. "You pull the van around back so we can load their bodies in without being seen." She then looked to Aileana. "Get their cellphones off them. We need to dump them before we leave, and we have to stop by the house to pick up the ruby and the spell book."

"This is rather exciting," Davina said. "I'm glad I let them in the store."

"Why do you say that?" Aileana asked. "This makes things more complicated."

Davina grinned at her sister. "Think about the opportunity to use a spell that allows us to get rid of someone we don't like, and there is no body or any evidence left behind. That opens up many interesting possibilities."

"Davina, go move the van," Bridget said impatiently.

"I'm just trying to look on the bright side," Davina said cheerfully.

Aileana knelt by the bodies, searching for the cellphones. After Davina left the shop, locking the door behind her, Bridget looked down at Aileana and said, "If Davina had been born four hundred years ago, they would have burned her at the stake."

Aileana laughed and then stood up, holding the cellphones she had discovered. She placed them on the counter and said, "I must admit, I about had a heart attack when Davina came walking in here with those two."

"The only thing I could think of, give them some cookies," Bridget said. "And I wanted to smack Davina."

"Fast thinking on your part. I just held my breath that Davina wouldn't do something else stupid, like grab a cookie for herself."

Bridget looked down at the three bodies and said, "We'd better get these guys tied up. They should be out for a few hours, but I would rather not take any chances."

FIFTEEN

Danielle let out a curse as she removed the quiche from the oven and burned the edge of her right pinky finger on the rack. Hastily, she set the sizzling pan on the stovetop and then put her injured finger under running cold water. Standing there a moment, letting the water soothe her pain, she looked over at the thin potholder now on the counter and told herself she needed to toss that thing. It was useless.

After a moment, she turned off the water faucet and glanced up at the wall clock. She stood in the kitchen, wearing a colorful apron over her blouse and jeans. It had been a birthday gift from Lily. Digging one hand in the apron's pocket, she pulled out her cellphone, checking to see if she had any missed calls from Walt.

"Where is he?" she muttered to herself, seeing she had no missed calls. She shoved the phone back in the pocket. Walt had promised to be back by now, when he had rushed out earlier, refusing to tell her where he was going. She set the kitchen table for two, grateful Walt didn't ascribe to the notion "real men don't eat quiche," and he actually enjoyed it occasionally for a light dinner. Of course, she typically served her double fudge chocolate cake for dessert on quiche night, which might have made him more amenable to a dish some men considered girly.

Fifteen minutes later, and still no Walt, Danielle walked out the side door and headed to the garage. Perhaps he had come home but got sidetracked talking to a neighbor. Once she reached the garage and looked inside, she found no Packard. Pulling her cellphone from her apron, she called him. It went to voicemail. Again.

"Walt, where are you?" Danielle said into the phone. "You promised you'd be home by now. Please call me."

After leaving a message, Danielle called Ian's phone number.

"Hi, Danielle," Ian answered a moment later.

"Hi, Ian. Have you seen Walt?" she asked.

"Not since this morning. Is something wrong?"

"There might be when he gets home," Danielle said with a laugh.

"What's going on?"

"He went to town to pick something up, and he was supposed to be back by now. He's not answering his phone," she said.

"He probably ran into someone and got talking," Ian suggested. "And you know how he forgets to charge his phone."

"Yeah, probably. Thanks. If you see him, let him know he risks being cut off from chocolate cake."

Ian laughed. "Will do."

Danielle walked back to the house and took a seat at the kitchen table. She glanced over at the stove where the quiche sat, uncut and cooling off. Taking out her cellphone again, she tried calling Chris. The call went to messages. She then tried calling Heather. Again, the call went to messages. She then called Adam Nichols.

"Hi, Danielle, what's up?" Adam asked when he answered the call a moment later.

"Hey, Adam, did you work today?" Danielle asked.

"This afternoon, why?"

"I seem to have misplaced a husband. You didn't happen to see Walt in the last couple of hours, did you?"

"I didn't see him. But I noticed the Packard parked by the museum when I was going home."

"What time was that?" Danielle asked.

"After five."

"Thanks, Adam."

"Is everything okay?" Adam asked.

"Yeah. It's just not like Walt. But he probably got talking to someone. And if he's at the museum, that's likely what happened." Danielle said goodbye to Adam and then tried calling Walt again.

When the call went to messages, she tried the museum. The call went to voicemail.

Danielle sat alone at the kitchen table for another ten minutes, growing increasingly annoyed. When the kitchen door finally opened several minutes later, she expected to see Walt, yet it was Chris.

"Oh, it's you," Danielle grumbled.

"Now you sound like Walt," Chris teased.

"I tried calling you a while ago, but you didn't answer."

"Yeah, I know. I was on the phone, and when I saw it was you, figured I'd just stop by instead. Have you seen Heather?" Chris asked.

"Heather? Is she missing too?"

"What do you mean?" Chris asked.

"It's just that Walt was supposed to be home over an hour ago. He knew when I planned to have dinner. But he's gone AWOL, and he's not answering my calls. But I know where his car is, so I suppose he isn't exactly missing. In fact, I was thinking of going down there and seeing what the heck is going on." Danielle paused a moment and asked Chris, "Am I turning into a nagging wife?"

Chris laughed. "Nah. So where is his car?"

"I talked to Adam; he saw the Packard by the museum. If Walt hadn't already sent his manuscript to the editor, I would assume he forgot the time and got lost in some research. I tried calling the museum, but they aren't answering."

"Come on, I'll take you down there. I'm looking for Heather anyway. And when you find Walt, you don't want to drive two cars home. How can you give him hell if you're in another car?"

"SO WHAT IS this about Heather being missing too?" Danielle asked as she sat in the passenger seat of Chris's car, on the way to the museum. "I tried calling her earlier when I was looking for Walt. She wasn't answering," Danielle explained.

"She told me she was going downtown to run some errands, and she offered to pick up some papers from Adam. But according to Adam, she never showed. And I haven't heard from her. I'm wondering if her car broke down again. She just got it out of the shop yesterday. And sometimes she can be a little careless about charging her phone."

"Walt too," Danielle said.

When Chris pulled down the main street, he drove straight to the museum, and to the Packard. But it was not alone in the parking lot. Next to it was Heather's car.

"We found them both!" Chris said. "What are those two up to?"

"We found their cars, at least," Danielle said as she got out of Chris's now parked vehicle and walked to the Packard. Hands on hips, she glanced up to the museum.

"Let's go get them," Chris said with a laugh. They walked to the museum, and when they got to the front door, they found it locked. When peeking inside, they saw most of the lights were off.

Not convinced they weren't inside, Danielle pounded on the door. When there was no answer, Danielle pulled out her cellphone.

"Who are you calling?" Chris asked.

"Millie Samson," Danielle explained. A moment later, Millie answered the call.

"Hi, Millie, this is Danielle Marlow. I was wondering if you had docent duty this afternoon…Did you see Walt, by any chance?…And he never came in?…What about Heather Donovan?…Did you notice Heather's car?" A few moments later Danielle said goodbye to Millie and hung up. She slipped her phone back in her pocket and looked at Chris.

"Well?" Chris asked.

"Millie was on docent duty this afternoon, and she closed up the museum. She said she didn't see Walt or Heather. But she noticed Walt's Packard in the parking lot when she was going home. She didn't notice Heather's car. Said it could have been there, but she really wasn't paying attention to that. The Packard sorta stands out."

"Where are they?" Chris said, glancing down the street. "You don't think the two ran off together, do you?"

Danielle laughed. "If so, I didn't see that one coming."

Chris chuckled. "Let's walk down the street and see what we can find out."

"Maybe they're at Lucy's. I think everything else is closed," Danielle said.

They started walking away from the parked vehicles when Chris paused and said, "By the way, nice apron. You want to leave it in my car?"

Danielle glanced down at the apron. "I forgot I had it on. But yeah, I think that might be a good idea." She removed her cellphone from her apron pocket, slipped it in a back pocket of her jeans, and then handed her apron to Chris. After Chris tossed the apron in his car, they started down the street on foot, heading for Lucy's Diner.

All the businesses between the museum and Lucy's Diner were closed. When they reached the restaurant, they went inside and talked to the staff. No one had seen Walt or Heather. When they went outside, Danielle glanced across the street and spied someone she recognized, Police Chief MacDonald.

"HI, CHIEF," Danielle greeted MacDonald after she and Chris crossed the street and got within earshot.

The chief, who stood by a car he had been checking out, turned to face Danielle and Chris. "Evening, Chris, Danielle. Have you seen Brian?"

Danielle glanced to the car the chief stood by. "Isn't that Brian's car?"

"It is. I've been looking for him, but I can't find him anywhere. Just his car. And he isn't answering his phone," the chief explained.

Danielle frowned. "This is just too weird. We're looking for Heather and Walt, for the same reason." Danielle then told the chief why they had come downtown.

"When did you start looking for Brian?" Chris asked the chief after Danielle finished her telling.

"I stopped by the station a while ago, and when I was down there, Brian's cousin called. She said Brian had gone out to get her some essential oils for a headache, but he never came back. She tried calling him, but he didn't answer his cellphone. She started getting worried. So I told her I'd come down here and see if his car broke down or something," the chief explained.

Danielle glanced over at Pagan Oils. "I wonder if Brian was going there. I know they sell essential oils."

"I went over there already, and the place is closed. I went around back. It's all locked up," the chief said.

"This is weird. All three of them going missing at the same time. Not answering their phones. Their cars all here." Danielle looked down the street at the museum parking lot.

"So are we talking alien abduction here, or has the Rapture begun?" Chris asked.

"This is not funny," Danielle snapped.

"Aw, come on, Danielle, I'm sure there is a logical explanation for all this," Chris said. "We can't lose our sense of humor."

"I'm afraid I have to agree with Danielle," the chief said. "I don't feel good about this."

Chris frowned. "Come on, Chief, I don't think there is a band of kidnappers snatching people off the streets of Frederickport, and then what, selling them into white slavery? And you forget, Walt comes with his own line of defense, Brian is a trained cop, and Heather…well, some kidnapper would just be stupid to mess with Heather. She can be mean."

"Maybe all of that is true, but unfortunately, I have a gut feeling. And my gut is rarely wrong," the chief said.

Chris was tempted to remind the chief that his gut had been wrong about Carol Ann but kept his mouth shut.

"What are we going to do?" Danielle asked.

"I would give it a little more time if it was just Brian I couldn't find. But with all three of them disappearing, I think I should begin with the security camera," the chief said.

"What security camera?" Danielle asked.

The chief pointed to a light pole across the street from Pagan Oils and More. "The one we installed there last year."

SIXTEEN

Joe Morelli's girlfriend, Kelly Bartley, offered to stay with the chief's two boys on Saturday evening while he investigated the missing persons. Joe, who had Saturday off, worked to help with the investigation.

Within an hour of locating the abandoned cars downtown, they got the footage from the security camera. Chris and Danielle stood with the chief in his office, waiting for Joe to see what was on the recording. The three stood behind the chief's desk, looking over Joe's shoulder at the computer monitor, while Joe located the timeframe of interest.

"There's the Packard," Danielle called out, pointing to the monitor. The vehicle drove past the camera's view and out of sight, presumably parking at the museum.

"And there's Heather. She's going into Pagan Oils," Chris said. They all continued to watch.

"There's Walt and Brian," Joe noted a few minutes later. They all watched as the pair stood on the sidewalk in front of Pagan Oils, talking. They then turned up the walkway and continued to the store.

"I figured that's where Brian was going," the chief said. "After Kitty told me he went to buy essential oils."

"Why is Walt going to the shop?" Danielle asked. "He's not into oils or witchcraft." She then let out a knowing, "Ah…I know why he's there."

"Why?" Joe asked.

"I bet he went back to get me that necklace I wanted," Danielle said.

"It doesn't look like they're going to get in," Joe noted. "Seems the door is locked."

Danielle frowned. "Why would that be? Heather's still in the shop."

"Oh, look, I think that's one of the shop owners," the chief said when he spied the redhead rushing up to the door and then unlocking it.

"I've seen her," Chris said. "Actually, there were three of them."

"Sisters," the chief said. "They own Pagan Oils. The Parker sisters."

"I saw one of them walking down the alley behind Heather's when I picked her up for work yesterday morning. They look like triplets," Chris said.

"Well, at least we know they all went into Pagan Oils. Now let's see where they go when they leave," Joe said.

They continued to watch. The redhead who had let Brian and Walt in the store left and then walked to her van and drove off.

"Why are they still in there?" Danielle asked a few minutes later.

Joe sped up the video, yet finally turned it off after Danielle and Chris showed up on the recording, when they walked past the camera on their way to Lucy's Diner.

THE CHIEF INSISTED Chris and Danielle go home and allow the police to handle the situation. He didn't want civilians to get in the way, giving him one more thing to worry about. He didn't know what they might walk in on.

They agreed Danielle and Chris would first stop at Brian's house and let his cousin know what was going on. After they stopped, Danielle talked Kitty into going home with them for the evening. Danielle didn't want Kitty to be alone in a strange town while the police were out looking for her cousin.

Back at Marlow House, Ian and Lily joined them with Connor

and Sadie. Chris picked up Hunny from his house, bringing her back to Danielle's, while they all held a vigil.

Danielle served the cold quiche to those who were hungry, and cut into the chocolate cake, offering everyone a slice, while Chris served beverages. Silently, she prayed for Marie or Eva to show up. She could really use their special help and guidance.

"WHAT DID YOU FIND OUT?" Danielle asked Saturday evening when she opened the front door for Police Chief MacDonald.

"Where is everyone?" the chief asked.

"In the living room," Danielle said anxiously.

"WE HAVEN'T FOUND THEM YET," the chief announced when he and Danielle walked into the living room. "Nor have we found anything—other than what we saw on that video—that might show foul play."

"Did you get in the store?" Chris asked.

"Yes. It was empty. Closed up for the night. Nothing to show there had been a struggle. Nothing."

"But we didn't see them leave the building," Danielle said as she went to sit on the sofa with Lily and Connor.

"We didn't see them leave through the front door, but that doesn't mean they didn't leave through the back door," the chief pointed out.

"Did you talk to the women who own the store? The one who let them in?" Chris asked.

"We drove to their house, but no one was there. We spoke to their neighbors. One told us they saw the three sisters all drive off together in the van several hours ago."

"Are there any cameras in the alleyway behind the shops?" Danielle asked.

"I'm afraid not," the chief said. "But I called the owners of the other businesses along that section, asking if anyone saw any of them late this afternoon or heard anything suspicious in the alley. But nothing."

"What about their phones?" Chris asked. "Can't you track them on their cellphones?"

"Joe is working on that right now. He's also trying to find the cellphone numbers for the Parker sisters, assuming they have cellphones," the chief said. "I also have some people doing a thorough search of that area, working on the premise they left from the back door."

"At least we know they're still alive," Danielle said.

"How do we know that?" Kitty asked.

Danielle, who had momentarily forgotten Kitty was with them, looked at the woman. She smiled softly and said, "I would just know if something happened to Walt. If he was dead, I would know. And if Walt is alive, I'm confident the others are too."

BRIDGET DROVE the van while Davina and Aileana shared the passenger seat, crammed uncomfortably into the small space. In the back, the three abductees remained unconscious and securely tied up. The van raced down the rugged dirt road leading them deep into the forest, sending the sisters bouncing wildly in their seats.

"Ouch! Slow down!" Aileana cried out when her head bumped the van's ceiling. She rubbed the injured spot and said, "We don't need a flat tire."

Bridget slowed down. "Sorry. I just want to get there before dark."

"According to the internet, sunset is 8:40. Which means about thirty-five minutes until nightfall after that," Davina said.

"What time is it now?" Bridget asked, never taking her eyes off the road.

"We have plenty of time," Aileana said.

"Once we get to the trailhead, I figure it's going to take us about twenty to thirty minutes to walk to the altar. I don't see how we can make it any faster, each one of us hauling one of them. It would have been easier if it was just Donovan," Bridget grumbled.

"You're the one who offered them cookies," Davina said.

"What was I supposed to do when you let those two walk in at the same time Donovan was about to keel over?" Bridget asked.

"How did I know what you were doing? You could have warned

me," Davina said. "Called me up, told me what was going on and not to just barge in the store."

"Oh yeah, right, and how would we do that with Donovan standing there?" Bridget asked.

"Enough, you two; stop arguing," Aileana snapped.

The sisters remained quiet for the rest of the drive. When they finally arrived at the trailhead, they got out of the van and went to work immediately, each knowing what she had to do. When first discussing Donovan as a sacrifice, they all knew where it would take place. They had been to the altar many times since moving to Oregon.

Aileana had originally suggested using a travois to transport Donovan's body from the van to the site. It was what the Native Americans had used when hauling goods or people any distance, she had told her sisters. Plus, it was something they could make themselves. Aileana had found instructions online on how to make one. She figured all they would need was rope, a tarp, a good ax, and maybe a hunter's knife. Those were all things they already had. They would also need long poles, but she figured those they could get from the forest.

Originally the plan was for Aileana to make a travois once they arrived at the trailhead. But now there were three people to transport, so they needed to make three travoises. There was not enough time to transport their prisoners one at a time using one travois. This meant they each had to make one; two sisters could not just stand around and watch Aileana, as would have been the case if they just had Donovan to transport.

It didn't take long for the sisters to realize it wasn't as easy to make a travois as they originally thought. But they had no other option, they had to persevere, and eventually they completed their task.

One by one they removed their prisoners from the van, rolling each one onto a travois. They had a few items they needed to take with them, such as battery-operated lanterns, which they tied to travois poles.

The sister witches dragged their unconscious prisoners over the narrow trail, with Bridget leading, Davina behind her, and Aileana at the rear of the procession. The sun was setting, yet there was still plenty of daylight making its way through the treetops for them to see where they were going.

They had put the rest of the rope and their ax back in the van, but Bridget shoved the hunting knife in her jacket's pocket for protection. While she might not fend off a mountain lion with the knife, having it gave her some comfort. She told herself that when she arrived at the altar, she would cast a protection spell to get them out of the forest safely and back home. Normally she would have done that before entering the forest, but everything had happened so fast. They did not have enough time.

PANICKED, he felt suffocated. Something filled his mouth, blocking the air. Survival instincts kicked in, and he took a deep breath through his nose, drinking in the unexpected scent of pine. He tried to open his eyes, but his lids felt heavy, and someone was jostling him around, like he was being pulled over a sandy beach on a sleigh while trussed up like a deer on the top of his grandpa's old jalopy.

He heard shouting, but he couldn't understand the words. It sounded like a woman. Heavy breathing replaced the shouting. Suddenly the jostling stopped, and then he felt himself drop, his head and shoulders bouncing against something hard. Someone rolled him onto the ground. He landed on his side. It wasn't sand. It was hard, and there was a rock jabbing his right hip.

It felt as if glue secured his eyelids shut. He struggled to open them and finally succeeded. Blinking several times, he tried focusing. Surrounded by shadows, he heard voices, more than one. Standing was not an option. He could feel his ankles tied together, as were his hands, securely at the wrists, at the front of his body.

A burst of light several feet away illuminated the space. None of it made any sense. Then he saw them, the three women with long red hair, and he remembered going into Pagan Oils to get Kitty something for her headache. But why had they brought him here?

He heard one of them say, "The cop first."

The next moment he felt hands grabbing him on either side of his body, taking ahold of his arms right below his shoulders. They began to drag him.

SEVENTEEN

Wherever they were, it appeared to be a circular clearing in the middle of the forest. The light he had seen earlier now came from the center of the circle. Instead of a bonfire, it looked like three LED battery-operated camp lanterns, each turned on. Lanterns were not the only source of light. The setting sun provided some illumination, making its way through the trees, but providing more shadows than light.

At least they don't plan to burn the forest down, Brian thought, adding cynically, *just kill us.*

They had him sitting on the ground, his legs stretched out before him, bound securely with rope. His back leaned against a tree. He looked down at his hands still tied together, now resting on his lap. He tried to move but then realized they had not just tied up his legs and wrists; they had also tied him to the tree. Apparently, they did not want him to jump up and hop over to them. What exactly did they expect him to do, escape by headbutting them with his hands and feet tied up?

When placing him by the tree the women said nothing, nor did they seem to notice he had regained consciousness and now watched them. Or perhaps they didn't care.

He looked across the clearing, beyond the lanterns, into a pair of terror-stricken eyes. They belonged to Heather Donovan. They had tied Heather up to a tree, as they had tied him.

His eyes shifted to the left of Heather and spied a third captive, Walt Marlow. Like him and Heather, the women had placed Walt against a tree, but his head was turned at an odd angle, with his eyes shut, suggesting Walt had not regained consciousness. Or perhaps he was dead.

If any of the captives wished to call out for help, it would be impossible with the gags the women had put in each of their mouths.

Brian looked from Walt back to Heather, and then to the three women now gathered by the lanterns. One woman held something in her hands, but he couldn't see what it was. It was relatively small, cupped in the palms of her hands. She held it up to the sky and chanted. The words sounded like senseless gibberish.

The woman placed whatever she was holding on the ground between the lanterns. The women then held hands, forming a circle around the lanterns, and chanted. Each turned her face to the sky, and together, while holding hands, they moved around the circle, reminding Brian of demented children in a horror movie, playing ring around the maypole.

He continued to watch, and he got the impression they had put themselves into a trance while still moving around the lanterns and chanting. Then he noticed something fall out of one of their pockets. Whatever it was, it glittered, but then disappeared, unnoticed by the women, who inadvertently buried it into the dirt and pine needles as they circled the lanterns, carelessly stepping on the fallen object.

THESE CRAZY WOMEN are freaking nuts, Heather thought as she watched the chanting redheads circling the lanterns. She kept looking over at Walt, silently urging him to wake up so he could get them out of this mess. She looked forward to seeing him send the crazy wannabee witches flying into a tree and knocking them out. After he did that, he could untie the ropes, and then they could start for home. Perhaps it would be best if Walt didn't knock them out too hard, so they could tell them how to get home. Heather had absolutely no idea where they were. The place was not familiar. But Walt could use the same powers of persuasion on them as Marie had used on Beau.

THE GHOST AND THE WITCHES' COVEN

Knowing Walt was just a few feet away from her was comforting, even though he had not yet come to. She knew he was still alive. If dead, she would expect his spirit to be lingering nearby, and she would see him. And if that was the case, she assumed he would still have his power to move things, as he had the last time he had been a ghost. Which would mean he could still help her and Brian escape. But Heather wanted Walt alive. Having him dead again would break Danielle's heart.

She tried wiggling out of her bindings, but each time she moved, they seemed to get tighter. So she stopped trying. Heather then focused on her gag. It was some disgusting piece of cloth covering her mouth and tied around her head. It smelled gross, and Heather wondered what they had used the rag for prior to rudely shoving it in her mouth.

Looking back to Brian, she noted he did not seem to be trying to get out of the ropes. Like her, he sat still. She suspected the ropes securing him tightened when he moved, as did the ones holding her. She looked from Brian to the redheads, cursing herself for ever stopping in their stupid shop.

The women obviously thought they were actual witches, the way they pranced around the lights. She wondered if it was kosher for witches to use LED lights. A respectable witch should use candles or a bonfire.

Turning her attention back to the gag, Heather got a piece of its fabric into her mouth and bit down, gnawing it with her teeth. While it might smell disgusting, she was happy to discover its fabric was old and brittle, easy to tear. She persistently continued to gnaw and tug, determined to chew through the gag. And if Walt didn't wake up soon, she would chew through the damn ropes on her wrists too, she told herself.

While working the fabric between her teeth, she suddenly remembered her dentist's admonishment about using one's teeth for tools. But wasn't that really the purpose of teeth? Heather asked herself as she continued to chew the now damp fabric.

DOZENS OF SCENARIOS flashed through Brian's mind. He detested feeling so vulnerable and unable to know what the women planned to do with them. But he doubted he would like it. Overhead the sun was quickly sinking, at least giving him some sense of direction of north, south, east and west. Although, he wasn't sure how that was going to help him if he remained tied up.

The women finally stopped chanting, and one leaned down to the lanterns, picking something up. He assumed it was the object she had placed there earlier. She carried it away from the light and disappeared into the shadows beyond the trees encircling the clearing. When she returned a few minutes later, there did not seem to be anything in her hands.

He watched as the women began picking up the lanterns.

One captor looked at her accomplices and said, "We'll come back tomorrow night and get it. It will be over by then."

"What about the travoises?" another one asked, pointing to something on the ground.

"No reason to haul them out. They got broken, and it's not like we'd reuse them anyway, and according to the spell, they'll be gone when we return."

The sisters walked together into the darkness, disappearing from sight. Listening, Brian could hear their voices as they talked amongst themselves. No longer discussing their captives, it was now burgers versus pizza. The voices grew fainter. He found it bizarre they would kidnap three strangers, haul them in the forest, and leave them as they returned home—while discussing what they intended to have for dinner.

Finally, he could no longer hear the voices. But then he heard the engine of a vehicle start, and the vehicle driving away, until he heard nothing more, beyond the sounds of the forest, where the three women had dumped them.

"Holy crap!" Heather called out, making several spitting sounds.

Brian looked to Heather, and fortunately, because of the setting sun cutting through a section of trees, he could see her. The women had taken the lanterns with them, and once the sun set and twilight ended, it would plunge them into darkness.

Heather had chewed through her gag, and she continued to spit, Brian assumed to rid herself of any loose fibers from the gag. Taking Heather's lead, Brian worked to chew through his gag, as Heather had chewed through hers. If they could talk to each other, perhaps they could come up with some plan to get out of this predicament. Although, he wasn't sure how, not unless someone heard their cries for help. Someone other than a mountain lion.

One plus, if the women were telling the truth, they were not planning to return until tomorrow night.

"Walt! Wake up!" Heather screeched, repeating it over and over.

Brian assumed Heather feared Walt was dead, which he might be. Yelling in itself was not a bad idea, but she should call for help as opposed to yelling at Walt to wake up. But the woman was clearly hysterical, which he understood. If he didn't have a gag shoved in his mouth, he might yell along with her.

"Darn it, Walt, wake up!" Heather yelled again. "Walt! Wake up and get these ropes off us before it gets dark. Walt!"

Heather continued to scream at Walt while Brian focused on chewing through his gag. When he finally freed his mouth from the restraint, he looked to Heather and said, "Heather, calm down."

"What do you mean, calm down? It's going to be pitch dark any minute, and I don't know about you, but I would like to be untied by then," Heather said. She then turned to Walt and yelled, "Walt, damnit, wake up!"

"Heather!" Brian snapped. "You're hysterical, and that will not help get us out of this. You need to calm down so we can discuss a rational plan. Yelling at Walt won't help."

"The sooner he wakes up, the sooner we can get out of these damn ropes. Walt!"

"Heather, they tied Walt up just like we are," Brian said, his tone overly calm. "You are hysterical. You need to stop. Walt can't help you right now. But maybe—"

"Oh, shut up, Brian," Heather snapped. "If you're not going to help me wake Walt, just shut up. You know nothing. And frankly, I do not have the patience to pretend right now." She turned back to Walt and screamed at the top of her lungs, "Walt!"

"Heather! Stop. I think Walt might be dead."

Heather stopped shouting. She looked to Brian and smiled. "You do?"

Brian frowned at Heather, uneasy with her odd expression. Was she about to laugh? Was this what a woman looked like who had been pushed over the edge of sanity? he wondered. "I know he's a friend of yours, but you need to face the possibility. He hasn't moved since we got here."

Heather laughed. "I told you, you know nothing. If Walt was dead, well, we would already be free by now." She turned back to Walt and started screaming again for him to wake up.

We are going to die, Brian thought as he watched Heather yelling like a deranged woman at the unconscious man. What did she expect him to do if he did wake up? Brian wondered. But the woman had clearly lost it, which did not bode well for their chances of survival. He had hoped they could put their heads together and perhaps come up with a plan, but she had been pushed too far, and if someone happened by and saved them, perhaps after hearing her shouting at Walt, he suspected she might end up in the psych ward when they got out of the forest.

"You're awake!" Heather shouted.

Brian looked quickly to Walt. He wasn't dead after all.

EIGHTEEN

Walt's eyes felt dry, scratchy as if the wind had blown sand into them. He wanted to wipe the sand away, but he couldn't move his hands. Blinking, he focused on his surroundings. A shaft of sunlight cut through the trees from the west, breaking through the shadows surrounding him. He knew it came from the west, because he instinctively knew sunset approached, not sunrise.

He heard someone shouting his name, demanding he do something. Turning his head toward the shouting, he saw it was Heather. He tried to call out, ask her what was happening, but something was in his mouth, preventing him from talking. He wanted to stand up, but he couldn't. Each time he moved, something—he assumed a rope—painfully cut into his body.

Glancing down, he looked at his wrists bound tightly together and resting on his lap. He tried raising his hands to remove the gag, but a rope wrapped around his arms below the elbows restricted his motion, only allowing his hands, bound at the wrists, to make it halfway to his chin.

Walt told himself to settle down. He needed to remove the gag from his mouth. Since he couldn't see how it was tied, it would be impossible for him to undo the knot with his energy. But perhaps it would be possible to will the fabric out, away from him, and pull it down, off his mouth and face. He focused, wincing a bit as the gag's knot cut into the back of his head. He pulled the fabric forward.

BRIAN WATCHED as Walt tried to make sense of his surroundings while Heather continued to shout at him. He looked from Walt to Heather and was about to tell her to stop yelling at the poor guy when he heard Walt say, "What happened?"

Brian turned back to Walt, whose gag now hung below his chin. He wondered how Walt got it pulled down with his hands bound like his, but assumed it must not have been as tightly knotted as his and Heather's, which they had literally chewed through to escape.

"It's getting dark. We need to get out of these ropes. Hurry," Heather begged.

"I don't understand. Where are we?" Walt asked.

Heather let out a sigh and then said, talking quickly, "As best I can figure, those redheaded psycho witches drugged us with those damn cookies. They brought us out here for some witch's ritual, where they have left us for the night, and they plan to return tomorrow night, probably to finish us off if the wild animals don't do it first. Now will you untie us?"

"Heather—" Brian began.

"Shut up, Brian," she snapped. "We don't have time. It's getting dark."

Walt looked down at his hands, staring a moment, and then looked back to Heather. "I can't do it without seeing the knot."

"What do you mean you can't do it?" Heather screeched.

"I need to see it so I know how to untie it," Walt said. "There isn't enough light."

"What are you two talking about?" Brian asked.

Heather looked at Brian and said impatiently, "Please, Brian, just stay out of this." She turned back to Walt and said, "Can't you just pull the rope until it breaks."

"That won't work," Walt said.

"Yes, it will. Just pull the rope off your wrists. You can see your wrists, can't you?" Heather asked.

"You don't understand," Walt said, looking at Heather. "But I can see your wrists too, so let me show you what the problem is."

The next moment Heather's wrists moved forward slightly as she cried out in pain. "Damn, Walt, that hurt!"

"That was what I was trying to tell you," Walt said impatiently.

"How about pulling the rope apart, but not against my wrists, in the opposite direction, away from the wrists," Heather suggested.

"I can't move in two directions at once," Walt told her.

Brian frowned. What were they talking about? Had their abduction caused them both to snap? Wonderful, he thought; it was bad enough being tied up and left in the middle of the forest, but to be tied up and left with two people who were obviously bonkers—this day was just getting worse and worse.

Heather and Walt continue to argue over ropes and energy, making no sense to Brian, when the raspy sound of a mountain lion's cry silenced the pair, yet not before Heather muttered, "Holy crap."

The three looked toward the darkness of the surrounding trees to the east, and from where the eerie cry had come. They all continued to stare, each of them remaining motionless. Brian found himself holding his breath.

Minutes ticked away, and Brian, who thought the danger had passed, began to relax when a mountain lion strolled leisurely into the clearing, again letting out a cry.

"Holy crap, holy crap, holy crap," Heather muttered. The mountain lion looked her way. "Do something, Walt!"

If the mountain lion was going to eat any of them, Brian figured it would probably be Heather, since she had just captured the big cat's attention. It strolled up to her and sniffed. Brian didn't feel especially comforted by the fact, even if it meant the mountain lion might get its fill and leave. As much as he found Heather annoying, he did not want to see her brutally ripped to shreds.

In the next moment, Walt said, "Over here."

The cat abandoned Heather and turned to Walt. Brian wasn't sure if that was the most heroic thing he had ever witnessed, or the most stupid.

He watched as the mountain lion pushed its nose into Walt's face. Because of the fading light, Brian could not see Walt's expression. He assumed it was that of terror, yet he would have been wrong. Walt's expression, had Brian been able to see it, was supreme calm.

Minutes ticked away, and Brian could hear his own heartbeat as the wild animal and Walt continued to stare into each other's eyes, just inches apart. Brian wanted to look away, but he couldn't.

The mountain lion stepped back from Walt and let out another cry. Brian watched as Walt lifted his bound wrists in what appeared to be an attempt to reach out to the mountain lion, yet the ropes limited his movement.

The mountain lion stepped up to Walt again, this time opening its mouth, showing its wicked teeth before biting down on Walt's wrists. Brian closed his eyes, expecting Walt to cry out in pain. Not only couldn't he watch, but he didn't understand. None of it made sense. Why would Walt offer his hands to the mountain lion? Did he imagine he could punch its nose and scare it away? Walt was as whacked as Heather, Brian thought.

Holding his eyes closed tightly, Brian waited for the scream that never came. Instead, he heard Walt say in a calm voice, "Thank you."

Confused, Brian opened his eyes. Walt's wrists were no longer tied together. Nor were they bloody. At least, not from what Brian could see in the fading light. Walt shook his wrists several times, as if to shake off any numbness along with pieces of the now shredded rope.

The cat circled Walt's tree, its head down, disappearing from sight. What Brian couldn't see was the cat now chewing at the ropes along the back of the tree, the ones securing Walt in place. When Walt leaned toward his ankles a moment later, his body no longer bound to the tree, Brian knew the cat had cut the ropes, as it had the ones around Walt's wrists. None of it made any sense.

Walt untied his ankles as the cat moved from behind the tree and watched him.

"Thank you, but I can get these," Walt said.

Brian wondered if their kidnappers had put some hallucinogens in those cookies. None of this could seriously happen. With his ankles now free, Walt stood and reached out to the mountain lion. The cat sniffed Walt's hand and then turned its head slightly and rubbed the back of its head against Walt's fingers. Brian could swear he heard a purr.

The next moment the cat turned from Walt and ran off, disappearing into the forest.

"Dang, Walt, I figured you would just toss that cat," Heather said.

"Why would I want to hurt a magnificent animal like that?" Walt asked. "We're intruding on her domain. Plus, her sharp teeth

THE GHOST AND THE WITCHES' COVEN

came in handy." He moved to Heather and began untying her wrists.

Wide-eyed, Brian stared speechless at Heather and Walt, who seemed unfazed that a mountain lion had just chewed through the ropes—without hurting Walt—and then simply left. Several minutes later Walt was by Brian, now untying the ropes around his wrists. The last of twilight was almost gone, and Brian could barely see Walt's face.

"What just happened?" Brian finally asked as Walt finished untying the ropes around his wrists.

"Does anyone have any matches?" Heather asked as she busily dragged the abandoned travoises to the center of the clearing. "I'm glad they left these; they'll make a good bonfire. And these tarps can keep us warm tonight."

"What just happened?" Brian repeated.

"I have matches," Walt said. "But we need to be careful. It's August, and not the best time to start a fire in the forest."

"This is survival, Walt. We'll be careful. Think you can break these into smaller pieces?" Heather asked, referring to the tree limbs the Parker sisters had used when making the travoises.

"What just happened?" Brian said again.

Much to Brian's frustration, Walt and Heather did not answer; instead each worked quickly before darkness completely engulfed them. When looking to Walt and Heather laying logs for a fire, he remembered seeing one woman drop something. He walked to the area and began feeling around on the ground. A moment later, he found what she had dropped buried beneath the dirt and pine needles, a hunting knife. Fortunately for him, a leather shield covered its blade, preventing Brian from cutting himself on its sharp edge while blindly groping in the dirt.

"I found something we can use," Brian said, holding up the knife.

"Where did that come from?" Heather asked.

"I saw one of them drop it," Brian said.

"I wish they would have dropped a bottle of water instead. I'm dying of thirst," Heather grumbled.

"My new friend told me there's a fresh stream not far from here," Walt said. "I don't think we'll die of dehydration."

THE HALF-MOON ROSE ABOUT twenty minutes after twilight. Yet even during the darkest phase of the night sky, the bonfire provided light and warmth. The three sat around the fire, each wrapped in a tarp recycled from the travoises that had brought them to this place.

They had just settled by the newly built fire when Brian asked, "Will you tell me now what happened with that mountain lion. Can you explain it, please?"

Heather looked to Walt and smiled. "I think you should tell him."

Walt let out a sigh. "Under the circumstances, I suppose you're right. If we're going to get out of here alive, I imagine that's not the only thing he's going to learn."

"Are you going to explain?" Brian snapped.

Walt looked to Brian, studying him a moment as the flames of the bonfire flickered and cast shadows. Finally, he said, "Remember when you were in the parlor, behind the sofa, picking up that picture that fell off the wall, and I walked in, and you caught me having a conversation with Max?"

Brian frowned. "Yes. What about it?"

"I lied to you. I didn't know you were there. I discovered later you'd overheard me, and that was only because it was caught on the security camera. I had forgotten they were there when I had my little conversation with Max. Chris told me later, when he watched that clip. He thought it was rather hilarious."

"I still don't understand," Brian said.

"I was talking to Max. And he was talking to me. Well, not talking exactly. Communicating telepathically. I have a habit of saying out loud what I'm conversing mentally with Max."

"Are you suggesting you talk to the animals?"

Heather laughed. "Yeah, Walt is our own Dr. Dolittle. I told him once he could make a fortune as an animal psychic."

NINETEEN

Brian did not respond to Heather's Dr. Dolittle comment. Instead, he stared into the flames while trying to process all that had happened to him since stepping into Pagan Oils. The women who had brought them to this site had transported them using homemade travoises, each one fitted with a tarp. Fortunately, they had left them behind. The branches from the travoises fed the fire, while the tarps gave them something dry to sit on. He pulled up the corners to provide extra covering and warmth. It might be summer, but the evening temperatures in the mountains could dip to chilly numbers. Hopefully, there would be no rain tonight, and by the clear sky overhead, Brian thought they might be lucky and stay dry.

"Were you surprised you could talk to the mountain lion like you do cats and dogs?" Heather asked Walt.

"A mountain lion is a cat," Walt reminded her. "Just a big one."

"But it is a wild animal," Heather said.

"True. But I have wondered about this scenario before," Walt said.

"What, you imagined you'd get kidnapped, left in the forest, and a mountain lion would show up and set you free?" Heather asked.

Walt chuckled and then said, "No. I wondered how a big cat, like a mountain lion or tiger, would respond. Would it differ from a domestic cat? But I always suspected it might be like it was tonight."

"Why is that?" Heather asked.

"Think about how Sadie and Max get along. If Max were a larger cat, maybe a panther—"

"Max looks like a mini panther," Heather said.

"Imagine him a full-grown panther, and he and Sadie ran into each other in the woods," Walt suggested.

"Max would probably eat poor Sadie," Heather said.

"But that isn't always true. I'm sure you've seen those videos online of big cats and domesticated dogs who are best friends," Walt said.

"Yes, but that's because they're introduced when the cat is very young," Heather said.

"Introduced when they can get to know each other—*communicate*—before the cat thinks of eating the dog. I suppose you might say it gives them time to develop their own language. And I believe one reason for war and strife is an inability to understand or communicate with each other."

"So you're suggesting once the mountain lion got to know you better, more than just potential dinner, she wasn't as apt to kill you?" Heather asked.

"Something like that," Walt said.

"What in the hell are you talking about?" Brian blurted.

Heather looked at Brian. "I thought you understood now. Walt can communicate with animals. Well, at least some animals. We don't know if he can with all of them."

"What did those crazy women put in those damn cookies? Were they spiked with some acid along with whatever knocked us out?" Brian asked.

"I doubt it," Heather said. "I certainly haven't seen anything weird."

Brian stared a moment at Heather, his expression blank. Finally, he said, "Seriously? You have seen nothing weird tonight? Nothing? A mountain lion chewing off Walt's ropes for him, that is not a bit unusual?"

Heather shrugged. "I said I was surprised. But it's not weird like acid-trip weird. Although, I admit, I have never taken acid. Drugs have never been my thing. And while I don't have personal experience with using drugs, I know each person's trip is different. We all saw the mountain lion chew off those ropes."

"All I know, when we get out of here and back home, if I was to tell anyone what I saw with Walt and that mountain lion, people would think I'm nuts," Brian said.

"Welcome to our world," Heather quipped.

"Maybe we should discuss how we plan to get back home," Walt suggested. "Instead of rehashing our encounter with the local wildlife."

"I assume we'll sleep here tonight, by the fire," Heather said. "And try walking out as soon as the sun comes up. I don't think it would be very smart trying to walk out now. We don't know where we are as it is. We'll surely get more lost if we take off in the dark."

"More lost?" Brian smirked. "Are there degrees to being lost?"

Heather glared at Brian. "Oh, shut up."

"You've told me to shut up a lot tonight," Brian said.

"I would stop saying it if you would just do it," Heather said.

"I don't think we need to bicker," Walt said. "If we are to get out of here, we need to work together. Unfortunately, I have absolutely no idea where we are."

"I came to when they were bringing us here," Heather said. She then pointed to one area along the trees encircling them. "We came through that way. There is a trail. We should probably just follow it."

"After they left, I heard a car engine start. I assume it belonged to them. It's hard to judge time, but I'm fairly certain it was about thirty minutes after they left us. So perhaps we're about a half hour from a road," Brian suggested.

Heather looked down at her jogging shoes and said, "I'm just glad I got kidnapped on a Saturday."

"There are preferable days for a kidnapping?" Brian asked.

"Yes. I jog every morning. And on Saturdays, I normally don't change out of my jogging clothes—like today. Who needs all that extra laundry?" Heather said.

"But doesn't that mean you're all sweaty and smelly?" Brian teased.

"Oh, shut up," Heather said, but she didn't sound angry. "On workdays I change out of my jogging clothes and often wear my boots to work. I would not want to wear those high heels while trying to walk out of a forest."

"I hope you shower before work," Brian said.

"Oh, shut up," Heather retorted.

Brian laughed.

"I'm glad to see you two have not lost your sense of humor," Walt said. "But I would like to know, why are we here?"

"Like I told you, I'm sure they drugged those cookies," Heather said.

"But why did they drug us?" Walt asked.

Instead of answering the questions, they all stared into the fire, each silently considering the true motivations of the women who had brought them to this place.

After a while, Brian said, "I don't think Walt and I were the intended targets. I think Heather was, and we just walked in at the wrong time."

"Why would I be the target?" Heather asked. "I don't even know those women. I'd never been in the store before. The only reason I went in there, Marie said they had a large selection of essential oils."

"Marie?" Brian asked with a frown.

Heather stared at Brian a moment and then shrugged. "Just a friend."

"Why don't you think we were targets?" Walt asked.

Instead of answering, Brian looked at Heather and asked, "How long were you in the store when we arrived?"

"I don't know. I walked in, asked about the oils. One of them showed me where they were. I looked for a few minutes, found what I wanted, went back to the counter, and they offered me a cookie. Then you guys walked in."

"Were they closing up when you got there?" Brian asked.

"Closing up? I noticed they put the blinds down when I came back to the counter with my oils. I asked them if they were closing up, thought maybe I should hurry. But they said I had plenty of time."

"When Walt and I got there, the door was already locked," Brian said.

"I don't know why they would lock the door; I was still in the store, and they said they weren't closing yet," Heather said.

"Exactly," Brian said.

Heather stared dumbly at Brian a moment before recognition dawned. "Oh...they locked the door and then offered me the cookie. Waiting for me to pass out."

THE GHOST AND THE WITCHES' COVEN

"Yes. And I don't think the one who unlocked the door and let us in the shop knew what was going on in there. But considering how fast those cookies worked, and you had already eaten one, I think they figured they didn't have any other choice than to drug all of us," Brian said.

"But why? What would they want Heather for?" Walt asked.

"You were still unconscious, but they performed some kind of ceremony," Brian said. "I have no idea what any of it meant. Sounded like a bunch of gibberish to me."

"They are obviously witches. Or at least, think they are," Heather said.

"Do you believe in witches?" Brian asked.

"I'm not sure what you mean by witches when you asked that question. There is the Wicca religion, where members consider themselves witches. But those are not broomstick-flying witches we think of at Halloween. I looked at their website. According to them, they aren't Wicca. They call themselves blood witches. Which I thought was nothing more than marketing. But considering what they did, I have a feeling they believe all that stuff," Heather said.

After they discussed the reasons for the witches of Pagan Oils abducting them, and not coming to any conclusion, they decided it was time to take a drink from that stream Walt had mentioned, and then take a nature break.

The half-moon provided sufficient light on their trip to the water supply, while the campfire helped guide them back. On the way, they each took turns relieving themselves while the other two turned their backs to the person for privacy while adding protection in numbers. Heather put aside any inhibitions she might have had about going in the woods while accompanied by two men, considering her desperate need to pee.

Once back at the campsite, they agreed to take turns sleeping while one stayed awake to stand guard. Brian kept the hunting knife close by for protection yet didn't realize Heather felt far more comfort knowing Walt was there, as opposed to a cop with a large knife. Walt volunteered to stand guard first, since he had been the last to regain consciousness after being drugged. Yet the real reason, he felt he was the one best suited to protect them.

Heather fell asleep first, leaving Walt and Brian awake. Brian added more branches to the flames, using the knife to cut them into small pieces. When he finally settled back by the fire, he told Walt, "If you want to sleep, go ahead. I'm wide awake."

"No, that's fine. I'm not sleepy either." Walt pulled the tarp tighter around him. "I can't imagine what Danielle is going through right now."

"And my cousin. I assume she called down to the station looking for me. I wonder if they've connected our disappearances," Brian asked.

"Perhaps." Walt stared into the fire.

After a few moments of silence, Brian asked, "How long have you had that gift?"

"I assume you mean communicating with animals?"

"Yes."

"Probably longer than I realized," Walt said, thinking of the decades he had spent as a ghost in Marlow House, never seeing a dog or cat, yet perhaps able to communicate with one had he seen any.

"Could you do it when you were a child?" Brian asked.

"No."

"I thought you couldn't remember your childhood."

Walt chuckled. "Trying to trick me?"

Brian shrugged. "Not really. I didn't consider your amnesia when I asked the question. But remembered it when you gave the answer."

"It's complicated, Brian. But believe me when I tell you I know nothing of Clint Marlow's life other than what I have been told."

"Can you communicate with Hunny and Sadie?" Brian asked.

"Yes. And with Bella, Heather's cat."

"If I hadn't seen you with that mountain lion, I would never believe it," Brian said.

"Remember when you and Danielle were in the garage with Beverly Klein before I walked in?"

"Yes," Brian said while silently thinking, *Another example of my poor taste in women.*

"I knew what I was walking into. One of the neighbors' cats told me," Walt explained.

"Who else knows you have this gift? Heather, obviously. I assume Danielle."

"Yes. Ian and Lily and Chris."

"According to Joe, Kelly always feels like she's an outsider. Like there's some secret the Beach Drive group shares, that she's excluded from."

"Beach Drive group?" Walt asked with a chuckle.

Brian shrugged. "It's what we call you. And now I know what that secret is."

You don't even know the half of it, Walt thought.

TWENTY

Danielle absently stroked Max's head and neck as she sat on the parlor sofa, her feet tucked under her and the cat on her lap purring. Bella slept curled up in a corner. They had picked up the cat from Heather's house earlier that evening. Chris entered the room carrying two glasses of wine. Everyone had gone home, except for Chris. He handed Danielle a glass of wine.

"It's the good stuff," he told her as he took his glass and sat in the chair facing her.

"We haven't had this for a while," Danielle said, taking a sip of the wine. She let out a little sigh as she savored her favorite and ridiculously expensive brand of wine.

"I had one last bottle at home. Thought we could use it." Chris took a sip, then reached down and gave Hunny, who had just curled up by his feet, a pat.

"I appreciate you staying with me tonight," Danielle said.

"No problem. I know Lily would have liked to have kept you company, but it's too much of a hassle with Connor. You'd almost need to stay over there. And I figured you'd want to sleep in your own bed. Plus, I'm more than comfortable in the downstairs bedroom here."

"I wish Marie or Eva would show up," Danielle asked.

"I'm not sure how much help they would be at this point," Chris said. "I'm sure if they knew something was wrong or where Walt and Heather were, they'd be here by now."

"At least we know they're alive," Danielle said.

Chris leaned back in the chair with his glass of wine. "I agree. Knowing Heather, if someone killed her, she would be here so quick, demanding one of us do something."

Danielle smiled sadly. "I just want them to stay alive."

"None of it really makes any sense," Chris said. "To be honest, my first thought was that they had walked into a robbery at Pagan Oils. If you think about it, someone locked that door after Heather entered, and then after Walt and Brian entered, they ended up going out the back door. But according to what the neighbors of the Parker sisters told the chief, all three left together in the van, and they seemed in high spirits, laughing. Not like someone had just held up their store."

"Something must have happened after everyone left out the back way. Maybe after the owners of the store drove off," Danielle suggested.

"If we could just talk to the Parkers. Those women were obviously the last ones to see them. They could tell us why they all left out the back door and if they saw anything," Chris said.

The doorbell rang and Hunny jumped up and barked. She ran from the parlor to the entry hall. Danielle started to push Max off her lap so she could stand up, but Chris told her to stay put, he would answer the door.

A few minutes later, Chris walked back into the parlor with the chief.

"Any news?" Danielle asked.

"Unfortunately, we still have no clue where they are, but we found these." The chief held up a plastic bag with three cellphones.

"Their phones?" Danielle asked. She gently shoved Max off her lap and stood up. The chief handed her the baggie for closer inspection. "That's Walt and Heather's cellphones, I recognize the cases. Where did you find them?"

"Along the highway leaving town," the chief explained. "It looks like someone pulled off on the side of the road, turned the phones off, wiped them down, and then pitched them out the window. I doubt we would have found them had they turned the phones off before they left town. Not unless someone just happened to find them."

"This doesn't sound good," Danielle said.

"It's beginning to sound like a kidnapping. And maybe Heather was the target," Chris said.

Danielle looked at Chris. "Because she works for the Glandon Foundation?"

"It wouldn't be the first time someone affiliated with my family was targeted, would it?"

"I have to agree with Chris," the chief said. "Maybe someone was watching Heather, followed her downtown, and planned to grab her. But when she didn't come out of the store, maybe they drove around back, saw her walking out, and instead of waiting for another opportunity after seeing Walt and Brian, they took them all. But I don't see how they would have taken them by force, considering Walt's gifts."

"What makes you so sure the women who own the shop aren't involved?" Danielle asked. "They were the last ones seen with them, and they left town before we even realized they were missing."

"We've done a little background check on the Parker sisters, and while they are unorthodox and apparently seem sincere in their belief that they're witches, they have no prior arrests—not even a traffic ticket."

"Why do they always say that about psycho killers?" Danielle grumbled.

"Say what?" the chief asked.

"Whenever a person without priors is arrested for some heinous crime, you always hear the police say something about how they didn't even have a traffic ticket. Heck, maybe criminals are more careful, and they're less likely to get traffic tickets because they don't want to attract attention to themselves," Danielle said.

"I'm just saying they don't fit the profile," the chief said.

"I don't know about that." Chris spoke up. Both Danielle and the chief looked at him.

"Why do you say that?" the chief asked.

"Remember, I saw one of them walking past Heather's house yesterday morning in the alley, when I was picking her up for work. Why would she be walking down the alleyway? Where do they live?"

The chief told Chris where their house was, and Chris then said, "That's the house we drove by, where the other two were standing outside by the van. Both Heather and I noticed how much they looked like the woman we saw walking down the alley. We suspected they were sisters, and we were right. But why was she walking by Heather's?"

"Perhaps we need to look in Heather's house," the chief suggested. "If she really was the target."

HAD they come downtown thirty minutes earlier, they would have seen the police cars parked along the street and alleyway near Pagan Oils, forcing them to abort their midnight mission. But there were no police cars, and they had no idea that minutes earlier the area had been thoroughly searched.

The three sisters dressed in black, from the knit caps covering their hair to their black leggings. The only things they wore not black were their shoes, each one wearing different color jogging shoes. Before parking, they drove down the desolate street. All the businesses were closed. They pulled into the alley behind one row of shops. When they reached the back of Pagan Oils, they parked, pulling off the road into some bushes to conceal the vehicle. When getting out of the car, one sister noted they looked more like cat women than witches, to which the other two sisters quickly hushed her. Now was not the time to chat.

Together they crept to the back door of Pagan Oils. The oldest of the three used the flashlight app to illuminate the doorknob. Minutes later the door opened and the three slipped into the store, closing the door behind them.

TWENTY MINUTES earlier Joe was surprised to find Kelly at home when he walked into their house. She sat on the sofa, wrapped in a blanket, while watching television, with no lights on. The moment Joe walked in, she turned on the lamp sitting on the end table and used the remote to turn off the television.

"Have you found them?" Kelly asked.

"Nothing yet. I'm surprised you're home. I thought you were sitting with Evan and Eddy?" Joe asked, dropping his keys on the coffee table and then leaning down to give her a quick kiss.

After the kiss she said, "His sister came over; she's spending the night with the boys. I'm surprised you're home."

"I just stopped by to grab something to eat. The chief called, and he wants us to go through Heather's house. So I'm going back out."

AFTER JOE GRABBED a quick bite to eat, he got back in his car, intending to meet the chief at Heather's house. Fortunately, Danielle had a key, so there would be no reason to break in. On the way over, he drove down the main street, not sure what he thought he might see, but it was the last place Brian, Heather or Walt had been seen, and he felt compelled to check it out again.

Just as he drove by Pagan Oils, he spotted something he hadn't expected to see—a light coming through the closed blinds of the front window. It wasn't like someone had turned the light on in the shop; it looked more like a flashlight moving around the store, and whoever was holding the flashlight appeared to be standing close to the front window. Joe immediately called the chief.

FEELING cocky at pulling off their reconnaissance mission during the dead of night, the three sisters slipped out the rear entrance of Pagan Oils into the darkness. They had just shut the door and relocked it when floodlights blinded them, and a voice called out, "Police, put your hands up!"

WHILE JOE and his team went through Heather's house, looking for anything that might give a clue as to their disappearance—perhaps someone had sent her a warning letter that she hadn't shared with Chris or her other friends—Chief MacDonald sat in the interrogation room with Finola Baird, while the police held her two sisters separately.

In the chief's hand he held a baggie containing a necklace, one made with a thin leather strap and a whalebone carving of a hawk. He looked from the baggie to Finola.

"You broke into a store in the middle of the night, just to steal a necklace that's priced less than twenty dollars," the chief said. "And you already have one." He pointed to the necklace around her neck.

Finola fingered the white hawk carving and then said, "May I see it, please? It was too dark in the store to get a good look. And if I have to go to jail for stealing something that's only worth twenty bucks, I'd like to at least see it."

The chief frowned at her request but slid the bag across the table to her. He didn't object when she removed the necklace from the bag and then took a closer look, studying it while turning it from side to side.

"What is this all about?" the chief asked.

"That's what I'm trying to find out," she said, placing the necklace back in the baggy and handing it to the chief.

He took the baggy and said, "What do you know about the disappearance of Brian Henderson, Walt Marlow and Heather Donovan?"

She frowned. "Disappearance? Walt Marlow, isn't he the one who owns Marlow House; some distant cousin of his founded Frederickport?"

"Yes."

"I met him and his wife the other day. He's missing?"

She seemed sincerely clueless, so he asked, "How well do you know the Parker sisters?"

"You mean the women who own the shop we broke into?"

"You admit you broke in?" the chief asked.

"You caught us red-handed, so it would be silly of me to deny it."

"How well do you know them?"

"I don't know them at all," she said.

"Why did you break into their store?" the chief asked.

She nodded at the baggie on the table and said, "To get that necklace."

"Why didn't you just buy it?" he asked. "In the long run, it would be much cheaper for you."

"Because I didn't want to step foot in that store while they were there," she said.

"Why is that?"

"Because the Parker sisters have been stalking us for some time now. If I'm to figure out why, I need to know more about that necklace."

TWENTY-ONE

The tarp made a crinkling sound as he rolled to one side. *I'm too old for camping*, Brian silently grumbled, his back killing him after spending the night on the hard ground. Opening his eyes, he sat up while rubbing sleep from them before looking around. The fire continued to burn, but without more fuel it would soon die. Brian glanced over to Heather, who snored lightly, and then to Walt, who sat bundled in his tarp, silently watching him while the sun rose above the treetops to the east. The three had taken turns standing watch—or more accurately, sitting watch—while the other two slept. Brian had taken over for Walt, and he had expected Heather to be on watch when he woke.

"Good morning," Brian said in a quiet voice. He nodded to Heather. "How long has she been sleeping?"

"About an hour," Walt told him. "I woke up, couldn't get back to sleep."

"Yeah, not the best accommodations," Brian said, twisting his body in a failed attempt to work out the kinks.

Walt stood up and said, "Now that you're awake, I think I'll walk down to the creek. When I get back, we should wake up Heather and get going."

"Agreed," Brian said, stumbling to his feet. "I'll go when you get back."

After Walt disappeared through the trees, Brian picked up his tarp and gave it a shake to remove the dirt and pine needles. When he felt the tarp was sufficiently clean, he folded it.

"I never figured you for a neat freak," Heather said, now sitting up.

Brian looked over to her. "You're awake. How did you sleep?"

Heather jumped to her feet. "I imagine better than you. I heard groaning last night every time you turned." She stretched and then touched her toes.

"Stop showing off," Brian grumbled, tossing his now folded tarp on the ground.

"Showing off how?" Heather asked, now jogging in place.

"Reminding me how old I am. You jumping around like that." Brian reached down and picked up another tarp; he began to fold it.

"Wow, you really are a neat freak," Heather said, no longer jogging in place.

"I just figure it'll be easier to carry them if they're folded," he said. "And we need to get going. No time to waste."

"Why would we be carrying them?" Heather asked. "I'm not normally a litter bug, but under the circumstances, isn't that a bit compulsive?"

"I'm thinking more along the line if we need them again," Brian said.

"Why would we need them again?"

"If we have to spend another night in the woods," Brian suggested.

"No! I refuse to spend another night out here! I need to shower. I have to wash my hair. I'm hungry."

"I don't want to be here in the first place."

Heather let out a sigh and picked up her tarp. "Now that I think about it, even if we don't have to spend the night in the forest, it would be crappy to leave these behind." She gave the tarp a little shake and then folded it.

"We also need to cover the fire," Brian said.

Heather looked at the dying embers. "Yeah. I don't want to burn the forest down. That would be worse than littering it with tarps. But we don't have a shovel. And it's too bad we don't have something to carry water in. We could douse it good."

Brian picked up the hunting knife from where he had left it the night before and said, "I can use this as a makeshift shovel."

Walt returned to camp a few minutes later to find Brian and

Heather kicking dirt on the embers. They explained what they intended to do before leaving camp.

"Why don't you walk Heather down to the stream first?" Walt suggested. "I'll work on covering the campfire while you're gone."

Heather grinned at Walt. "Oh, that is an excellent idea." She grabbed Brian's right hand and started dragging him from the camp.

"Wait!" Brian stubbornly refused to be dragged along by Heather. He tried handing the hunting knife to Walt, who refused to take it.

"No," Walt said. "You might need it."

Brian looked at the fire, which was no longer flaming, just red embers. "We don't have a shovel."

"Go ahead, and take the knife with you for protection. We'll finish up when you return."

Before Brian could argue the point, Heather dragged him from camp.

Now alone, Walt stood silently, looking down at the dying campfire while listening to Brian's and Heather's voices fade off down the trail to the creek. Confident they would not be returning in the next few minutes, he willed the hot embers to lift into the air and then set down on the ground several feet away. Where the fire had just been, his energy removed dirt, forming a deep hole. The dirt landed several feet away. Walt watched as his energy pushed the campfire into the hole he had just formed. He looked to the pile of dirt and then willed it to cover the embers. When Walt completed his task, all evidence of a campfire had vanished.

He smiled and said, "Much easier than doing it manually."

HEATHER KNELT by the creek while cupping her hands and taking a drink of water. Brian stood next to her, glancing around and thinking of all that had happened since he had regained consciousness.

"What made you believe Walt could really communicate with animals?" Brian asked.

Heather stood up and wiped her wet mouth off on her sleeve. "What do you mean?"

"If I hadn't seen that encounter with the mountain lion, and then the fact Walt knew right where this stream was because supposedly the mountain lion told him, well, what made you a believer?"

Brian stood with his back to the stream while he talked to Heather. As she listened to his question, she glanced past him and the water. Instead of answering his question, she reached out and grabbed his wrist, giving it a squeeze. Without letting go, she said, in a wavering voice, "Yes, that mountain lion knew all about this place because it's obviously her watering hole."

Brian frowned at Heather and then slowly turned to the stream. There, standing on the other side, was the mountain lion—he assumed the same one that had the encounter with Walt. The lion's eyes met his as she drank some water, and a minute later she turned and ran away in the opposite direction, quickly disappearing from sight.

Heather glanced to Brian's other hand, not the one whose wrist she had been clutching, but the one holding the hunting knife. She noticed his knuckles, now white from clutching the knife's handle over tightly.

"Were you planning on a knife fight with the cougar?" Heather asked.

"Damn. Let's get back to camp," Brian said.

Heather didn't argue. Together they quickly made their way back to Walt.

When they stepped into the clearing a few minutes later, Brian came to an abrupt stop when he spied the campfire—or more accurately, the lack of one.

"Where did it go?" Brian blurted.

"I covered it," Walt said with a shrug.

Brian looked at Walt's hands. They were clean. Impulsively, Brian grabbed hold of Walt's right hand and looked at it. Even Walt's fingernails were fairly clean.

"You'll have to excuse Brian," Heather said, swatting him away from Walt and breaking up the fingernail inspection. "We just ran into your friend by the stream. I think Brian is a little jumpy."

"I just don't understand how you did it—so quick. You don't have any tools," Brian said.

"Walt is always full of surprises," Heather said. "Better not to overthink it." She walked over to her tarp and picked it up.

Confused, Brian shook his head and then picked up his tarp and Walt's. He handed Walt's to him and said, "I thought we should take these with us. Hopefully, we'll get back to civilization before nightfall, but if we don't, we'll need these."

"I agree," Walt said, tucking his folded tarp under one arm.

"Walt!" Heather squealed. Both men looked her way and found her pointing behind them. "Do something!"

Both men turned around and saw a snake slithering into the clearing—a rattlesnake.

"Um…can you talk snake?" Brian asked nervously. By reflex, they began backing away from the snake. In reaction to their movement, the snake coiled, its rattler now buzzing loudly.

"I don't think so," Walt said, his eyes never leaving the snake.

"Walt, do something. I read once they only strike when coiled, and that damn thing is coiled!" Heather said.

The next moment the snake flew into the air—but not because it decided to strike. It went straight up, a good twelve feet above the ground, hovering there a moment before it flew from the clearing, traveling a considerable distance, well out of sight.

"Did you hurt it?" Heather asked.

"Now you're worried about me hurting the snake?" Walt asked. "I thought you wanted me to take care of it."

"I just wanted you to get rid of it," Heather said. "I don't want to kill the poor thing."

"That's what I did," Walt said.

"I know. But I hope you didn't kill it. Not really the snake's fault. We're on its turf," Heather said.

"I put it down gently," Walt assured her.

"What is going on?" Brian shouted.

Walt and Heather turned to Brian, who looked as if he was ready to explode.

"What is going on? Ever since those crazy witches drove out of here, Heather started yelling at Walt to wake up, to get us out of this. I thought she was just being hysterical."

"Me hysterical? I think you're the hysterical one right now," Heather said calmly.

Brian glared at Heather. "Talking to animals, making snakes fly, and disappearing campfires!"

"Which only proves I was not being hysterical," Heather said. "I knew Walt's special gifts would come in handy."

"Someone explain what is happening!" Brian asked.

"You understood about the mountain lion," Walt said calmly.

"I don't think understand is the correct word," Brian snapped.

Walt almost expected to see steam coming out of Brian's ears at any moment. He glanced over to Heather, who seemed to derive pleasure from Brian's confusion. "Stop snickering, Heather," Walt told her.

Heather shrugged. "Oh, come on, Walt, it is amusing, if you think about it. I remember all those stories Danielle told me about Brian, when they first met. This is sort of karma."

"And Danielle considers Brian a friend now," Walt reminded her.

"Hello? I am still standing here," Brian said.

Walt turned to Brian and said, "I'm sorry, Brian. I'm sure this is all very confusing, especially considering what happened to us since last night. I will explain, but please, take a deep breath and calm down first."

Reluctantly, Brian did as Walt suggested and then waited for an explanation.

"Do you remember the time you ran into me in the grocery store, and cereal boxes fell off the shelf, but instead of falling to the floor, the boxes went back on the shelves?" Walt asked.

Brian stared at Walt but did not respond. He had convinced himself it had all been his imagination.

"And how you recently saw Danielle fly around our living room on a broom?"

"You said that was a trick with wires," Brian said expressionlessly.

Walt smiled at Brian. "I lied."

TWENTY-TWO

"Danielle calls it telekinesis," Heather told Brian. "It's the psychic ability to move objects."

"Who all knows about this?" Brian asked.

"Everyone who knows about my ability to communicate with some animals," Walt said.

"Except for snakes," Brian added.

"Honestly, I'm not hundred percent certain of that. I may have been able to, but the snake seemed to be a little too upset to listen to what I had to say." Walt paused a moment and then added, "Police Chief MacDonald, he knows about it too. I don't think I included him before when I told you who knew of my abilities."

"Why am I not surprised?" Brian muttered.

"I think we should get going," Walt said.

Heather pointed to the opening where the Parker sisters had left through. "We need to go that way and follow the path. It should lead us to the road."

"Did either of you see the road?" Walt asked.

Heather shook her head. "No, I came to right before we entered this clearing."

"I didn't either. They were tying me to the tree when I woke up. But I saw them leave that way. And I heard the car about thirty minutes later," Brian said. "I just assume they parked it on a road. Not necessarily a paved road."

The three headed for the opening leading to the pathway that had brought them to the clearing. They walked side by side down the path, with Heather in the middle.

"So how long have you had this tele-whatever ability?" Brian asked after about five minutes of walking in silence.

"I'm fairly certain that prior to the car accident, Clint Marlow did not move objects mentally or communicate with animals," Walt said.

"You talk as if that's another person, not you," Brian said.

"It might as well be. I know nothing of his life before the car accident, beyond what I've been told," Walt said.

"It's because of the coma," Heather said.

Both men glanced briefly to Heather.

"The reason he has these powers," Heather explained.

"Why do you say that?" Brian asked.

"A coma is like a near-death experience. You read about these sorts of things. Someone almost dies, maybe they see a white light, talk to angels, and then when they come back, they have some special powers, like Walt."

Brian glanced to Walt and asked, "Did you see a white light or angels when you were in the coma?"

Walt chuckled. "Not that I recall."

"Do you agree with Heather that the coma brought on these powers of yours?"

"I prefer to think of them as gifts as opposed to powers," Walt said.

"Whatever. But do you think the coma caused it?" Brian asked.

Walt glanced over to Brian and smiled. He looked back down the path as they continued to walk. "I honestly don't know why I have these gifts. But I am fairly certain that the man who walked in this body prior to that car accident didn't have them."

"I THINK it's going to take longer than thirty minutes to get to the road," Heather said after they had been walking about twenty minutes.

"Why do you say that?" Brian asked.

"I was thinking about how it sounded after they left us. I think they were walking fast. It might take us an hour or more to get to the road," Heather said. "Unless we want to walk faster or run."

"I seriously doubt they ran for thirty minutes," Brian said.

"I don't know why. I jog for longer than that each day," Heather said.

They picked up their pace; the path wound around several massive boulders and then came to an abrupt stop. The path they were following broke into three pathways. They could continue straight or go right or left.

"Which way do we go?" Heather asked.

"I would expect it to be obvious, considering some of the ruts in the path we've come across, which I'm sure were from them dragging us out here," Walt said, looking from path to path.

"Those contraptions they used could have been hauled over any of these," Heather grumbled.

"I would think we'd want to continue west," Brian suggested. "We know that takes us to the ocean."

"I want to get to a road, not the ocean," Heather said.

"It looks like the path to the right winds around and may take us back to where we were," Walt said. "So, my guess, keep going straight or take the pathway to the left. Plus, the one straight looks more like something has recently been dragged over it."

"So does the one to the left," Brian said.

Heather groaned. "I'm hungry. I want a nice cup of tea. When I get out of this, I am marching over to Pagan Oils with Marie to show those Parker sisters the damage a real witch can do!"

Brian frowned at Heather while Walt chuckled and said, "Now you're claiming to be a witch?"

"Why not? Anyone can claim to be a witch," Heather said.

"Why don't we keep going straight?" Brian suggested. "That path seems more traveled than the other one."

"You're probably right," Walt agreed.

They continued down the path, Walt taking the lead while Brian and Heather walked side by side, trailing behind him.

"Are you okay?" Brian asked Heather.

Heather looked to Brian and smiled. "You sound sincerely concerned."

Brian shrugged. "This has been hard on all of us. And a minute ago, I thought maybe you had reached your limit."

"Nah, I haven't even begun to flip out yet."

Brian chuckled. "I suppose I should be grateful; if we have to be stranded in the middle of the forest, at least someone like Walt is with us."

Now it was Heather's turn to chuckle. "You thought I was just being hysterical when I was trying to get him to wake up after we came to."

Brian grinned. "You could have told me."

"Yeah, right. Like you would have believed me," Heather said.

Brian watched the back of Walt's head as he led them down the path. He then glanced to Heather and said, "I always knew there was something different about Walt. Of course, this isn't exactly what I expected."

"I have to say, I am rather proud of you," Heather told him.

"Why do you say that?"

"Some people would either freak or go into total denial mode, desperately searching for some rational explanation. Take Joe, for example. I don't think he would ever believe it, even if he was the one Walt sent flying around on the back of a broomstick."

THEY HAD BEEN WALKING for over forty minutes when they began worrying. Had they chosen the wrong pathway? No one said anything, each hoping they would come to a road, reminding themselves they were probably traveling at a slower pace than the Parker sisters, who had wanted to get out of the forest before nightfall. They stopped fifteen minutes later when a small river blocked their way.

"Holy crap," Heather muttered. She glanced around. They had come to the end of the trail.

Brian let out a sigh. "I guess we need to turn back and take the pathway to the left."

"I don't mean to be a pain," Heather groaned. "But maybe we can look for wild berries or something first? I haven't eaten since lunch yesterday, and I barely had any lunch."

As if to prove her point, Heather's stomach growled.

"I'm hungry too," Brian said. "But if it makes you feel any better, we can go without food for longer than water, so I suppose we should be grateful we keep finding water."

Heather frowned at Brian. "I seriously never pegged you for a Pollyanna."

Brian shrugged.

"I don't think there's reason for us to go hungry," Walt said as he stood by the side of the river, looking into the crystal-clear water. He could see fish swimming around, searching for smaller fish.

"Why, do you see some berries?" Heather asked hopefully.

"Even if we find berries, do you know which ones are safe to eat and which ones are poisonous?" Brian asked.

Hands on hips, Heather turned to Brian. "I liked you better as a Pollyanna as opposed to a Debbie Downer."

Ignoring the exchange, Walt said, "I wasn't thinking of berries. How does fresh fish sound?" A trout flew out of the water and landed on the ground by Heather's and Brian's feet. A moment later a second fish flew from the water, followed by a third.

Walt grinned at Brian and Heather, who stared down at the flopping fish. Walt looked at Brian and said, "You have the hunting knife, so you can clean them, since I caught them. I have the matches; I'll start the fire. I'm not in the mood for raw fish."

THE THREE SAT around the small fire, enjoying their morning feast. And it looked like a feast. Brian had gutted and beheaded each fish. He speared each one with a long sharpened stick before cooking them over the fire. But it wasn't just fish for breakfast, they had berries on the menu.

"Are you sure these won't kill us?" Brian asked before taking some berries in one hand.

"In answer to your question earlier, yes, I know the difference. I took a class at the museum, on natural plants in the area. These are huckleberries," Heather explained. "And they are edible."

"They look like blueberries," Brian said before popping several into his mouth.

Ravenous, the three stopped talking and focused on the meal before them. When they finished, they each stood up and walked to the water for a drink and to wash their hands, now sticky from eating berries and fish.

"That was pretty good," Heather said, wiping her clean yet wet

THE GHOST AND THE WITCHES' COVEN

hands off along the sides of her jogging pants. "I didn't even miss the tartar sauce."

"It's amazing how good food tastes when you're starving," Walt said.

"I almost forgot, that's one reason why I used to enjoy camping trips," Brian said.

Heather looked to him and asked, "What do you mean?"

"This morning, when I woke up, it reminded me how I'm too damn old for camping. Missed my bed," Brian said.

"That has nothing to do with age," Heather said. "I missed my bed too."

"But our breakfast reminded me of something I enjoyed about those camping trips I used to take. Freshly caught fish cooked over an open fire. Always tastes better, I think. Although, I remember fishing used to be a little different. Involved poles, hooks, and bait." Brian flashed Walt a smile.

"One has to improvise when you don't have a fishing pole," Walt said.

Brian looked down at the small fire Walt had built for cooking the fish. "I guess we need to do something about that before we leave. Walt?"

Walt let out a faux sigh and said, "You guys are going to make me do all the work, aren't you? Last time I invite you two on a camping trip with me."

The next minute water splashed from the nearby river, dousing the fire. Brian watched in fascination as Walt did his magic, first forming a hole for the doused fire, moving the fire into the hole, and then covering it with dirt. Heather watched Brian, getting as much enjoyment from observing him as he was getting watching Walt.

"How's that?" Walt asked when he finished covering the fire.

Brian shook his head in awe. "And I can't even tell anyone about this when we get back. They would think I'm nuts."

"You can tell the chief," Heather reminded him.

TWENTY-THREE

After leaving their sacrifices at the altar in the forest, the Parker sisters had spent the night at a motel instead of driving all the way home. The decision was a spur-of-the-moment one. Drugging their victims with tainted cookies and then dragging them out to the forest had been exhausting.

But when they woke up in the morning without a change of clothes, they headed back to Frederickport, before returning to the forest that night. They pulled into their driveway a little after nine in the morning. The first order of business after parking their van, showers and a change of clothes, and then breakfast. Although tired, accompanied by sore muscles from lugging around the bodies, the Parker sisters felt both excited and optimistic about their future.

Wrapped in exhilarated optimism and a clean robe, Davina fairly skipped to the kitchen to start breakfast while her sisters finished their showers. She had just filled the coffeepot with water when the doorbell rang. Considering the modesty of her floor-length, green flannel robe, she didn't consider not opening the door. When she opened it a few minutes later, she found two police officers standing on the doorstep. One was a woman, the other a man. The man introduced himself and his fellow officer. His name was Joe something, but she didn't catch the woman's name or Joe's last name. But she had seen both of them around town. He asked if she was one of the Parker sisters, owners of

Pagan Oils and More. She said yes, gave her first name, but didn't ask him in. She remained standing behind the door, inside, looking out.

"We need to speak to you and your sisters," the one named Joe said. "May we come in?"

"What is this about?" she asked.

"We're investigating a missing persons report, and we understand you may be one of the last ones to see them," Joe said.

She frowned, still clutching the edge of the front door. "Who's missing?"

"Walt Marlow, Brian Henderson, and Heather Donovan."

"I don't know who they are," Davina said. "I can't help you."

Joe then said, "And your store was broken into last night."

"It what?"

"May we come in?" Joe repeated. "We really need to speak to you and your sisters."

Hesitantly, Davina swung the door open wider. "My sisters are upstairs taking showers. They should be down in a few minutes." Clutching the front of her robe, she motioned toward the living room. Once in the living room, Davina took a seat on the sofa and motioned to the nearby chairs for the officers. Instead of sitting down, Joe walked over to the sofa and laid three photographs on the coffee table before Davina; one was of Heather, one of Walt, and the third of Brian.

Davina looked down at the photos. "What am I looking at?"

"Do you remember seeing them yesterday?"

She shrugged. "No."

"What's going on here?" a woman's voice asked.

Joe and his fellow officer turned to the voice and saw Bridget and Aileana Parker standing in the open doorway. Unlike their sister, they were dressed for the day, each wearing a dark kaftan, their long red hair flowing free down past their shoulders.

"They said something about the store being broken into last night," Davina told her sister, ignoring the photographs still on the coffee table before her.

Once again Joe made introductions and then said, "Before we discuss the break-in, we need to ask a few questions about our missing persons."

"Is our store okay?" Bridget asked.

"Yes, everything is fine. But first, I need to find out what you know about the disappearance of one of our officers, along with Heather Donovan and Walt Marlow," Joe said.

"Why would we know anything?" Bridget asked.

Davina pushed the photos, still on the coffee table, away from her and told her sisters, "They showed me these pictures, but I told them I don't recognize them. I don't know who these people are. I haven't seen them."

"That's interesting," Joe said, looking at Davina. "We have you on the surveillance camera letting Walt Marlow and Brian Henderson into your store shortly before closing last night. The footage also shows Heather Donovan going into the store a few minutes earlier." He turned to Bridget and Aileana and added, "The footage has you two entering the store before that, and not leaving. In fact, the footage doesn't show any of you leaving," Joe paused a moment and then turned to Davina and said, "Except you."

"What surveillance camera?" Bridget asked.

"The one across the street from your store," the woman officer said.

Davina frowned and then looked back down at the photos Joe had placed on the coffee table. Hastily she pushed them back into view and looked at them.

"I guess these could be the two men who I let into the store. I didn't recognize them by the pictures," Davina lied.

"I'm afraid my sister's facial-recognition skills are poor," Bridget said. "I remember once an old boyfriend of hers stopped by the house, and she didn't even recognize him at first. Thought he was trying to sell something." Bridget smiled at the police officers and then strolled to the coffee table and looked down at the photos.

"Do you remember them?" Joe asked.

"Of course," Bridget said smoothly. "The woman, she came in first. She bought some essential oils. Then the men came in. They all seemed to know each other. We were getting ready to close up and had a couple of heavy boxes we needed help carrying out to our van, and the two gentlemen were kind enough to offer to carry them for us. I honestly don't remember their names. When we drove off, they were still standing at the back of the store, talking."

Joe glanced from Bridget to Davina. Davina nodded and said, "Yes. That's what happened."

"What did the men buy?" the woman officer asked.

Bridget stared at her a moment and then said, "They didn't buy anything. They got to talking to the woman. I told you they all seemed to know each other. And when we mentioned we were about to close up and something was said about having to carry the boxes out, they offered to help. I just assumed they came into the store to talk to their friend."

"Did you notice anyone else behind the shops when you were leaving?" Joe asked.

Bridget appeared to be considering the question for a moment, and then shook her head. "No. I didn't see anyone. Now, what is this about our store being broken into?"

"Late last night, when I was driving down the business district, I noticed a light in your shop. It looked like someone walking around with a flashlight. We caught them coming out the back door," Joe explained. "The only thing they took from the store was a necklace."

Bridget's eyes widened. "A necklace?"

"Yes." Joe reached into his pocket. He pulled out a plastic baggie containing the hawk necklace. He showed it to Bridget.

Bridget smiled at Joe and said, "We don't want to press charges against the women."

"I didn't say the burglars were women," Joe said.

Bridget looked up into Joe's face, her eyes wide in faux innocence. "Didn't you? I guess I just assumed it was women. That necklace doesn't seem like something a man would take. Who were they?"

"While I made the initial arrest, Police Chief MacDonald interrogated them. I think it would be best if you spoke to him directly. But nothing seemed to be disturbed in the store, and the only thing they had with them when I found them leaving out the back door was this necklace. And you were right, they were women. Three of them."

"How did they get in?" Aileana asked.

"Apparently one of them is rather skilled at picking locks. You might consider having a locksmith change your locks—something a little more challenging for criminals. But as I said, nothing was disturbed. No broken windows, no vandalism. And according to them, all they wanted was this necklace."

"Thank you, officer. I don't think I need to talk to the police chief. And I have no desire to press charges. Sounds more like a prank to me."

"Prank?" Joe asked with a frown.

"Yes. You know, when someone does something for the thrill? The necklace itself isn't of great value. And you said they had nothing else with them. If they wanted to take something of value, they would have filled up a sack with essential oils. Some of those bottles go for over a hundred dollars." Bridget smiled at Joe and then turned the smile at the woman at his side.

CHRIS LET the chief into the parlor on Sunday morning. Danielle sat on the sofa, staring off blankly as Max snuggled by her side. The moment MacDonald walked into the room, she looked up hopefully, her red-rimmed eyes revealing the countless tears she had cried.

"I'm sorry, nothing yet," the chief said quickly, not wanting to give her false hope. He took a seat across from her while Chris sat on the sofa next to her.

"But we finally talked to the Parker sisters," the chief began before recounting Joe's conversation with the sisters.

When he finished, Danielle said, "I can't believe Walt and Brian left without buying something. Maybe Walt, if he felt they were just closing up and he could come back later, but Brian was there to get something for Kitty's headache. I don't see him leaving without it, since he was already in the store."

"I agree," the chief said. "What Joe found odd; they didn't seem interested in knowing more about our missing people. I would expect them to ask some questions, but they weren't curious. Unfortunately, we have nothing substantial on them. We have been through their store twice, once after we looked at the surveillance video, and again after the break-in. Found nothing to indicate foul play. And their explanation about leaving through the back door is plausible."

"But you said the one sister denied knowing anything when looking at the photographs," Danielle reminded him.

"True. But it is possible she didn't connect the faces in the pictures with the customers in her store. Some people aren't observant and have poor facial-recognition skills."

"Did you find anything at Heather's last night?" Chris asked. He and Danielle had wanted to go through the house with the police, but the chief said they couldn't. Instead, Danielle had handed over Heather's spare house key and waited to hear if they found anything. With all the extra commotion of the break-in at Pagan Oils, no one ever got back to them with the search results.

"We found nothing," the chief began. "But there was one thing I wanted to double-check on. Heather's security cameras."

"What security cameras?" Chris asked.

"The cameras Heather had installed in her house," the chief said.

"Heather doesn't have any security cameras," Chris said.

"My team found three of them," the chief argued.

"If you found security cameras hooked up in Heather's house, she didn't put them there," Chris insisted.

"I agree with Chris," Danielle said.

"The cameras didn't raise any red flags," the chief began. "Not unusual for someone who has a pet to have cameras monitoring them."

"Heather takes Bella to work with her," Danielle said.

"I understand, but like I said, home security cameras in themselves are not unusual these days. But what we found unusual, there wasn't an app for the cameras on Heather's phone. That's why I wanted to ask you about it. Typically, people monitor security cameras on their cellphones with an app," the chief explained.

"Find who put those cameras in Heather's house, and I bet you find who knows where they are," Danielle said.

"And one of the Parker sisters was behind Heather's house the day before they went missing," Chris added.

TWENTY-FOUR

"I know you've already looked through Pagan Oils, twice, but can you get a search warrant for the Parker house?" Danielle asked.

"On what grounds?" the chief asked. "They don't deny Heather, Walt and Brian came in the store; and we have no reason to believe they didn't leave out the back door. According to the neighbors, they saw the Parkers pulling up to their house not long after they locked up the store. The neighbor said one of them went into the house while the other two stayed in the van. She came back a few minutes later, carrying a sack, and then got back in the van, and they all drove off. The neighbor said she wondered where they were going, because they seemed in high spirits. And according to her, it was only three of them."

"How do they know they weren't in the back?" Danielle said.

"It's an old Corvair van, with windows in the back," the chief said. "If someone was sitting in the back seat, they would likely see them."

"Unless they were tied up on the floor," Danielle said.

"You're grasping at straws," the chief said. "If someone tied them up, then that would mean Walt was unconscious. I can't come up with a plausible scenario where those women incapacitated all three of them minutes after entering the store. We are talking about a seasoned officer and someone with Walt's abilities. And like you say, there is no reason to believe they aren't alive considering none of their spirits have shown themselves to you or Chris."

"What about the women who broke into their store?" Danielle asked.

The chief frowned. "What about them?"

"A coincidence they broke into the store a few hours after they go missing. If nothing else, maybe they were casing the place and saw something," Danielle suggested.

"I thought of that already," the chief said. "But according to them, they weren't downtown during that timeframe, and we didn't see them on the security camera."

"We didn't see anyone on the security camera," Danielle grumbled.

"So what's the deal with the women you arrested?" Chris asked.

"Looks like I'll probably be letting them go without filing charges. I doubt the DA will be interested in prosecuting, since Pagan Oils refuses to press charges."

"Why don't they want to press charges?" Danielle asked.

"I'm not sure. But I suspect the Parkers know who broke into their store, although Joe said he never mentioned the names of the burglars. Yet they guessed they were women, and they didn't seem surprised at the only item taken. Which was strange in itself."

"What do you mean?" Chris asked.

"They entered through the back door, picked the lock. All they took was a leather necklace with a hawk whalebone carving. The odd thing, the woman who took it wore one just like it. At first Joe thought she had taken both of the necklaces. But, after looking closer, he could see her leather strap was different and well worn. Her hawk also looked much older, and she claimed hers was a family heirloom. Plus, before they broke in the shop, she'd had the clasp on her necklace repaired locally, and we were able to verify it with the shop."

"Are you saying the Baird sisters broke into Pagan Oils?" Danielle asked.

"You know them?" the chief asked.

"I met them briefly. They rent a house from Adam," Danielle said. "And they claim to be witches, like the Parker sisters."

"None of the Baird sisters claimed to be witches when I interrogated them. Of course, I didn't ask. But they said one thing I found interesting. They claimed the Parkers had been stalking them, and that's why they broke into the store. They wanted a closer look at the necklace that matched theirs. After they looked at it in the bright light, they seemed perfectly happy turning it over to me."

"What did they mean the Parkers stalked them?" Chris asked.

"They refused to elaborate. And it doesn't look as if the Bairds have ever filed a complaint," the chief said.

"They have to know something," Danielle said. "Something they know about the Parkers that they're not telling you."

"You really think the Parkers have something to do with the disappearance?" the chief asked.

"They might know something that could help. Walt and the others walked into that store and disappeared. And one of the Parkers was by Heather's house the day before. Maybe the Bairds know something about the Parkers that could help us," Danielle said.

"Thankfully, they're still alive," Chris reminded her. "Which is the one positive in all this."

"We just need to find them before their ghosts show up," Danielle said.

"I promise to talk to the Baird sisters again before I release them," the chief said.

After the chief left fifteen minutes later, Danielle looked to Chris and said, "We need to find Marie and Eva."

"How will that help?" Chris asked.

"Some people install cameras in someone's home to spy on them. I prefer using ghosts," Danielle said.

THE THREE BAIRD sisters sat quietly around the interrogation room table, their hands folded on the tabletop in front of them. The chief's first thought when walking into the room and seeing their eyes all focused on him, *I wonder if they are going to cast a spell on me.* His second thought, had this been three hundred years earlier, they would have more to worry about than a breaking and entering charge.

Without saying a word, he took a seat at the head of the table, remembering how they had all forfeited their right to an attorney the night before, saying they would wait in the cell until they learned what charges were going to be charged.

"It seems the Parkers will not press charges," the chief began.

Finola stood while saying, "Then we can go?"

"Please sit down, Ms. Baird," the chief said.

With a sigh, Finola sat back down.

"While the Parkers do not want to press charges, that does not mean the DA won't press charges. You broke into a business, and when arrested, you were in possession of stolen merchandise."

"Does the DA seriously want to waste resources on such a petty crime?" Ina asked. "We already gave the necklace back, and we hurt nothing."

"It's still at the discretion of the DA to press charges, not the Parkers," the chief reminded them.

Finola studied the chief a moment and then asked calmly, "What do you want?"

The chief arched his brows. "Excuse me?"

"You clearly want something. I don't believe for a moment the DA intends to pursue this case. You obviously want something from us," Finola said.

The chief leaned back in his chair and studied Finola. Finally, he said, "I want you to tell me all you know about the Parkers, and why you said they were stalking you."

Finola and her sisters exchanged glances. She then looked back to the chief and let out a sigh. "I was not trying to be secretive last night when I didn't elaborate on my stalking claim. To be honest, I wish I never said it, but sometimes I speak before I think."

"Are you saying they didn't stalk you?" the chief asked.

"No. We believe they were stalking us, but under the circumstances, going to someone like you about this rarely works out for people like us," Finola said.

"Someone like me?" the chief asked.

"A cop. And you aren't just a regular cop, you're the police chief," Finola said.

"I find it hard to believe you're suggesting you've had past issues with the police," the chief said. "When I ran a background check on you, nothing came up on any of you. No priors. So when exactly have you had a problem with the police?"

"It's not just who you are, it's what we are," Finola said.

"Is this because you claim to be witches?" he asked.

Finola stared at him a moment and then smiled. "So, you know."

"Frederickport is a small town. And you haven't exactly been secretive about it. But the last time I checked, we no longer burn witches at the stake, so I'm not sure what the problem is."

Finola reached up and absently fondled the hawk carving hanging from her neck. "There are some things difficult to put behind us."

"I'm not really sure what you're talking about, but I would like to know more about this stalking, and if you would be a little more open, perhaps we can get you out of here, with no charges filed."

Once again Finola exchanged glances with her sisters. She let out another sigh and then said, "We have never formally met the Parkers. At first, we thought it was a coincidence."

"Coincidence?" the chief asked.

"The first time we noticed them was during college. They lived in the apartment across the street from us. It was strange; it felt as if they were always watching us. And then, one day, someone broke into our apartment. Our neighbor, a guy we were friends with, came home unexpectedly, and we're certain he interrupted the burglars. They had ransacked the place, but nothing was missing. One of our other neighbors said she spied a redhead leaving out the back of our apartment around that same time. We didn't really connect it to the Parkers until we realized they had moved out in the middle of the night. They were no longer living across the street."

"You never found out who broke in?" the chief asked.

"No. But the cop didn't even take fingerprints. While they no longer lived across the street from us, we saw them around town. We finally decided their sudden move had nothing to do with our break-in. A couple of years later, when we moved from California to Ohio, we were surprised when they moved into a house down the street from us. We thought it was such a bizarre coincidence, but we were sure it was them."

"And then we moved to Nevada, and they followed us there," Kenzy said.

"I can't honestly say back then we believed they followed us, but it seemed to push the coincidence thing," Finola said. "When we moved to Oregon, we said if they showed up, we would know they were following us."

"And they showed up," the chief said.

"Yes. Funny thing, I don't think we were really serious about the possibility of them showing up here," Finola said. "But they did."

"And now they're witches," Ina said.

"They weren't witches before?" the chief asked.

"To be honest, we've never met them. And if they considered themselves witches before moving to Oregon, we don't know. But after they moved here, they open Pagan Oils and practically shouted it to the world they're witches, with their store and YouTube channel," Finola said.

"I couldn't believe that article about them in the newspaper," Ina said. "They call themselves blood witches. And that ridiculous YouTube channel. Frankly, it's women like them who got our ancestors burned at the stake!"

"You're open about being witches," the chief said. "How is that different?"

"They're exploiting something they know nothing about," Finola said. "And the spells they include on their YouTube channel, it's irresponsible."

"What exactly did you hope to accomplish by breaking into the store?" the chief asked.

"I needed a closer look at that necklace, and I didn't want to do it when they were in the store," Finola said, touching her hawk carving.

TWENTY-FIVE

It had been over an hour since Walt had covered the breakfast fire. They made it back to the fork in the trail, took the left pathway, and after walking over ten minutes found themselves confronted by a new fork in the trail.

"At least there are only two choices this time," Brian said.

"Back to Pollyanna?" Heather grumbled.

"Are you hungry again?" Brian asked. "Should I offer you a Snickers bar?"

Heather looked to Brian, her expression stern, and then she broke into a laugh. "I'm not sure which side of you surprises me the most, Mr. Sunshine or the comedian."

"At least I got you to smile," Brian said.

"Yeah, but don't you know, it's never a good idea to tease a woman with imaginary chocolate," Heather said.

"Chocolate, I'd love a piece of Danielle's chocolate cake right now," Walt said with a sigh.

"When it comes to chocolate, Walt, you can be such a girl," Heather teased. The three remained standing at the fork in the trail, not yet deciding which way to turn.

"I would happily take any cake. It doesn't even have to be chocolate," Walt said.

Brian glanced at his watch. "It's not even lunchtime. Too early for cake."

"Oh, Walt has a major sweet tooth," Heather said. "If we wander around in this forest much longer, don't be surprised if he starts tracking bees so he can find their hive."

"I wouldn't mind seeing that," Brian said. "Watching Walt get the honey away from the bees using his powers. Think he would try talking them out of the honey or take it forcibly?"

Heather laughed. "You also have a silly side. You surprise me, Brian Henderson."

"I hate to disappoint you two, but I doubt I'm about to wrestle any bees for their honey quite yet. I'd rather we figure out which path we should take."

"Such a spoilsport, Walt." Heather then looked down the path and said, "Brian called the last one, which was wrong."

"But we got breakfast out of it," Brian reminded her.

"True. Extra points for that," Heather said.

"I say we keep going straight," Walt suggested.

"Agreed," Brian said.

Heather started down the path in a slow jog, leaving Walt and Brian to trail behind her.

"So what is the deal between Chris and Heather?" Brian asked Walt. While they could see her up ahead, she was out of earshot.

"They are friends; he is her boss," Walt said.

"Just friends?" Brian asked.

Walt glanced briefly to Brian and then looked back down the path as they continued to walk. "Surprised you're asking a question like that."

Brian shrugged. "Just curious. I've heard different people suggest they're an item. Seems like an unlikely pair."

"Until recently, Heather was dating someone. I don't know what happened, but she's no longer seeing him and doesn't seem upset about it. As for Chris, he's been doing his share of dating, yet not with anyone locally. I don't think he's found the person he feels safe enough with to share his actual identity."

"But Heather already knows, and they seem to spend a lot of time together," Brian said.

"True. But I see them more like siblings than a couple. Which includes trying to set the other one up on dates."

"Really?"

Walt nodded. "Really."

ASIDE FROM HAVING BEEN DRUGGED, kidnapped, and left tied up in the middle of the forest, Heather felt rather chipper. Sleeping on the ground hadn't been as bad as she made it out to Brian. Before going to sleep, she had placed her tarp over a bed of pine needles, softening the hard ground. Breakfast of freshly caught fish and berries had sat well with her, and she wanted desperately to break into a brisk jog yet knew it would not be wise to get too far ahead of Brian and Walt.

Drinking in the fresh air, she took a moment to count her blessings. She didn't know why the Parker sisters did this, but she knew that if Walt and Brian hadn't walked into the store after her, she would have woken alone in the middle of the forest, tied to a tree. Heather didn't want to consider what would have happened to her when that mountain lion showed up. The thought gave her chills.

Another thing to be grateful for was knowing Chris and Danielle would realize she was missing and then take care of Bella. She didn't have to worry about Bella going hungry or thirsty.

While merrily counting her blessings, while jogging at a slow pace so as not to get too far ahead of the men, Heather turned a corner and came to an abrupt stop.

"Oh crap," Heather muttered, coming face-to-face with a bearded man aiming a rifle at her.

"Stop right there," the man ordered.

Heather's eyes widen as she took in the unexpected sight. His plaid flannel shirt and denim pants, both well-worn and faded, with boots on his feet and a floppy hat on his head painted a picture of someone who had been in the forest for some time. The gray beard covered much of his face, and she wasn't sure if he was in his fifties or eighties.

Nervously putting her hands in the air, she said, "Please don't shoot."

"What are you doing here?" he barked.

"I...I'm lost. I just want to find the way to the road out of here. That's all," Heather said.

"I know what you're doing here, snooping around. But I don't have a problem shooting you like I did the others. I don't care if you are a woman. You are a woman, aren't you? Hard to tell in that getup."

Before she could call out a warning to Walt and Brian, she heard them behind her, and the next moment she heard Walt let out a curse as he came to a stop next to her.

"Get the rifle," Heather whispered to Walt, her hands still in the air, her eyes never leaving the man aiming his weapon at her.

"Why are your hands in the air?" Brian asked Heather.

"Why do you think?" Heather snapped.

The man waved his rifle from Walt to Brian and said, "Get your hands in the air, both of you!"

From the corner of her eye she saw Brian just standing there, looking at her. "Brian, do as he says! Walt, hurry!"

Walt raised his hands in the air, his eyes on the bearded man.

"Now you, put your hands up," the man ordered, his rifle aimed at Brian.

"Walt!" Heather hissed under her breath.

"It's not working," Walt said calmly. He held his hands in the air while looking from the old man to Brian. Brian now looked from Walt to Heather.

"What are you two doing?" Brian asked.

Walt nodded toward the old man, whose agitation increased with Brian's failure to comply. "Brian, what do you see over there?"

Brian frowned and then looked toward the old man. "Am I supposed to see something? I don't get it."

Walt let out a sigh and lowered his hands. "Heather, I think you can put your hands down."

Heather glanced from the old man to Brian and then said, "Oh…you mean…"

Walt nodded. "First clue, I couldn't get his rifle away from him. Second clue, Brian doesn't see him."

"I said put your hands up!" the old man screeched, now wildly waving his rifle.

"What don't I see?" Brian asked.

"The man pointing the rifle at us," Heather said, regaining her calm.

The man started shooting, but when no one fell to the ground after being shot, he disappeared.

"Or should I say, the man who just shot at us and disappeared," Heather said. She walked to the spot the apparition had been on and looked around.

"I wish one of you would please tell me what the hell you are talking about!" Brian raged.

Heather looked to Walt. "Do you want to tell him, or should I?"

Walt shrugged. "You might as well. I think I'm going to look for the guy. It's what Danielle would do."

Brian watched as Walt continued down the path while Heather stood a few feet from him, smiling like she was about to tell him some unpleasant news, yet wasn't particularly sorry about it.

"Are you going to tell me?" Brian asked.

"Do you remember when I claimed to see ghosts?" Heather asked.

Brian's eyes narrowed. "Yes. Why?"

"I didn't lie. Also, Walt can see them too. So can Danielle and Chris. And Evan."

"Evan?" Brian asked.

Heather nodded. "Yes. The chief's youngest son. The chief knows about this too. He knows about all of it."

Brian said nothing, but just stared.

"I thought he was real," Heather began.

"You thought who was real?" Brian asked.

"The old dude with the rifle. He was just here a minute ago, pointing it at me. That's why I put my hands up—that's why Walt put his hands up. He thought he was real too. But when he couldn't take the rifle away—"

"Wait a minute, are you saying a ghost was just here? And you and Walt saw it?"

Heather nodded. "Yes. And I'll admit, scared the crap outa me when I thought he was real. But a ghost can't hurt you. Not if you're an innocent, anyway. And frankly, I consider myself an innocent. I'm not a bad person."

"I have no idea what the hell you're talking about."

"I can't find him," Walt said when he returned. He looked at Heather and asked, "Did you tell him?"

"Yes, but I'm not sure he understands," Heather said.

Walt looked at Brian, "Normally we would probably come up with some story about why Heather was holding up her hands. We'd engage in some double talk to explain this all away. But frankly, considering our situation, we're past all that, don't you think?"

Brian stared at Walt yet said nothing.

"It's about ghosts. They exist, and we can see them." Walt started to list off the local mediums, but Heather stopped him by saying she had already told Brian who the mediums were.

After a moment, Brian took a deep breath and said, "Okay, let me get this straight. Walt can communicate with animals—"

"We don't know if it's all animals," Heather interrupted, to which Brian raised his hand as if to stop her from saying more.

Brian then said, "Walt can communicate with *some* animals, he can also move objects with his mind, and he can see ghosts."

"He is not the only one who can see ghosts," Heather grumbled.

Ignoring Heather, Brian looked at Walt and asked, "Is there anything else? Any more secrets about you I don't know?"

Walt shrugged. "Not sure what they would be. Isn't that enough?"

"What about the fingerprints?" Brian blurted.

"Excuse me?" Walt asked.

"Your fingerprints. Why are they the same as the original Walt Marlow's? And your handwriting, why is it the same as the original Walt Marlow's? Even your signature is the same. Why is that? And why, when I brought this up with the chief months ago, he brushed me off and didn't want to discuss it?"

Heather watched as the two men stared intently into each other's eyes.

"Do you really want to know?" Walt asked in a quiet voice.

"Yes. I do," Brian said.

Heather's eyes widened, unable to believe Walt would actually tell him the truth.

Walt smiled at Brian and said calmly, "Because I am the original Walt Marlow. My ghost lived at Marlow House for almost a hundred years. Danielle saw it. Chris saw it. Heather saw it. Even Evan saw it. You felt it a few times, like when you grabbed Lily and I decked you. Or when I made you spill beer on yourself at Ian's bachelor party. But I did bring you a towel. And then there were the cigars I used to smoke. You could smell them. But I gave cigars up for Danielle."

Brian's eyes widened, but he said nothing. He continued to listen.

"When my distant cousin Clint Marlow, who looked just like me and shared my name, came to visit and almost died in a car accident, his spirit did not want to return to his body. He wanted to move on with his fiancée, and the universe let him. And I was given a second chance in life, in my cousin's body. I don't know why the fingerprints of Clint's body changed into my own. But when one dies and then is reborn, it doesn't mean that person has all the answers."

TWENTY-SIX

"I'll get it," Lily called out to Ian when she heard the doorbell ring. He was in the living room on the floor, playing with Connor, while she was in the kitchen, fixing them both a glass of iced tea. Sadie the golden retriever followed her to the front door, her tail wagging.

When Lily opened the door a minute later, she found Danielle standing on her doorstep. By her expression, she knew Walt and the others hadn't returned. Lily opened her arms, and before exchanging any verbal greetings, Danielle accepted the offer, and the two friends hugged while Sadie tried pushing her way between them, vying for attention.

The hug ended and Lily took Danielle by the hand, leading her into the living room, while Danielle gave her a quick update. Sadie followed the pair, her tail still wagging.

When they entered the living room, Ian looked up at the women. "Any news?"

Danielle shook her head and immediately set her sights on Connor, whose eyes lit up when he saw her, opening his arms for her as his mother had done. Needing love and comfort, Danielle scooped up the baby, holding him close and breathing in his scent—a mixture of milk and animal crackers, while Lily conveyed to her husband what Danielle had told her.

"You haven't seen Marie?" Danielle asked as she set Connor back on the floor with his father.

"We never see Marie," Lily reminded her.

"You know what I mean."

"Sorry. I don't think she's been here since before they went missing. Connor has not acted like she's been around, and she usually lets me know by writing hello on the board," Lily said.

"Still no sign of Eva or Marie?" Ian asked.

Danielle shook her head. "No. I could really use a Casper right about now."

Lily frowned. "Casper?"

"Yeah, it's a term Chris coined this morning," Danielle explained. "You know, Casper the Friendly Ghost. That's what we could use, a friendly ghost."

"Where is Chris?" Ian asked.

"That's sort of why I'm here," Danielle began. "We'd like to find Eva and Marie. I think they could help. Eva always seems to know more than anyone else—as in any other spirits. And if those women from Pagan Oils had something to do with their disappearance, or know something that they aren't telling, the quickest way to find out is to have Eva or Marie over at their house, listening in on what they're saying. But we need to find them first. Chris left Marlow House a little while ago, heading down to the cemetery. Sometimes they go there to visit. And I'm going over to Adam's house. I know Marie likes to hang out with him."

"Is there anything we can do?" Lily asked.

"That's one reason I stopped by. I'd like to write a message for Marie on the dry-erase board in Connor's room, just in case she stops in while he's napping and doesn't let you know she's here. I also left a note for her and Eva at Marlow House, if they stop by while I'm out."

ON THE DRIVE over to Adam's house, Danielle tried to think of what she wanted to say. While she frequently dropped by his office to say hello, she didn't normally drop by his house. But it was Sunday afternoon, and she knew he wouldn't be at the office. If she wanted to find Marie, one of the first places to look was at Adam's.

While the chief seemed to believe the Parkers were not

responsible for the disappearance, she had a gut feeling he was wrong. She then thought of the Bairds and what the chief had told her about his last conversation with the sisters before releasing them without filing charges. Just as she pulled into Adam's driveway, she knew what excuse she would give him for stopping by.

"Danielle," Adam said with surprise when he opened the door a few minutes later, "any news?"

"I'm afraid not," Danielle said.

Adam opened the door wider, welcoming her inside. He didn't notice when Danielle glanced around, looking for any sign of Marie.

"You just missed Mel," Adam said. "Can I get you something to drink?"

"No, I just stopped by to ask you something."

Adam led Danielle into the living room, and they both sat down.

"Sure, what did you want to ask me?"

"Those women who rent a house from you, the ones who lost the necklace I returned?" Danielle began.

"Ahh, my witches? What about them?"

"I'd like to talk to them. I was hoping you could tell me where they live."

"You don't think they have something to do with the disappearance, do you?" Adam asked.

"No. But I'd like to ask them some questions about the owners of Pagan Oils. From what I understand, they sort of know them," Danielle explained.

"Well, I suppose it makes sense all the witches in Frederickport know each other," Adam snarked. "But frankly, all that witch stuff is just goofy. Mel says it is like those people who start sleeping in coffins and call themselves vampires. Actually, there was a guy in town who got a dentist to put fake fangs in because he wanted to be a vampire. Nuts. So, tell me, you really think the women who run Pagan Oils are responsible for their disappearance?"

"I just think they know more than they're saying."

Adam told Danielle where the Bairds lived and then asked, "When I was downtown a while ago, I noticed the Packard and Heather's car were no longer by the museum."

"Yeah, I dropped Chris and Ian down there last night, and Chris drove the Packard to Marlow House while Ian drove

Heather's car back to her house. We had extra keys, and the chief okayed it," Danielle explained.

"YOU ARE NOT GOING THERE ALONE," Chris insisted when Danielle told him she was on her way to see the Baird sisters. She had just said goodbye to Adam and called Chris on her cellphone while walking to her car.

"Why?" Danielle asked while opening her driver's side door.

"I just don't think it's a good idea. Let me go with you."

Holding the cellphone by her ear, she laughed at Chris while getting into the car. "No way, you are too much of a distraction."

"What is that supposed to mean?" Chris asked.

"The Baird sisters, there are three of them. My guess, all in their twenties. If you come with me, they will never be able to focus on my questions."

"Funny." By his tone, it didn't sound as if Chris really thought it was funny.

"Anyway, you need to keep looking for Marie and Eva. Find us a Casper, will you?"

THERE WERE no cars parked in front of the Bairds' rental house, not in the street or in the driveway. But that didn't mean no one was home, Danielle told herself. Their cars could be in the garage. She parked along the sidewalk in front of the house and turned off the ignition. A few minutes later she stood on the front porch, ringing the doorbell.

Danielle waited for someone to answer the door. When no one did, she rang the bell again.

"No one is home," Danielle heard a woman's voice say. Danielle turned around quickly and found herself looking at the woman she had talked to downtown—the one who had seen the necklace drop —a necklace that matched the one she wore—the woman Danielle thought looked like a hippy. The woman wore the same outfit she was wearing the last time Danielle had seen her, and she wondered if she was homeless.

"You were the one I talked to downtown," Danielle said.

"Yes. And thank you for returning the necklace to Finola. I would have done it, but I'm afraid I was in a hurry."

"So you know the Baird sisters?" Danielle asked.

The woman smiled. "We haven't met. But I know who they are. I've seen them around. I saw them not long ago when they were getting ready to leave. I overheard them say they were going to Pier Café for an early dinner, if you're looking for them."

"Um…thank you. Do you live around here?" Danielle asked.

"I'm staying with some friends. But I need to be going now." The woman turned and hurried away. Danielle watched as she disappeared down the street. With a sigh, Danielle pulled out her cellphone and dialed Chris.

"Everything okay?" Chris asked when he answered the call.

"Any luck finding Casper?" Danielle asked.

"I'm afraid not."

"How does Pier Café sound for an early dinner? I'll meet you there."

"Sure. What happened with the Baird sisters?" Chris asked.

"I'll explain at the pier."

CHRIS ARRIVED at the pier first, and when Danielle spied him sitting in the parking lot, she pulled her car next to his. After they both got out of their vehicles, they started walking toward Pier Café while Danielle told him one reason for being there.

"I thought you didn't want me with you when you talked to the Bairds?" Chris asked.

"I'm hungry, figured you could use something to eat too. And if Carla is working today, I'd sorta like to talk to the Baird sisters without her hovering about. You can keep Carla distracted while I do."

"What's the real reason you don't want me with you when you talk to the Baird sisters?" Chris asked.

"I told you, you're a distraction," Danielle said.

"Knock it off. What is the real reason?"

Danielle let out a sigh. "I just think I'll have more luck with them opening up and telling me something that they might not have told the chief if it is just me."

"If they have anything to tell," Chris reminded her.

"I know it's a long shot. But it's easier to confide in one person than two people. Because later, if you regret being candid, it's easier to change your story. But with two people—two people you don't know—listening to what you have to say, people are more cautious. I want candid, not cautious. And, when I met the Bairds, they were pretty standoffish. They only got friendly after they realized I had something they wanted."

CARLA RUSHED to Danielle and Chris the moment they walked into the restaurant.

"Has there been any news?" Carla asked, giving Danielle a hug.

"No, I'm afraid not," Danielle said, not bothering to ask Carla how she knew about the disappearance. Not only was it a small town, where news traveled fast, the disappearance had been the front-page story of the morning newspaper.

"No ransom demands?" Carla whispered to Chris.

"No. Nothing," Chris said.

When they pried themselves from Carla's questions, they headed for an empty booth while Danielle scanned the café, looking for the sisters. She spied the three sitting at a table for four along one window.

After Carla took their order a few minutes later, Danielle stood up, and by all appearances it looked as if she was headed for the women's restroom, when she was in fact walking towards the Bairds' table. When she reached their table, she stopped, standing silently for a moment until the three sisters noticed her.

"You're the one who returned my necklace," Finola greeted her with a smile.

"Yes, I'm Danielle Marlow."

"I heard about your husband. Is he still missing?" Finola asked.

Danielle nodded. "Yes, along with Brian Henderson and Heather Donovan, both friends of mine."

The sisters each expressed concern, and then Ina Baird asked, "Have there been any leads?"

"Well, actually, that's why I'm here. I was wondering if I could have a few minutes of your time. Please. It's very important," Danielle said.

"Um, I'm not sure how we can help," Finola said.

"I understand you know the Parker sisters," Danielle said.

By reflex, Finola touched the hawk carving hanging from her neck. "We don't know them, exactly."

"I think they are someway involved in my husband's disappearance. Please, can you spare me just a few minutes," Danielle begged.

The sisters exchanged glances, and then Finola reached out to the empty chair next to her and pushed it out slightly. She nodded to the chair and told Danielle, "Sit down. I'm not sure how much we can help. But we'll try."

TWENTY-SEVEN

Danielle sat down on the offered chair. Finola, who had just finished her meal, pushed her empty plate away while her sisters listened to what she was about to say and quietly finished their food.

"This is a small town, so I imagine you'll hear about our recent arrest," Finola began, with no hint of embarrassment. She then repeated what Danielle had already heard from the police chief.

Danielle silently listened, occasionally glancing at the two sisters, who said nothing while eating their meal.

When Finola finished her telling, she cocked her head slightly, studying Danielle. Finally, she asked, "Why do I think you already knew everything I just told you?"

Danielle blushed and then said, "I confess, I knew some of it. That's why I'm here. I wanted to know what you didn't tell the police."

"I heard the Marlows were pretty chummy with the local police department," Finola said.

"They have arrested me a few times," Danielle said.

Finola laughed. "Nice to hear it. So we aren't the only ones?"

Danielle grinned. "No. But the police chief is a good guy and someone who tries to do the right thing. My husband is one of the people who are missing, so naturally he is a little more open with me on this case than he would be with someone else."

"Does he know you're talking to us?" Finola asked.

Danielle shook her head. "No."

Finola eyed Danielle and asked, "What do you want to know?"

"Do you think the Parkers could be behind the disappearance?" Danielle asked.

"Like I said, we've never actually met them," Finola said. "But yeah, I think it is entirely possible."

Danielle did not respond.

"You looked shocked?" Finola asked.

Danielle shrugged. "I suppose a little."

"We just believe the Parkers are irresponsible and potentially dangerous," Finola said.

"How so?" Danielle asked.

"Have you checked out their YouTube channel?" Finola asked.

"I looked at it a little last night, but it didn't really tell me anything. At least nothing I felt might be helpful in finding out what happened to my husband and the others."

"That's because you don't understand what you were seeing," Finola said.

"How do you mean?" Danielle asked.

"For one thing, they claim to be blood witches, which I don't believe for a minute. My sisters and I are blood witches." Finola paused a moment and then asked, "Do you know what that means?"

"Someone descended from a line of witches," Danielle said.

Finola nodded. "Yes, that's correct. One of our direct ancestors, Gavenia Tolmach, was a witch. They burned her at the stake."

"In Salem?" Danielle asked.

Finola shook her head and said, "No, in Scotland, about four hundred years ago." She then touched the hawk carving and said, "This belonged to her. The leather strip, of course, has been replaced many times over the years. But the carving, it belonged to Gavenia. She gave it to her daughter just days before they burned her at the stake. In our family it's passed down to the eldest daughter."

Danielle leaned toward Finola a moment, taking a closer look at the hawk carving again, and then sat back in her chair. "It's very similar to the one they sell at Pagan Oils."

"You mean the one we stole," Finola asked with a smile.

"Why did you steal it?" Danielle asked.

"We saw it in the store's window. It looked so much like this one. We couldn't believe it. It made little sense. Gavenia's husband made it. There is only one like it. Or so we thought."

"I saw another one. When I found your necklace after you dropped it, a woman who was walking down the street pointed it out, told me she saw you drop it, but she was going the other way and asked if I would give it to you. When she walked away, I noticed she had one like it around her neck."

"She probably bought it at Pagan Oils," Finola suggested. "I guess you thought I was pretty foolish when you asked me where I bought it, and I went on about it being a family heirloom and one of a kind. I imagine you thought I was lying."

Danielle shrugged in response.

Finola touched the carving again and asked, "Do you know what Gavenia means in Scottish?"

"No," Danielle said.

"White Hawk. That's why her husband carved her a hawk. The eldest daughter in our family who receives this is sometimes called a White Hawk."

"So you're called a White Hawk?" Danielle asked.

Finola shook her head. Her hand dropped from the necklace and then reached for her glass of iced tea. She picked it up, took a drink, and then said, "The last White Hawk was my grandmother's great-grandmother. The White Hawk has special powers. Someday, I hope to have a daughter, and she will be the White Hawk."

"Special powers?" Danielle asked.

"That's not important. I'm telling you this so you can understand why we believe the Parker sisters are not what they seem. They are not blood witches, but they say they are to lend credibility to their website and to sell more merchandise from their store. And to be honest, I think they have convinced themselves it's all true. Their website, it's littered with half-truths. Dangerous information that in the wrong hands could cause harm."

"What do you mean half-truths?" Danielle asked.

Finola considered the question a moment and then said, "They claim a blood witch can't be killed. Which is true."

Danielle arched her brow. "Are you saying you never die?"

Finola laughed. "Not exactly. If someone walked in here and shot me through the heart, for those around me it would appear that I died. But my essence and magic would take another form."

"I suppose some might say that is true for all of us," Danielle suggested.

"No. It's not the same thing," Finola insisted. "During the witch trials, many people were falsely accused of being witches, and they were brutally murdered for the imaginary crime. But there were some genuine witches, like my ancestor, who they burned at the stake. Do you know why they were burned?"

"To kill them?" Danielle suggested.

Finola shook her head and said, "Many were already dead when burned. But people believed the only way to destroy a witch's power was to burn her body. That was not true. And the Parkers are correct when they say that."

"Um...if witches never die, then what happens to them? Your ancestor, for example. If they burned her at the stake, what happened to her?"

Finola smiled. "A witch can return in many forms. After Gavenia's arrest, her daughter, Blair, just a child, hid in the forest for days, waiting for her mother, until they killed Gavenia and burned her body. Gavenia returned to her daughter in human form, and she helped Blair escape the village, and stayed with her, teaching her the magic of our ancestors."

"So you're saying Blair was a witch like her mother?"

"Yes."

"If they never really die, where are they now?" Danielle asked.

"I don't know. The last one to see Gavenia was my grandmother's great-grandmother," Finola explained.

"You are getting off topic," Ina told her sister.

Finola glanced to her sister back to Danielle while saying, "She's right. I was just pointing out an example of something that they get right on their website. However, there are other things, such as spells they include, which are dangerous and ridiculous."

"How so?" Danielle asked.

"One spell caught my attention. It's a spell on how to vanquish a blood witch. Utter nonsense. Of course, they claim it is one of the more powerful and dangerous spells. They don't include the incantation the spell requires; instead they talk in general terms."

"It's all fake," Kenzy said. "You can't destroy a blood witch with a spell."

WHEN DANIELLE RETURNED to the table with Chris, her hamburger was already waiting for her and getting cold. As she sat down, she glanced over to the Baird sisters and watched as they walked from their table to the exit door.

"Did you learn anything?" Chris asked.

"A little." Danielle's eyes still on the sisters, she noticed someone by the door, the hippy woman she had seen earlier by the Baird house. The woman stood by the door, as if waiting for the Bairds, and then left with them.

"I thought she didn't know them," Danielle said as the four went outside.

"Who?" Chris asked, looking in the same direction as Danielle.

"Did you see that woman following them out the door?" Danielle asked.

"Yeah, what about her?" Chris looked back to Danielle.

"That's who I ran into at their house. She's the one who told me where they were. And she claimed not to know them."

"Then how did she know where they were?" Chris asked. Danielle told him about her two encounters with the woman. After the telling, he said, "It didn't really look as if she was with them. It looked more like she just happened to be leaving out the door at the same time. They didn't even look at her when they got to the door."

"I suppose. But still, it is weird. Why was she here?" Danielle turned her attention back to her plate and looked down at the burger. Using the tip of her right index finger, she gave the burger a poke, testing its warmth.

"So what did you learn?" Chris asked.

"This witch thing of theirs is really out there. They claim blood witches—which they profess to be—never really die. I guess they die, but then they come back in some other form."

"Like a black cat?" Chris asked.

Danielle frowned. "Didn't there used to be a TV show like that once?"

Chris shrugged. "Not that I remember."

Danielle picked up her burger. "Yes. *Sabrina the Teenage Witch*, or something like that. I think it was a comic series too."

"Sounds vaguely familiar. So you're saying they come back as cats?"

"They didn't mention cats." Danielle then shared what she had learned about the history of the Bairds' ancestor, burned as a witch, yet who reportedly returned in human form to her daughter.

"Does any of this help us?" Chris asked.

"The takeaway from my conversation, the Parker sisters are a little strange. Although the Baird sisters are pretty strange themselves, considering what they told me." Danielle took a bite of her burger. A moment later she continued. "The Bairds claim they are the real deal, but the Parkers aren't. Witch wise. They believe the Parkers want to be them."

"Like in take over their lives want to be them? Or just copy them?"

"I'm not really sure. But they believe it all started when they first moved next door. I think it was in California. On one hand, they practically call the Parkers charlatans, but in the next minute they talk as if they feel the Parkers actually believe they're witches. Although Finola never really explained how the Parkers knew she and her sisters were witches. According to Finola, they never met, and back then they didn't discuss their family's history with strangers."

"And what does it mean for us?"

"Nothing specific. Just that the Bairds believe the Parkers are not above doing something that might hurt someone, if they feel if benefits them."

"And how would it benefit them? I haven't even received a ransom note," Chris said.

"I know. But the Baird sisters also said they don't believe the Parkers' motivation is money."

"Then what is it?"

"I have no idea." Danielle finished eating her burger while Chris considered all that she had told him.

Finally, Chris said, "That woman leaving with them, didn't you say she was wearing the same necklace as Finola?"

"Yeah. I'm sure she got it at Pagan Oils."

"Maybe not. Maybe she's a ghost," Chris suggested.

"Whose ghost?" Danielle asked.

"The ghost of this ancestor burned as a witch. The necklace was originally hers, and if she came back to help her daughter, maybe it was her ghost that came back."

"And her daughter was like us, a medium?" Danielle asked.

Chris nodded. "Yes."

Danielle considered the suggestion for a moment and then shook her head. "No. I don't believe she is this Gavenia's ghost."

"Why not?"

"I talked to her. Gavenia died in Scotland—some four hundred years ago. The woman I spoke to didn't have an accent. And Scotland four hundred years ago, I don't think they spoke English. And even if they did, well, I worked with a woman from Scotland once, and it was very difficult for me to understand her. No. She isn't a ghost. Remember Saint Nicholas? His ghost still had his accent, and he died over fifteen hundred years ago."

TWENTY-EIGHT

"They've been missing almost twenty-four hours now," Danielle said after she and Chris walked into the kitchen at Marlow House late Sunday afternoon. Hunny greeted them while Max and Bella stood by the door to the hallway, meowing.

"I wish there was something more we could do," Chris said, leaning down and scratching Hunny behind the ears.

Danielle opened a can of cat food. The next moment snow fell from the ceiling, and both Danielle and Chris stopped what they were doing and called out, "Eva!"

The falling snow swirled and then faded. In its place, the apparition of Eva Thorndike appeared. "What a friendly welcome," Eva said, waving her hands in a flourish.

"Where's Marie?" Danielle asked, quickly abandoning the open can of cat food on the counter.

"I thought you were happy to see me," Eva said with a pout. In the next moment Max let out a meow, and Eva looked to the cat. A second later, she looked to Hunny and then back to Max and then to Bella.

"We are happy to see you," Danielle said.

Eva looked up to Danielle with a frown and asked, "Where is Walt? Heather? Is something wrong?"

"First, where is Marie?" Danielle asked.

"I imagine at Adam's. She was stopping over there for a little while, and then she's meeting me here. We've been in Portland at a film festival. What is going on?" Eva asked. "Hunny and the cats are quite concerned."

Several minutes later, the three sat at the kitchen table while Danielle and Chris filled Eva in on what had been going on. Eva conveyed the information to Hunny, Bella and Max, who wondered where Walt and Heather had gone.

"Do you have any idea where they might be?" Danielle asked when they finished with the telling.

"No more than you," Eva said. "As you know, being a ghost doesn't mean I know everything that's going on in the living world. Or with the dead, for that matter. But if you haven't seen their spirits, we can be fairly certain they are still alive. I can't imagine Walt or Heather not coming back here."

"That's what we think too," Danielle said. "But Walt's not defenseless. Which makes us wonder, has he been knocked out? Is he unconscious somewhere? Or is it something like when Walt and I were trapped in the tunnel, and his powers were practically useless?"

"How can I help?" Eva asked.

"We were hoping you or Marie might hang out at the Parkers' house and see if they say anything that might lead us to where they are," Danielle said.

"You believe those women are responsible for the disappearance?" Eva asked.

"Maybe not responsible directly, but they might know something," Danielle said. "Something they don't want to tell the police."

"It might also be a good idea to do some ghost sleuthing with other shops along that strip," Chris suggested. "See if they know something they aren't telling the police. Someone had to have seen something."

"Which do you want me to do first?" Eva asked.

"Go to the Parkers'," Danielle said. "And when Marie gets here, I'll have her check on you, and then maybe one of you can stay with the Parkers, and the other one can do some sleuthing like Chris suggested."

EVA ARRIVED AT THE PARKERS' in time to see the three women getting into their van.

"Where are you going?" Eva called out to deaf ears. The next moment she sat in the back of the van with one of the Parker sisters while the other two sisters sat up front.

"Aren't any of you concerned about what the police asked us this morning?" the sister sitting next to Eva asked.

"What was that?" Eva wondered aloud, knowing they could not hear her.

"Calm down, Davina. The only reason they spoke of Heather is because the spell wasn't finished. You'll see, when we get there, Heather and the others will be gone, and when we return to Frederickport, no one will even remember she existed," the sister sitting in the driver's seat said. She then slipped a key in the ignition and turned on the engine.

"What do you mean no one will know who Heather is? You know where they are!" Eva said. She wanted to tell Danielle and Chris what she had just overheard, yet she also wanted to continue listening. Looking out the car window, she hoped to see Marie, who could relay a message to Danielle and Chris, but she was nowhere in sight. Eva didn't know if Marie was still with Adam, or had she arrived at Marlow House? Even if she had, Eva imagined it would take her a while before she made it to the Parkers', assuming Danielle and Chris would need to fill her in first on all that had happened in the last day.

"Are you sure, Bridget?" Davina asked.

"Yes, that has to be it. We know the spells work. They brought us the ruby and Heather. This one will work too. We did everything right. In a couple of hours, we'll get to where we left them and then be able to start back home before it gets dark," Bridget promised.

"What did you do?" Eva asked. "What spell?"

DANIELLE SAT in the living room with Chris, watching television, neither of them able to focus on the program, when Danielle's cellphone rang. She picked up her phone from the coffee table while Chris muted the television. Before answering, she looked to see who was calling.

"Hey, Lily," Danielle greeted her.

"By your tone of voice, doesn't sound like you have any news," Lily said.

"No. But Eva showed up, and she went over to the Parkers' to do some eavesdropping. Marie's at Adam's, but I expect her to be here soon."

"Then would it be okay if I take the note for Marie off the dry-erase board?" Lily asked. "Joe and Kelly are coming over in about an hour, and I really don't want them to see it."

"No problem. Think maybe you can wait until they get there before you take it down? Just in case she goes there first?"

"Sure."

The next moment Danielle said, "Never mind. Marie, don't move!"

"I take it Marie just showed up?" Lily asked.

"Yes. Talk to you later." Danielle hung up the phone.

"Goodness, what is this all about?" Marie glanced around. "Where's Eva? She was going to meet me here."

"Something's happened," Danielle began. She and Chris then told Marie the events of the last twenty-four hours.

"Oh my!" Marie said after hearing what had happened. "Let me pop over there now and see if Eva has learned anything."

"I KNOW this is the right house," Marie muttered as she wandered through the rooms of the Parker house. Danielle had mentioned they owned a van. While there was a Volkswagen parked in their garage, along with a Jeep, there was no van.

The house appeared to be empty, and there was no Eva in sight. She wondered if she was at the wrong house, but when she walked by the desk in the family room a moment later, she spied a stack of bills addressed to Bridget Parker.

"I'm at the right house," Marie said aloud. She continued through the rest of the rooms, calling for Eva, but there was no answer. She returned to Marlow House.

"No one is there," Marie announced when she appeared again before Chris and Danielle. Chris immediately turned off the television.

"Not even Eva?" Danielle asked.

"No one," Marie said. "I went through the entire house. There were two cars in the garage, but I didn't see the van you mentioned."

"Maybe you were at the wrong house," Chris suggested. He started to tell her the directions to the house again, but Marie stopped him.

"I was at the right house. I found mail addressed to a Bridget Parker."

"That's one sister," Danielle said.

"They must have gone somewhere, and Eva went with them," Chris said.

EVA DIDN'T KNOW how long they had been driving or where they were going. Not long after their cryptic discussion of Heather, the sister in the passenger seat had turned on the car radio, and since then the three had been merrily humming along to the music.

In her boredom, Eva looked around the back of the van, when something caught her attention. A fingernail—one painted dark purple. Eva remembered Heather's nails had been painted the same color the last time she had seen her—just the day before she had disappeared. Unable to pick up the broken nail, as Marie might with her energy, Eva looked closer at the nail and then turned her attention to the hands of the women in the van. None wore nail polish.

"Heather was in this van," Eva murmured.

Later, Eva would regret not paying attention to where the Parkers drove or when they turned off the highway. At some point they turned onto a dirt road, and it was then she realized her error. While she would be able to will herself back to Marlow House, and from Marlow House will herself back to her current location, giving directions to Danielle was another matter.

Eventually the van parked along the side of the road, and the Parker sisters got out from the vehicle. Eva joined them.

"We need to hurry. I want to get back before dark," Bridget said. "I hate driving over this dirt road after nightfall."

"At least we don't have to drag anyone along with us," Davina said. They all laughed.

"You had Heather. That cop, he was a big dude," Bridget said.

"What did you do?" Eva demanded. With unease, she followed

the sisters as they made their way down a footpath. They walked for about twenty minutes and then came to a clearing.

The minute they stepped into the clearing, Davina squealed, "It worked! It really worked."

"I told you," Bridget said smugly.

TWENTY-NINE

While the Parker sisters listened to music and sang along during the ride from Frederickport to the middle of the forest, they had engaged in some conversation, which enabled Eva to figure out the sisters' names. Keeping those names straight had nothing to do with physical or facial differences. If Eva didn't know better, the pale-skinned, green-eyed, twenty-something women with long curly red hair could be triplets. On closer inspection, she could tell a slight difference between each one.

Yet the easiest way to keep them straight, Bridget wore a green kaftan, Davina a navy-blue-print kaftan, and Aileana's kaftan was made from fabric in reds, blues and orange. Eva found all three dresses equally hideous.

Eva stood akimbo at the opening to the clearing, watching as the sisters ran silly circles around the open area, one following another while waving their hands up and down like birds about to take flight, and chanting, "We did it, we did it!" What they did, she was not sure, but she knew it had something to do with her missing friends.

"I can't believe it. It worked. Everything is gone," Davina said, running up to a tree and kneeling down to its exposed trunk. She ran her hand over the bark. "The spell took them away. Even the rope vanished and—" Davina gasped and looked closer at the trunk.

Eva narrowed her eyes, glaring at Davina.

"What is it?" Bridget asked. She and Aileana rushed to Davina's side and looked down at the trunk.

Davina rubbed her fingertips over an indentation on the bark. "Look here. This was where we tied the rope. It left a mark. I thought the spell would remove everything—leaving it as it was before we brought them here."

Bridget looked at the tree and then inspected two other trees. A moment later she returned and said, "There are no marks where we tied up Donovan, which tells me the spell did what it should. If there are marks on the tree where we tied up Walt Marlow, that really means nothing. The spell won't make people forget Walt Marlow and Brian Henderson ever existed, but it will make the world forget about Heather Donovan. And we don't really know if those marks are from Marlow. They could have been there before, and we didn't notice."

"You tied them up here and left them?" Eva gasped.

"Let's get the ruby and go home," Bridget said.

"Ruby?" Eva frowned.

"I hope it's still there," Davina said.

"Of course it's still there. Stop doubting the spell!" Bridget snapped.

Eva watched as the three sisters rushed to the other side of the clearing, along the edge of the trees. Bridget knelt down and began digging up something from the ground while her sisters stood over her, watching anxiously. A moment later Bridget squealed as she pulled something from the dirt and stood up, holding whatever she had unearthed up over her head.

The sisters began jumping up and down like excited children, clapping their hands and again chanting, "It worked. We did it!"

When the spontaneous celebration ended, Bridget lowered her hands, holding the unearthed object in one hand while she used the other hand to brush off the dirt. Curious, Eva moved closer for a better look. To her surprise, Bridget held a ruby ring.

"This ruby holds the power of the blood witch Heather Donovan," Bridget said in awe.

"What do we do now?" Aileana asked.

"Now we must finish the ceremony, transferring the power of Heather Donovan to our coven," Bridget said solemnly.

Eva frowned. "Why does all that sound familiar?" She watched as the sisters moved to the center of the clearing. Bridget set the ring on the ground and then joined hands with her sisters, forming a circle. They moved around the ring, chanting what would sound like nonsensical ramblings to most people, yet to Eva, the words were eerily familiar.

"I've heard that before," Eva murmured. She watched as Bridget picked up the ruby ring a moment later and slipped it on one of her fingers.

"You can't wear it," Aileana said.

"I don't want to lose it," Bridget said. "I'll put it in the safe when we get home."

Eva watched as the sisters gave the clearing one last inspection before heading back in the direction they had come, down the path leading to their car. Eva followed the three, carefully listening. They were far more talkative on their walk back to their car than they had been the entire trip.

By the time Eva reached the van, it had confirmed her suspicions. The women had drugged her friends and then dragged their bodies out to the clearing, tied them to trees, and attempted to cast a witch's spell. From what the supposed witches were saying, all three were alive when brought into the forest—and still alive when the witches returned home. According to what they said, Heather and one man had regained consciousness by the time the Parkers left. Eva suspected it was Brian who had regained consciousness and not Walt, or he could have kept the women from abandoning them in the forest.

Eva understood the women believed the spell they used was responsible for the three vanishing, along with the ropes, tarps, and travoises that they had brought with them. But Eva didn't believe that for a minute. She suspected Walt had finally regained consciousness and used his telekinetic powers to free them. Which meant her friends were wandering around the forest, and by the position of the sun, it would be dark soon.

Instead of driving with the Parkers back to Frederickport or using her own energy to travel there—which was much quicker—Eva decided to find her friends, which would make it much easier for Danielle to pick them up. She just hoped they were still okay.

EVA STOOD on the side of the dirt road and watched as the Parkers drove out of sight. Tempted to return to Marlow House to tell Danielle and Chris what she had learned, she resisted the temptation. She would rather return with news that she had found them, and that they were alive. Now that she knew the Parkers had drugged them, Eva wasn't a hundred percent certain that something hadn't happened to them after getting untied from the trees. She understood the absence of their appearance at Marlow House did not mean they were still alive. If killed while still under the influence of a narcotic, not clearly understanding how they had arrived at a strange location, it would make for a confused spirit. That spirit, even one who understood such things when alive, such as Heather and Walt, might spend eternity wandering through the forest. Eva had to find them, dead or alive. In either case, she needed to get them back to Marlow House.

Walking down the dirt road, Eva called out for Heather and Walt. Overhead, the sun quickly slipped from sight. Soon it would be dark, and being a ghost didn't give a spirit night vision. Until the moon came up, it would soon be difficult to see where she was going.

Eva stopped and glanced around, trying to decide which way to go. She froze when she heard something behind her, stealthily approaching. She was fairly certain what it might be. Not moving, she waited. Whatever it was grew closer. The next moment she looked down just in time to see the paws of an enormous cat flying through her torso and landing several feet in front of her—with the rest of the mountain lion attached. The big cat did a little roll before landing back on its feet, and then looked up at Eva.

"Was that very nice?" Eva asked.

The mountain lion, now sitting, looked Eva in the eyes. Of the two, the cat was better equipped to see in limited light, yet it didn't mean Eva didn't understand what the cat was thinking, despite the fact it looked more like a shadowy figure.

"What do you mean, you knew I was a spirit? How did you know that?" Eva asked.

She then laughed at the response and asked, "And you have seen many ghosts?"

After the mountain lion answered the question, Eva said, "I'm looking for three friends of mine. Two men and a woman. Someone brought them out here, tied them up to a tree, and—" Eva paused a moment and arched her brows. "Really? That would have to be Walt. You don't know where they are, do you?"

THEY WERE LOST. Although technically, they had been lost since the minute they woke up after being drugged by the witches. Brian didn't think the term *witch* was strong enough. Mentally he replaced the *w* with a *b*.

When they realized they had to spend another night in the woods, they backtracked to the last place they had seen the river. Walt did a little fishing while Brian and Heather set up camp nearby before it got dark. By the time Walt returned to the camp with fish, Heather and Brian had made a campfire.

Before they finished dinner, the moon lit the night sky. They made another trip to the river to wash up. After returning to camp, they each placed a tarp on the ground around the fire, getting ready to settle in for the night while discussing their next course of action.

Brian was about to say something when they heard a rustling sound from the nearby bushes. He turned to the sound, as did Walt and Heather, and saw a mountain lion strolling casually toward them. Frozen in place, his heart beating erratically, Brian expected Walt to talk to the animal or throw it from camp. What he didn't expect was Heather saying, "Eva? Are we glad to see you!"

Brian frowned. *Since when was the mountain lion's name Eva?*

THIRTY

"I would hug you if I could," Heather said, now standing.

"Glad to see you're all alive. I was beginning to wonder if you weren't," Eva said. She glanced down at the mountain lion by her side and said, "But your friend here told me what happened. And she has been keeping an eye on you. Tells me you have been wandering around in circles since she helped you. I believe she was getting a little concerned."

Sitting, his heart now racing, Brian looked from Heather to the mountain lion and then to Walt.

Walt stood up and said, "I'm with Heather. You have no idea how glad we are to see you."

The next moment the mountain lion made a snarling sound and turned, disappearing through the bushes.

"Can we go home now?" Heather asked.

Instead of answering the question, Eva looked over at Brian and smiled. "I believe Officer Henderson is a little confused at the moment."

"He's been running into a lot of confusion this weekend," Heather said.

"I just want Danielle to know we're okay," Walt said.

"That's fine for you, but I want a dang shower! And something to eat besides fish," Heather whined.

Brian stood up and said, "I understand the mountain lion

helped free Walt, but when did we start calling her Eva? And she's gone, so why are you two still talking to her? And, Heather, since when did you start talking to animals like Walt?"

Heather looked at Brian and rolled her eyes. "Eva is not the mountain lion's name, you weirdo. It's the ghost's name."

Brian looked around. "There's a ghost here? Where?"

"Why even ask that question?" Heather asked. "You can't see ghosts."

"Eva Thorndike," Walt said.

Brian looked from Heather to Walt. "Eva Thorndike? As in the silent screen movie star?"

"Oh, how sweet, he knows me!" Eva gushed.

"The one whose portrait hangs in the museum? The one who owned the Missing Thorndike?" Brian asked.

"You get a prize for all the correct answers," Heather said. She pointed to Eva. "She's standing right there."

Although Brian was not capable of seeing or hearing Eva, he looked anyway and continued to stare blankly, seeing nothing but trees cast in moonlight.

"Most spirits move on after they die," Walt explained. "Eva is one who has decided not to move on yet."

Brian looked to Walt and arched his brows. "Does Danielle know about this?"

"Of course Danielle knows," Heather said impatiently. "She can obviously see Eva."

Brian continued to stare at Walt, not looking at Heather, his mouth turning into a smile. He asked, "And she's okay with this?"

Walt studied Brian for a moment and then laughed. "Yes, she is fine with it."

"And why wouldn't she be?" Eva asked, sounding insulted.

"Oh...I get it," Heather said. "Because Walt had such a thing for Eva."

"We were just good friends," Walt insisted.

Eva smiled.

"Okay, I'm cool with this," Brian said, trying a little too hard. "Hey, a mountain lion chews off Walt's ropes without leaving a scratch. I watch a rattler fly away from us. A ghost shoots at me—although I have to admit I didn't see that. I just have to take your word it actually happened, and Walt catches fish without a pole. You say the ghost of Eva Thorndike is standing here, I'm good with it." Exhausted, Brian dropped to his tarp, again sitting.

"Oh my, it sounds like you have all had quite the adventure," Eva said.

"Can we go home now?" Heather asked.

"It's a little more complicated than that," Eva said.

"Complicated how? You found us. Now have Danielle and Chris come get us," Heather said.

"Eva, how did you find us?" Walt asked.

"Danielle felt the Parker sisters knew more than they were telling the police, so I went over to their house." She then explained what had happened since going to the Parkers' house and finding them.

"They used us in some spell?" Heather asked. "What kind of spell?"

"I'm not entirely certain, but I have an idea. Yet, first we need to get you home," Eva said.

"I thought you said it would be complicated?" Heather asked.

"You don't know where we are, do you?" Walt asked.

Eva shook her head. "No. I don't. I'm afraid I didn't pay attention when they drove here. There's no way for me to give Danielle directions on finding you, at least, not in the dark."

"I don't understand, Eva, are you saying you're lost?" Heather asked.

"Wonderful," Brian muttered. "Still stuck in the forest but now with a lost ghost."

Eva glanced over to Brian and smirked, "Someone is cranky." She looked back to Heather and said, "I'm not lost in that I can't find my way back to Marlow House."

"I don't understand," Heather said.

"There are different ways a spirit can travel from place to place," Walt told Heather. "Some ways are different from how you or I move about."

"Well, I know that. Ghosts randomly barge in my house. Never use the door," Heather said.

"What I mean," Walt began, "it's possible for a spirit to move by thought alone. Eva can think about a specific place, and she can go to that location. But if she has never been there, or is unfamiliar with the location, thought alone may not take her where she wants to go."

"I don't understand," Heather said.

"Think about when Clint was in the hospital, in a coma. While I knew the location of the hospital, I was unable to simply will myself to his room. Now, had I been to his room before—"

"Which obviously was impossible since you were under house arrest," Heather reminded him.

"My point being, since I had never been there before and was not certain of its location, it was impossible for me to simply will myself there. Getting to the general location of the hospital would be possible if I knew where it was located on a map, yet to his specific room, no. Not without having been there before."

"What does that have to do with Eva and us?" Heather asked.

"Eva didn't pay attention to where the Parkers were driving when she hitched a ride with them tonight, so she isn't sure where we are, not in the way necessary to give someone directions. Now that she has been here, she can will herself to Marlow House and then come back here."

"Then we are rescued," Heather argued.

"No, we aren't." Brian spoke up from where he sat on the tarp, listening in to Walt and Heather's side of the conversation.

"Why not?" Heather asked Brian.

"If I'm getting this right, how it works, Eva here"—Brian looked over to where he imagined Eva stood—"wherever she is, might be able to pop back and forth between us and Marlow House, but she can't really bring anyone along with her."

"Correct, almost," Eva said. "I could bring another ghost with me."

"And if she doesn't know how to get here, as I take it that is what she told you two, then she can't tell Danielle or Chris how to drive here," Brian finished.

"Then what are we going to do?" Heather asked.

"The only thing we can do," Eva said, rising into the air. Both Walt and Heather looked up as Eva hovered overhead.

"I don't understand," Heather said.

"In the morning, after the sun comes up, and I can see things clearer, I can get an idea where we are, but I have to do that above the treetops."

"I think we can hold out another night," Walt said. "Just please, go back to Marlow House and tell Danielle what is going on. I know she's worried sick about us."

"I'll be back later," Eva vowed. "And don't worry, our mountain lion friend is keeping an eye on you."

"Not sure if that makes me feel safer or not," Heather grumbled under her breath.

CHRIS AND DANIELLE sat in the library with Marie. Danielle had just gotten off the phone with Lily, and Marie had just returned from the Parkers', again checking to see if they or Eva had returned.

Marie was about to offer a suggestion on what they should do next when fireworks—minus the loud booming—began going off in the library, startling all three. The next moment Eva appeared, her arms outstretched, as she shouted, "I found them! They are alive!"

Danielle jumped from the sofa with Chris. Since it was impossible to hug Eva for the welcome news, she turned to Chris, and the two hugged, jumping up and down.

Several minutes later, Danielle, Chris and Marie sat together on the sofa, listening while Eva told them all that had happened since they had last seen her.

"And we can't go get them now?" Danielle asked.

"I wish we could, but frankly I don't know the location—not in terms I can translate into driving directions. But it might be a good idea if I take Marie out there, and she can keep an eye on them. Walt looked as if he could use a good night's sleep. I imagine he stayed up most of the night, feeling he was best suited to protect the others."

"You said Brian knows about—ghosts?" Chris asked.

"Apparently. It sounds as if this adventure has been rather enlightening for him," Eva said.

"I need to call the police chief. He has to arrest the Parker sisters for kidnapping," Danielle said.

"He can't really do that now. Where is the evidence?" Chris asked. "It sounds to me like that'll need to wait until they get back here and can press charges."

Danielle let out a sigh. "I guess you're right. He can't really arrest them because of what Eva tells him."

"I'm not so sure about that," Eva said.

"What do you mean?" Danielle asked.

"There is some evidence in that van," Eva said.

THE GHOST AND THE WITCHES' COVEN

"What kind of evidence?" Chris asked.

"A broken fingernail. Heather's broken fingernail. I know it's hers. She wore that same color of nail polish the day before the abduction, and I know they transported them up to the forest in the back of the van. She must have broken the fingernail then," Eva said. "I didn't remember to ask her about her nails when I saw her. Frankly, I forgot about the nail until Chris mentioned evidence."

IT WASN'T difficult to get a search warrant for the van on Sunday night in spite of the fact there was no evidence of foul play, and Walt, Heather and Brian had only been missing for twenty-four hours. But the last time anyone had seen them, they had been together inside Pagan Oils and More.

When the police first arrived at the Parkers', no one was home. One police car parked down the street a bit, waiting for them to return. When the van finally pulled into the driveway on Sunday evening, the parked police car waited for backup before serving the warrant.

THEY HAD JUST STARTED for the front door after returning from the forest, when the police car pulled into their driveway. Bridget stood with her sisters, almost at their front door, and looked out to the street, wondering why there were two police cars pulling in front of their house and another one in the driveway. She hadn't noticed the one parked down the street when they first got home. A moment later they found out why when Joe Morelli served a warrant to search their van.

JOE WATCHED as the team went through the van, looking for any clues. When one of them yelled, "Found something," and then showed him a broken fingernail with purple polish, he remembered what the chief had told him when sending him out on the call.

"The last time we saw any of them was when they walked into Pagan Oils. The Parkers claimed they all left out the back door, where they drove off and Brian, Walt and Heather were left standing in the alley. But what if they drove off with them in the van? Look for anything that might prove they were in that vehicle. For example, Heather has long nails, nails break. Danielle mentioned she was wearing purple nail polish that day."

Joe looked at the broken nail and frowned. "This is too weird," he mumbled.

THIRTY-ONE

Crackling firewood and forest night sounds broke the silence as the flames danced erratically, confined in the recently constructed rock border. Sitting on her tarp with its edges pulled up over her shoulders, Heather quietly studied Brian, who stared into the fire. Walt had fallen asleep on the other side of the campfire from her and Brian. She doubted he got much sleep the night before.

"Are you okay?" Heather whispered to Brian.

Brian, who sat on his own tarp, glanced to Heather, his expression unreadable. "Why do you ask?"

Heather shrugged. "A lot has happened to you in the last day."

Brian let out a snort. "Not how I expected to spend my weekend, that's for sure."

"I have to say, I'm rather impressed with how you're processing all this."

Brian studied Heather for a moment and then asked, "When did you know you could see spirits?"

"I had feelings—intuitions—growing up. Things that happened with my family. But my first vivid experience was the ghost at Presley House."

Brian stared at Heather but said nothing.

"Oh, there really was a ghost there. Haunted the place every

Halloween. He trapped Danielle and then later Lily in the basement. I could talk to him."

"At first, I just thought you were crazy," Brian confessed.

Heather laughed and then asked, "Just at first?"

Brian shrugged. "I started seeing too much—experiencing too much—to not start wondering if there was more going on than I understood."

"You know, I didn't see Walt at first. I mean, when he was a ghost. I would catch glimpses of him sometimes. But then my sensitivity got stronger and stronger, and I suspect I am as sensitive as Chris and Danielle now. They've been able to see spirits since they were kids," Heather explained.

"Does this ability—does it bother you? I mean, do you see it as a blessing or curse?"

Heather considered the question a moment and then said, "I always felt—well, sort of like an outsider. But since coming to Frederickport and developing this gift—or curse—of mine, I guess I feel more at home, more comfortable with who I am, than ever before."

"Kelly claims you all share some secret," Brian said with a chuckle.

"Kelly may be Ian's sister, but she can be a pain in the butt."

"If Ian knows, why doesn't he tell Kelly? They're close."

"It's not as easy as you think. Heck, Lily knew about Danielle's gift, and Walt haunting Marlow House when I moved here, and she was dating Ian then. But Ian knew nothing about it at the time. It's not that simple to tell someone, no matter how close you are to them, without them thinking you're nuts or trying to make a fool of them."

"Is that one reason Chris hired you? You have that in common?" Brian asked.

"No. I think he hired me because I ran into his car and didn't have the money to fix it."

"I imagine there are a lot of women who would kill for the chance to work for Chris Glandon."

"Why, because he has stupid good looks and is obscenely rich?" Heather asked.

Brian grinned.

"At first I thought he was super annoying."

"Annoying how?" Brian asked.

"His looks, for one thing. When we go places together, and how women often react, I seriously want to barf. Sometimes I want to hang a sign around his neck announcing he's gay so they'll back off."

"He's gay?" Brian asked.

Heather laughed. "Not even close."

"You get jealous over the other women?"

"Now you're really not close. No, the fawning is just annoying. Maybe it wouldn't be so much if it wasn't so predictable. Actually, I would be happy if he would find someone and settle down, then I could just tell the women to back off, he's already married."

"Are you sure you aren't interested in him?" Brian asked.

Heather shook her head. "Nah, we're just good friends. I respect him. He really wants to help people. But he's just not my type."

"What is your type?" Brian asked.

Heather mentioned a couple of men she had dated since moving to Frederickport and asked Brian if he knew them.

"I know who they are. Aren't they a little old for you?"

Heather shrugged. "Why? Aren't they about your age?"

"My point exactly," Brian said.

"Didn't you have a thing with Darlene Gusarov? What was she, in her twenties?"

"Please don't remind me," Brian groaned.

"I'm sorry, but you have crappy taste in women," Heather said. "I don't think you're in any position to play matchmaker."

"Who's playing matchmaker?"

"Sounds like that's what you were doing with me and Chris," Heather said.

"No, I wasn't," Brian argued.

"Anyway, sometimes both Danielle and Chris are a little too nice. I just want to smack them."

"Too nice?" Brian chuckled.

"Seriously. If Danielle runs into some annoying ghost, she feels compelled to run after it and help it move on. And Chris, he really was quite goofy over Danielle, but gallantly stepped aside for Walt. It would have been more interesting if they'd duked it out a bit. Of course, considering Walt's abilities, maybe Chris did the smart thing." Heather shrugged.

"Don't tell me you were the high school cheerleader getting the two guys into a fight?"

Heather laughed at the idea. "Seriously? What, do I look like the cheerleader type? Hardly. I was the girl ditching class to join a protest."

"What kind of protest?"

"Usually something to do with saving the environment or animals. But now I work for the Glandon Foundation, I can do more than carry signs."

"You like your job?" he asked.

"Best job ever. It's like this was the job I was meant to do. I tell you what, every day I thank God for running into Chris's car."

Brian laughed. Heather joined him and then quieted and looked up.

"Eva is back," Heather announced.

"Where is she?" Brian glanced around.

"She's not here yet," Heather said, pointing upward and saying, "But the snow."

"What snow?" Brian frowned.

"Oh, well, you can't see it. But Eva likes a little drama with her entry."

The next moment Eva and Marie appeared, hovering over the fire, the snow vanishing.

"I am so glad to see you!" Marie gushed.

"Hey, Marie, I'm rather glad to see you myself. Heck, you can barge in anytime," Heather said. "I just want to get back home so you can do it there."

"Marie?" Brian frowned.

Heather looked at Brian and cringed. "Oh, we didn't tell you about Marie, did we? You know, Adam's grandma, Marie Nichols."

"What about Marie?" Brian asked hesitantly.

"So this little camping trip has been a learning experience for Brian," Marie said brightly.

"Like Eva, Marie has stuck around," Heather explained.

"Who else?" he asked.

Heather frowned. "Who else what?"

"What other ghosts are hanging around?" Brian asked.

"Currently, there is just Eva and Marie that I know," Heather explained. "And that guy who was shooting at us, but I don't know his name. Some stay for a while and move on, like your old girlfriend Darlene. She hung around for a while before moving on."

Brian rubbed his right temple with the heel of his right hand.

"Walt seems to be sleeping," Marie said, now hovering over Walt.

"He didn't get much rest last night. We're supposed to wake him when we're ready to go to sleep," Heather explained.

"No need to wake him," Marie said. "I'll look over you, so whenever you want to go to sleep, go ahead."

"I need to get back to Marlow House in case they need me," Eva said. "I'll see you both in the morning, and we'll figure out where you are." The next moment Eva vanished.

Heather looked at Brian and said, "Eva left, but Marie is staying so we don't get eaten by the wildlife."

"She'll wake up Walt if she needs him?" Brian asked.

"No reason to do that," Heather said. She looked at Marie and said, "Show him."

The next moment the hunting knife Brian had set on a nearby rock floated up in the air.

"See, she can move things like Walt can. And, if it is another mountain lion, she can communicate with it like he and Eva did."

Brian watched as the hunting knife floated back down to the rock. "So you're saying Marie Nichols's ghost is here. Really here?"

Heather nodded. "Yes."

"Does Adam know she's still here?" Brian asked.

"No. We already told you who the mediums are," Heather reminded him.

"But the chief knows, right?" Brian asked.

"Of course Edward knows," Marie said before tweaking Brian's ear.

Brian let out a yelp, grabbed hold of the injured earlobe, and said, "Damn, I believe Marie really is here." She tweaked his ear a second time, making him yelp again.

"I don't think Marie appreciated you swearing," Heather said with a giggle.

THIRTY-TWO

Eva arrived back at Marlow House in time to see Chris lead Police Chief MacDonald into the parlor. Danielle sat on the parlor sofa with Max on one side of her and Bella on the other, while Hunny trailed behind the chief and Chris, her tail wagging.

"Did they arrest the Parkers?" Eva asked.

"Hi, Chief," Danielle greeted him. "Eva just arrived. Did your people find Heather's broken nail?"

"Yes, we did," the chief said.

"And did you arrest them? What did they say? Did they tell you where they are?" Danielle asked in a rush.

"I'm afraid not," the chief said with a sigh. He started to sit down, but then paused and asked if Eva was sitting on the chair.

"No, she's over there." Danielle pointed to her left and then asked, "Why didn't you arrest them?"

"If you'll recall, the Parkers claimed one reason they left out back was because Brian and Walt offered to help carry boxes to the van. They didn't deny the nail belonged to Heather but said it must have broken when they put the boxes in the van."

"How does Heather's broken nail get in the van when Walt and Brian were the ones to take the boxes out?" Chris asked.

"They claim Brian was carrying several boxes, and when he started to put them in the van, one began to fall, so Heather grabbed it and put it in the van. They say the nail must have broken then," the chief explained.

"I bet there were no boxes," Danielle grumbled.

Chris looked at Eva and asked, "Did they tell you how the Parkers got them into the van?"

"No. We didn't discuss it. From what I overheard from the Parkers, they were all unconscious when they tied them up. But I could find out." The next moment Eva vanished.

"What is she saying?" the chief asked.

"She just left," Danielle explained. "She didn't know how the Parkers got them in the van, just that they were unconscious when they tied them to the trees."

"When we get them back tomorrow, I hope they remember enough about their abduction that we can press charges," the chief said.

"If not, they can always embellish what they know with what Eva found out," Danielle said.

"You mean lie," Chris said with a snort.

"I do not want to hear this," the chief groaned. "I did not hear you just say that."

"It would not be the first time," Danielle reminded him. "But at the moment, I'm more concerned about getting them home safely."

The discussion shifted to how they planned to locate the three in the morning. After about ten minutes of discussion, Eva reappeared, again not announcing her arrival with glitter or snow.

"Eva is back," Danielle said for the chief's benefit.

"According to Heather, she went into the shop to buy essential oils. When she brought her purchases to the counter, she noticed they had closed the front blind, but didn't think much about it. They offered her chocolate chip cookies, telling her they needed a taste tester because they wanted to sell them in the store. She had just eaten one cookie when Walt and Brian came into the shop with one of the other sisters."

"I can see where this is going," Chris said. "Walt and chocolate chip cookies."

"Chocolate chip cookies?" The chief frowned. Danielle held up her hand, silencing him so Eva could finish.

"They offered some to Walt and Brian. And the next thing Heather remembers is being carried through the forest on a travois and then tied up to a tree. They tied them each to a tree, performed some chanting ritual, and then left. Brian woke up in time to see them leaving, but Walt was still unconscious. There were no boxes. They all passed out while still in the store."

"Good news," Danielle told the chief.

"What?" he asked.

"You don't have to resort to giving false testimony to charge our kidnappers," Danielle said.

THE HOUSE LIGHTS had been turned off. A horror movie played on the big-screen television, providing the only illumination in the living room. Brad and Kathy lounged on the sofa, watching the movie, their bare feet propped on the coffee table and a large bowl of buttered popcorn sitting on the sofa between them. They had already taken their showers, and each wore a pair of flannel pajama bottoms and a T-shirt.

Eerie music played from the television while its screen flickered and darkened. Kathy shoved more popcorn in her mouth, a reaction to the scary scene before her. She gasped a moment later when she heard rattling by the front door.

Brad hadn't heard the rattling, but he heard the gasp, jolting him from the trancelike focus he had put himself in while watching the movie. He jumped and then snapped at his sister, "I hate when you do that!"

"Shh, didn't you hear it?" Kathy whispered, setting her feet on the floor. She picked up the remote from the coffee table and muted the television. Again, she heard a rattle. This time, Brad heard it too.

"Someone's breaking in," Brad whispered, jumping from the sofa and looking for something to use as a weapon.

The next moment the front door flew open, and what walked in was more terrifying than anything else they could imagine.

"Mom?" Kathy squeaked as she stood by the sofa.

"Why is it so dark in here?" Mrs. Stewart asked. She breezed into the room and flipped on the overhead light after slamming the door closed behind her. She carried an overnight bag, and a purse hung from one arm.

"What are you doing here?" Brad asked.

Mrs. Stewart dropped her suitcase on the floor, snatched the remote from Kathy, and turned off the television. She tossed the remote on the coffee table and looked at her son and daughter. "I need to talk to you two. I will be staying for a few days."

"You came all the way out here to talk to us…and this late at night?" Kathy asked.

"Yes. It seems my ruby ring has gone missing. Snatched right from my jewelry box."

Licking her lips anxiously, Kathy exchanged a quick glance with her brother and then looked back to her mother.

"I…I don't understand," Kathy stammered.

Mrs. Stewart opened her purse and pulled out her cellphone. Brad and Kathy watched as her finger made hasty swipes over the phone's screen.

"I guess you didn't know, I installed some security cameras at the house after your father—well, after he went off to his little retreat." The next moment Mrs. Stewart shoved the phone up to Brad and Kathy so they could see a video captured from one of the security cameras. It was of Kathy taking the ruby ring from her mother's jewelry box.

"I STILL DON'T UNDERSTAND what happened," Davina said for the tenth time. She sat with her sisters on Bridget's king-sized bed, each one leaning against the headboard, while Bridget sat in the middle, the spell book opened on her lap as she searched through its pages, looking for answers.

"Those police, they asked about Heather. Obviously, they didn't forget she existed. That damn fingernail is proof of that! The spell didn't work after all!"

"It worked," Bridget insisted. "I must have misunderstood. You saw it yourself. All traces of them vanished. It was like they had never been there. I don't believe someone happened across them in the woods and set them free. And if that had happened, then they would have been back by now, wouldn't they?"

"So you're saying the spell worked, just not exactly as you thought it would?" Aileana asked.

"Yes. It got rid of them. I'm sure of that."

"Doesn't this also mean when we vanquish the Baird sisters,

people will notice they're missing? Doesn't that defeat the purpose of doing all this?" Aileana asked.

Still focused on the pages in the spell book, Bridget shook her head and said, "No. I think I just misunderstood. The spell did what it promised. But to take away any memory of Donovan, along with her physical being, I think it required more than the ruby—it required the ruby as it is now, enriched with Donovan's powers."

"So when we use this on Finola, people won't remember her, like they do with Heather Donovan?" Davina asked.

"Yes. And to play it safe, we should probably deal with one sister at a time. That way, the ruby will continue to grow in power. Fortunately, we won't need to drug them like we did Heather." Bridget slammed the book close and tossed it to the end of the bed.

"What now?" Davina asked.

Bridget nudged Davina and said, "Get up."

Reluctantly Davina got up from the bed, followed by Bridget, while Aileana got up from the other side of the mattress.

"Now we're going to deal with the Baird sisters," Bridget announced.

"You don't mean now, like right now?" Aileana asked.

"Yes. According to the book, the spell we want to use on the Bairds works best close to sunrise. We need to get started now."

"Are you serious? It's late. We drove all the way out to the forest and back tonight, and I'm exhausted," Davina whined.

"Unlike you two, I was quick on my feet tonight, coming up with an explanation for that damn nail they found. I don't want the police to come snooping around again. And when we're finished with the Bairds, we'll have enough power to wipe the memories of Heather Donovan, Walt Marlow and Brian Henderson from the mind of anyone who ever knew of them or heard of them," Bridget said. "And we will have the Leabar."

MRS. STEWART SAT on the sofa, her son on one side and her daughter on the other, silently listening to Kathy explain why she had taken the ruby. When Kathy finished with the telling, none of the three said a word, while Mrs. Stewart stared blankly ahead, considering all she had been told, her two children expectantly watching her.

When Mrs. Stewart failed to comment, Kathy finally asked, "Mother? Say something."

Mrs. Stewart let out a deep sigh and asked, "You aren't serious?"

"I'm afraid she is. I told her it was a stupid idea," Brad said.

"Oh, shut up, Brad," Kathy snapped. She and her brother began bickering while their mother sat between them. Their voices each increased in volume, and finally Mrs. Stewart shouted for them to both shut up. The room grew quiet, and Mrs. Stewart stood up and walked from the sofa. Brad and Kathy remained sitting, looking up at their mother.

"I swear, Kathy Jane Stewart, you are crazy like your father's side of the family!" Mrs. Stewart said.

"I told her it was a stupid idea," Brad repeated.

"Oh, shut up, Brad," both Kathy and her mother shouted. Brad slunk back on the sofa and remained quiet.

"I want the ruby ring back. You have to go get it," Mrs. Stewart told her daughter.

"I can't. They already used it to get rid of Heather Donovan."

"Are you seriously telling me you paid for a hit on Heather Donovan? And in this little transaction, they threw in Brian Henderson and Walt Marlow? Because on the drive over here, it was all over the radio about how those three went missing together. Please don't tell me you are responsible for that," Mrs. Stewart asked.

Kathy shook her head emphatically. "No. I didn't pay them to kill anyone. I…I just gave them the ruby to use in the spell to make Heather disappear. I told you it was for Dad. It was the only way to break the spell she had over him. Don't you understand?"

THIRTY-THREE

Evan MacDonald and his older brother, Eddie, spent several weeks each summer with their grandparents, who had planned to come pick them up on Wednesday. Yet after one of Chief MacDonald's officers and two notable Frederickport citizens went missing, Edward MacDonald's in-laws offered to pick the boys up early on Sunday so he could focus on the investigation.

Chief MacDonald arrived at the office early on Monday. He hadn't heard from Chris and Danielle yet regarding the location of their missing persons. He had to leave that one to them, as he could not communicate with spirits, and the medium in his family had left with his grandparents the night before. According to the plan, when there was sufficient light, Eva and Marie would work with Danielle and Chris to figure out on a map where to pick up Walt and the others.

The chief was on his first cup of coffee, sitting at his desk, when the front office called to tell him he had a visitor, Francine Stewart. While he knew her son and daughter were currently staying at the old Barr place, he hadn't expected her to drop by. He told them to send her back, and a few moments later she walked into his office and sat at the chair facing his desk.

MacDonald found Francine Stewart to be an attractive woman, yet suspected she was probably high maintenance. Tall and slender, she wore what appeared to be a designer pantsuit, and she looked as if she had just stepped from the beauty shop, with her impeccably coifed hair and manicured nails.

"How may I help you, Mrs. Stewart?" MacDonald had always wondered how much she had known about what her husband and her children had been up to when they had kidnapped Walt and Danielle, almost killing them.

"I want to report a stolen ruby ring. It's very valuable." She opened her purse, removed a photograph of the ring, stood up, placed the photograph on his desk before him, and sat back on the chair.

"When did it go missing?" he asked, picking up the photograph and looking at it.

"It was taken from my jewelry box at home," she explained.

With a frown, he tossed the photograph on the desk and leaned back in his chair. "Mrs. Stewart, that is out of my jurisdiction. You will need to talk to your local police department."

"I know who took it. And the people who have it are in your jurisdiction," she said primly. "I don't know their first names. But their last name is Parker, and they own a store in Frederickport called Pagan Oils and More."

Upon hearing the Parkers' name, MacDonald sat up abruptly. "Can you please elaborate, beginning with who took the ring, and how you know the Parkers have it."

With a dramatic sigh, Mrs. Stewart dropped her purse on the floor beside her feet, sat back in her chair, and primly crossed her legs. "I'm not sure if you are aware, but my daughter, Kathy, is a troubled young woman, ever since her father's breakdown. They were very close." She then uncrossed her legs, setting both feet on the floor, and leaned toward the desk. "I hate to admit this, but mental issues run in my husband's side of the family, and I'm afraid Kathy may have inherited more from her father than I hoped. Very unstable girl. In fact, when I leave here, she has agreed to check into a private hospital and get the help she needs."

"What does all this have to do with the missing ring?"

Mrs. Stewart leaned back in the chair again and said, "Kathy took it and gave it to the Parkers. They manipulated her, exploiting her vulnerabilities to get the ring. They knew they were accepting stolen merchandise when they took it. In fact, they're the ones who persuaded her to take it."

"How did they do that?" he asked.

"I'm sure you've heard about my husband's rantings since his incarceration, about Heather Donovan and how she's a witch and cast a spell on him?"

The chief nodded. "Yes."

"Unfortunately, dear Kathy believed her father. And she desperately wanted to help him. She read the Parkers' advertisement in the newspaper for their store, and how they claimed to be witches. Foolishly, she went to them, asking if there was some way they could remove whatever spell Heather Donovan had put on her father. They said they could, but it would cost her. She told them she didn't have much money. I'm afraid that's true. I cut Brad's and Kathy's allowances after their father was committed; I just felt they needed to learn to stand on their own."

"So your daughter took your ring to pay them for removing the spell?" he asked.

"Yes, but it was actually their idea. When she told them she didn't have that kind of money, they suggested she come to me. She told them I would never give her the money, which was true. So they said something like, *'I'm sure your mother has some jewelry of value. We'll take that.'* And, in Kathy's diminished capacity, she foolishly took the ring and gave it to the Parkers."

"How did you find this all out?" he asked.

"Kathy didn't realize I had installed cameras at the house. When I watched the recordings, I saw her take the ring. I confronted her, and she broke down and confessed it all. I just want my ring back. I won't even press charges against the Parkers."

"Do you realize Heather Donovan has gone missing, and the last time anyone saw her, she was going into Pagan Oils?"

"I heard something about that on the radio, driving in to Frederickport last night. But you have to understand, my daughter only gave them that ruby so they would remove a spell, not remove Heather Donovan."

AFTER FRANCINE STEWART left his office, Joe walked in a few minutes later. "Was that Francine Stewart?" Joe asked the chief. In response, the chief recounted his conversation with her. When he finished the telling, he showed Joe the photograph she had left behind.

THE GHOST AND THE WITCHES' COVEN

Holding the photo in his hand, Joe studied it a moment and then said, "I saw that ring last night. Bridget Parker was wearing it."

"WHAT HAPPENED?" Brad asked when his mother got into the driver's side of the car. He sat in the back seat while his sister sat in the front passenger seat.

"I'd better get my ring back," Mrs. Stewart said as she slammed the door shut and put on her seatbelt.

"Do I really have to stay at that place?" Kathy groaned.

"Yes. Fortunately, the insurance will pay for it. Consider it a little holiday, like your father." She shoved the key in the ignition and turned on the engine.

"What did you tell him?" Brad asked, leaning forward, sticking his head between the two front seats.

"Exactly what I told you I would. And, Kathy, you need to thank your stars I put those cameras in. You do not understand what kind of trouble you could face," Mrs. Stewart said.

"What do you mean?" Kathy asked.

"After talking to the chief, he obviously suspects the Parkers of having something to do with his missing people. If they find some evidence on those women, do you think they won't hesitate to throw you under the bus for a plea deal, when caught?" Francine asked as she drove out of the parking lot.

"I don't understand," Kathy said.

"No. You don't. Which has always been your problem. What motive did those women have to take Heather Donovan? They would probably say you paid them to get rid of her, and the ring would be proof of that."

"But I never told them to touch Walt Marlow or Brian Henderson!" Kathy argued.

"Do you think anyone will believe you? They arrested your father because he tried to kill Walt Marlow, and Brian Henderson was one of the arresting officers. And it is entirely possible those women have killed the three of them, and if they tie you to something like that, then you could face the death penalty. So, young lady, you can thank me."

"But, Mom, now the police know I'm connected to all this! Why did you have to say anything to the cops? Is that ring really worth more than me?" Kathy whined.

"Don't be foolish, Kathy. No one is going to come after a mentally disturbed girl who paid some witches to cast a spell. Which is why you need to spend time showing you're seeking mental help before this blows up. Sometimes, young lady, you have to get ahead of these things before they become a problem."

"I don't understand. Why would they take Marlow and Henderson?" Brad asked.

"According to what I heard on the news," Francine said, "they were captured on a security camera going into Pagan Oils shortly after Heather Donovan. That was the last time anyone saw them. I suspect they walked into something they were not supposed to see. Probably Heather getting killed."

"I didn't tell them to kill Heather," Kathy said.

"I thought you told me they promised Heather would disappear," Mrs. Stewart asked.

"Well…yeah…but I didn't say to kill her. And they promised the spell would erase everyone's memory of her," Kathy said.

"Do not repeat that to anyone. Keep to the story you just paid them to remove the spell Heather placed on your father. Nothing more. Unless, of course, you want to go to prison and face the death penalty," Mrs. Stewart warned.

Kathy quietly sank back in the car seat, crossing her arms stubbornly over her chest. She looked out the window as her mother drove the car down the road out of town. Brad sat quietly in the back seat. After about fifteen minutes, Mrs. Stewart asked, "Kathy, have you learned anything from all this?"

Kathy didn't answer immediately, but finally grumbled, "Yeah."

"What did you learn?" Mrs. Stewart asked.

"Security cameras really suck," Kathy replied.

THIRTY-FOUR

Joe Morelli parked the police car along the sidewalk in front of the Parkers' home. The chief assumed the Parker women were involved in the disappearance. Now Francine Stewart claimed the women promised to put some spell on Heather Donovan—or were they removing a spell? He wasn't sure how all that worked. What he knew, too much crazy in this world.

Since the chief believed the Parker women were involved, he didn't want Joe going to their house alone or just with a partner, which was why two other police cars pulled up behind him. He noticed the van was not parked in the driveway, but it could be in the garage. He walked up to the house while the other officers waited by their cars. A minute later he rang the bell.

Across the street, one of the Parkers' neighbor stepped out onto her front porch and observed all the commotion. Wearing her bathrobe and clogs, her hair still wrapped in the toilet paper she used to preserve her hairstyle while sleeping, she hurried across the street to speak to the officers standing by their vehicles.

"What is going on over here?" she asked when reaching them. "Police cars have been coming and going all weekend."

"Ma'am, please go back to your house. It would be safer for you over there," one officer said.

"Why? They aren't home, anyway. I saw them leave before daybreak this morning. Had to take my dog out and saw them driving away in that hippy van of theirs. All three of them. What are they doing over there, anyway? It's drugs, isn't it? I bet it's drugs."

Up on the Parkers' front porch, Joe rang the doorbell for the second time. When no one answered the door and he didn't hear any motion in the house, he walked to the garage and looked in its window. There were two cars parked inside. But not the van.

Ten minutes later, Joe sat alone in his police car, calling the chief. When MacDonald answered, Joe said, "They aren't here. According to a neighbor, they all left together before daybreak. What do you want me to do now?"

"WHY COULDN'T they have used duct tape?" Ina Baird asked herself. She had watched the YouTube video on how to break out of duct tape, but if there was a similar video on some trick to break free from rope, she hadn't seen it. Tied to a chair in her bedroom, her ankles and wrists bound, she had stopped trying to wiggle free. Doing that had caused the ropes to tighten, and they now dug uncomfortably into her skin.

The fact the intruders had not tried to conceal their identity did not comfort Ina. Plus, she knew who they were—their stalkers, the owners of Pagan Oils and More and professed witches.

"What is this, some witches' turf war?" Ina grumbled to herself. None of it made sense, from the time they awoke her after daybreak with a gun to her head and some squeaky voice telling her not to make a sound.

But the most bizarre part was when one of those redheaded maniacs stuck a ruby ring in her face and said, "I warn you, we have this, so none of your witch's magic will work. It's fully loaded!"

"Loaded?" Ina muttered. "I can guess who's loaded."

Fortunately, she heard no gunfire, and while she was not a firearms expert, she was fairly certain the one they had shoved in her face hadn't been fitted with a silencer. She assumed her sisters were currently tied up as she was, considering she now heard loud voices coming from another part of the house, and they didn't belong to her sisters.

IF IT WASN'T for the morning sunlight slipping through the edges of the closed curtains, Kenzy Baird would be sitting alone in the dark. Tied to a chair in her bedroom, she tried to listen to what was going on, but all she could hear was a bunch of strange chanting and gibberish, presumably coming from those witch terrorists who had ripped her from bed at gunpoint. Or more accurately, wannabe witches. It sounded as if they were in the living room.

She had been trying to figure out why they had shoved a ruby ring in her face, when it came to her—their YouTube channel. Weeks earlier she had watched a few of their YouTube videos, but soon found them utterly ridiculous and stopped watching. However, there had been something about a ruby—not a ruby ring—but the gemstone. On the video they claimed a ruby held special powers that could block and steal a witch's magic.

Remembering that, Kenzy stared at her closed door and wondered if her sisters were all right.

THE INTRUDERS HAD PUSHED ALL the living room furniture to the walls, opening the center of the room. They had tied her to a kitchen chair placed in the middle of the room, encircled with votive candles, all flickering with tiny flames. They had gagged her after she kept asking about her sisters and demanding they tell her what they wanted. Whatever they wanted, it wasn't to engage in dialogue.

With a gag shoved unceremoniously into her mouth, Finola watched as the Parker women continued to chant while walking around her in a circle. There were not enough of them to hold hands to make a circle that would fit around her and the candles. To solve this problem, the women had brought along three pieces of red rope, all the same length. In each sister's hands they held an end of rope, thus forming a circle large enough to walk around her and the candles. She silently wished their dresses were a little longer; perhaps then one of them might catch a hem in a flame, considering how close they walked by the candles.

Finola wondered how long they planned to keep this up, and what exactly did they hope to accomplish? She guessed she had been tied to the chair for well over two hours. This was the third time they had done this chanting, only to disappear into the kitchen before returning. Each time they returned, they seemed a little more agitated than before. It was as if they expected something to happen that had not happened yet, and were getting frustrated.

They finally finished and once again stormed out of the room and marched off toward the kitchen, taking their red ropes with them. Finola did not know if she should be relieved they left again or afraid. One thing she was grateful for—minutes before they had broken into her house and dragged her from bed, she had returned from using the bathroom. "At least I don't have to pee," Finola told herself.

"WHY ISN'T IT WORKING?" Davina demanded, throwing the piece of rope she had been carrying onto the kitchen table.

"Because the Bairds are powerful witches," Bridget said. "We're just lucky we have this ruby to protect us. Can you imagine what they could do to us if free to unleash their magic?"

"Bridget is right," Aileana told Davina. "The fact we have them utterly helpless proves how powerful the ruby is."

"We did have a gun," Davina reminded her.

"When does a gun have actual power over a witch's magic?" Bridget asked.

Davina picked up the piece of rope and said, "We know this has power over a witch. Hang them all."

"But it won't really kill them. It didn't kill Gavenia, not even after they burned her at the stake," Bridget reminded her.

"This isn't about just killing them," Aileana reminded her.

"Then don't you think we should find the Leabar first? Before we vanquish them?" Davina asked.

Bridget considered the question for a moment. "Perhaps that's why this is taking so long."

"What do you mean?" Davina asked.

"According to the book, part of the power of the ruby is knowing what is best for its master," Bridget explained.

"And we're its master," Aileana said proudly.

"It's waiting for us to find the Leabar. We just assumed we would look for it after we take care of the Bairds, but what if it isn't here? Maybe they keep it somewhere else," Bridget suggested.

THE GHOST AND THE WITCHES' COVEN

THEY RETURNED SOONER than the last time. Finola watched as the one who seemed to be their leader marched to her and ripped off her gag.

"Where is the Leabar?" the woman demanded.

Finola's eyes widened. "What do you know about the Leabar?"

"I know you have it. You stole it from my family. I want it back."

Finola silently studied the woman and finally asked, "Who are you?"

"I don't believe you don't know who I am," the woman countered.

"I know you're all sisters. I know you own Pagan Oils and More. I know you claim to be blood witches. I've read your names in the newspaper, but I have no idea which one you are. And I know you and your sisters have been stalking us for years."

"I'm Bridget Parker. Where is the Leabar?"

"I'm not telling you. And I don't know why you claim we stole it from your family. It's been in my family for generations."

Bridget reached out to the necklace around Finola's neck. As her fingertips touched it, Finola jerked back, trying to distance herself.

"You aren't the White Hawk, are you?" Bridget whispered.

"Oh, my gawd, Helena was your great-great-grandmother, wasn't she?" Finola gasped.

THE WOMAN HAD BEEN WATCHING them since they had returned yesterday. After overhearing their plans, she had stowed away in the back of their van, confident they would drive that when they left in the morning. She had been correct. When they arrived at the house, she waited until they went inside before getting out and standing in the bushes so she could look in the windows. She had only been in the bushes for a few minutes when one had returned to the van and moved it into the garage, concealing it from view.

None of the blinds were open at the house, yet fortunately the ones in the living room had not been drawn completely, so she could look inside. Not long after arriving, she witnessed them performing some ritual in the living room, with Finola tied to a chair. Periodically they would stop, and then return, repeating it all over again. This seemed to go on for hours.

Concerned about the welfare of the other Baird sisters, she had walked around the house, peeking in windows. Although all the blinds remained closed, she could still see into rooms, along the edges of the curtains that had not been drawn completely. She spied Ina in one room, tied to a chair. In another room she found Kenzy, also tied to a chair. Unlike their older sister, neither wore gags.

She had returned to the living room window. Finola sat in the center of the room, tied to a chair, dozens of candles flickering around her in a circle. A few minutes earlier Bridget had marched into the room, followed by her two sisters. She had walked up to Finola and jerked the gag from her mouth. Bridget asked Finola something, but she couldn't hear what they were saying. It was when Bridget reached for Finola's necklace—the one that matched the necklace she wore—that she muttered, "What have I unleashed?"

THIRTY-FIVE

Sunrise came just minutes past six on Monday morning. Over two hours before Francine Stewart showed up at the chief's office, the three reluctant campers were awake, having wild berries for breakfast and watching the sun come up. Marie, who had watched over the three during the night, made a quick trip back to Frederickport to get Eva and to go over the plans with Chris and Danielle.

By the time Marie returned to the camp with Eva, Walt was burying the campfire while Heather and Brian folded the tarps.

"Eva and Marie are here," Heather told Brian as she took his folded tarp from him and placed it with the other two. She then looked at Eva and asked, "Did they find my broken fingernail in the van? Did they arrest the Parkers?"

"Yes, they found it. But I'm afraid the Parkers came up with a plausible explanation." Eva then recounted what the Parkers had told the police.

"I guess this means I get to be in on the arrest," Brian said after Heather repeated what Eva had just said.

"You'll enjoy that, won't you?" Heather teased.

"I will. So what happens now?" Brian asked.

"We need to find the road," Eva said. Heather repeated Eva's words for Brian.

Eva and Marie rose high into the air, over the treetops. Walt, who had finished covering the campfire, stood next to Heather while they both looked up into the sky.

"What are you looking at?" Brian asked.

Heather pointed upward. "Eva and Marie, what did you think?" She used one hand to shade her eyes from the morning sun.

With a frown, Brian looked up to where Heather and Walt looked, yet only saw the treetops and clouds in the blue sky.

A few minutes later, Marie and Eva returned to the ground.

"I think you have been walking in circles," Eva told them.

"Why do you say that?" Heather asked.

Eva pointed in one direction and said, "Because the clearing where the Parkers took you is that way, and just beyond it is the road."

"That's impossible," Walt said.

"What's impossible?" Brian asked.

"We have been walking in circles," Heather explained.

Brian frowned.

"I'm fairly certain I know what highway that road leads to," Marie said. "I'm going to go check it out and then let Danielle and Chris know. It's going to take them a good hour to drive here. Eva will stay and lead you to the road."

"Wait, Marie!" Heather called out.

"What's going on?" Brian asked. Heather hushed him.

Marie, who had risen in the sky again, looked to Heather. "Yes?"

Heather picked up the three folded tarps and offered them to Marie.

"What am I supposed to do with those?" Marie asked.

"I don't want to carry them. I don't want to leave them here, either. You're going that way, anyway. Can't you just drop them off by the road, and we'll pick them up there?" Heather asked.

Marie let out a sigh but focused on the tarps.

Brian watched as the three tarps floated out of Heather's arms and drifted into the air, moving over the treetops and out of sight. He continued to watch even after they were no longer visible. Finally, he muttered, "Nothing unusual about that."

"YOU'RE AWAKE?" Marie said with surprise when she popped into Marlow House on Monday morning and found Danielle and

Chris in the kitchen. Chris sat at the table with a map book and a cup of coffee while Danielle busily made sandwiches.

"Morning, Marie," Chris said between sips of coffee.

"Of course we're awake," Danielle said, adding slices of cheese to the open sandwiches laid out on the counter. "Eva said once the sun was up, you could figure out where they are. Did you figure it out?"

"Yes, I know where they are," Marie said brightly. She looked to Chris and said, "Good, a map book. I'll show you." The next moment the book opened.

After Marie showed Chris where Walt, Brian and Heather would be waiting, she looked over to Danielle, who was now wrapping sandwiches in waxed paper. "I do believe they'll appreciate that."

"I know you said they had fish, but I thought they still might be hungry," Danielle said.

"They didn't have fish this morning. Just wild berries. I don't think it appealed to them three meals in a row. Plus, they were a little excited to get going."

Danielle placed the wrapped sandwiches in a box. "Let me get the brownies I made, some chips and the water, and then we can leave. I can't wait to see Walt!"

"I'm more curious to see Brian," Chris said with a snicker. "Wonder how he's taking all this."

"He seems to have accepted all his new knowledge in stride," Marie said. "And it appears he and Heather have formed a bond. They were up for hours last night, whispering."

"Whispering about what?" Chris asked.

Marie shrugged. "I don't know. But when she fell asleep, she snuggled up to him all night. I was tempted to move them apart a bit—didn't seem quite right—but it was probably cold up there. I imagine they were taking advantage of the body heat."

"No other reason Heather would cuddle up to Brian Henderson," Chris said with a snort.

"Hey, it's totally understandable for two very different people to form a bond after a shared traumatic experience. And getting kidnapped and left in the forest would be traumatic," Danielle said. She then asked, "What about Walt? How did he do last night?"

"He slept soundly, on the other side of the fire. I think he was pretty exhausted, and with me there, he didn't feel compelled to be on guard," Marie explained.

IT TOOK them half an hour to reach the dirt road, with Eva leading the way. They had been walking along that road for almost an hour, heading towards the highway, with Brian and Heather trailing some distance behind Eva and Walt.

"It looks like Walt is talking to himself," Brian noted. Although Walt's back was to him, he periodically turned his head and said something.

Heather laughed. "No, Eva's walking next to him."

"So Danielle never gets jealous of Eva? Is it because she's a ghost?" Brian asked.

"I don't think Walt ever felt about Eva like he does about Danielle, and I think Danielle knows that," Heather said.

"I've seen her portrait. She was quite beautiful," Brian said.

"She still is." Heather continued to walk alongside Brian, watching Eva and Walt lead the way.

"So how did this all work? Walt and Eva just hung around as ghosts together, and then Danielle showed up?"

"Nah. Walt didn't even realize he was dead until Danielle moved in. And he didn't learn Eva had stuck around until much later. Chris likes to say Walt was on house arrest at Marlow House. He couldn't leave."

"Why was that? Was he being punished for something?" Brian asked.

Heather shrugged. "Being able to see ghosts doesn't mean I understand why things happen the way they do. I can only speculate. Personally, I think the universe had plans for Walt."

"The Universe? Are you talking about God?" Brian asked.

"Whatever you want to call it."

"So what plans did the Universe have for Walt, do you think?"

Heather stopped walking for a moment and looked at Brian. He stopped too and looked at her.

"What do you think?" she asked. "Danielle, of course. They're soul mates." They started walking again.

"You really believe that? People have soul mates?" Brian asked.

"I didn't before Walt and Danielle. But I do now."

After a few moments of silence, Brian asked, "Do Eva and Marie know things you don't?"

"I'm pretty sure they know more than they can tell us. In fact, Walt even says he feels there are certain things he forgot when he came back over to this side. But all the answers? I don't think you learn those until you go through the next door."

"And what door is that?" Brian asked.

"I guess whatever door Marie and Eva have refused to walk through."

"I have another question."

"Sure. What?"

"Why can Marie move things, but Eva can't?"

Heather shrugged. "I don't know. But I'm sure the Universe has its reasons."

The dirt road went up a slope, and when Brian and Heather reached the rise, Walt and Eva were already heading down. In the distance was the highway, and Heather spied Danielle's Ford Flex driving in their direction. Brian spied the car at the same time. Relief flooded over the pair. Heather jumped up excitedly while Brian let out an exuberant cheer. In their shared excitement, they turned to each other, and Heather flew into Brian's open arms.

"We're rescued!" Heather cried as Brian twirled her around in a circle. Both laughing and relieved, the twirl ended, and as Brian let Heather slide down so her feet again touched the ground, neither pulled away but looked into each other's eyes, and without thought —they kissed.

When the kiss ended, they abruptly released hold of the other, stepped back, their eyes wide in shock, and stared a moment at the other one.

"We'd better catch up with them," Heather finally said.

"Yes," Brian agreed, his expression unreadable.

DANIELLE COULDN'T HELP but think, what if someone made a movie about my life? Would this scene come across as dramatic or comedic? Considering the way her stomach had been churning since Walt first went missing, and how her heart now raced in anticipation of seeing him again, it felt high drama—high emotion. But would that come across in a movie? She had let Chris drive her car;

she was too edgy to be behind the wheel. Since leaving Frederickport, they had been following Marie, which was basically like driving behind an elderly version of the Flying Nun, minus the habit.

When Danielle saw them standing along the side of the highway, she phoned the chief to let him know they were about to pick them up. When Chris pulled over a few minutes later, Danielle was already opening her car door and practically outside. Chris yelled at her to be careful, but she wasn't listening. He remained sitting in the driver's side of the car a moment and watched as Danielle ran to Walt—who was already running to her, leaving Eva behind him, and behind Eva trailed Brian and Heather.

Danielle flew into Walt's arms, and the two were still kissing when Heather and Brian walked past them, each pretending to ignore the embracing couple and clearly relieved to be rescued. Chris got out of the car and met Heather, whom he gave a brief hug, and then he turned to Brian. He started to shake Brian's hand, but was surprised when Brian didn't accept the handshake, but insisted on a hug.

CHRIS DROVE BACK TO FREDERICKPORT, with Brian in the passenger seat, Heather in the seat behind them, and Walt and Danielle in the rear seat. Eva and Marie had vanished after they piled in the car and started back to Frederickport. Danielle passed around sandwiches, chips, brownies, and bottled water.

"I knew we could count on you," Heather said, diving into the brownie first. "I need this—and a good shower."

"The last time I had chocolate, it got me in trouble," Walt said while unwrapping his sandwich.

"Does this mean you're cutting down on sweets?" Danielle asked.

"I just won't be taking chocolate chip cookies from strangers again," Walt said before biting into his sandwich.

"So what happens now?" Heather asked.

"Arrest the Parkers," Brian said.

THIRTY-SIX

They had been driving in silence for about twenty minutes, each reflecting on the recent series of events. Danielle glanced toward the front of the car and found Brian turned in his seat, staring at her. When their eyes met, he gave her a smile.

"You really didn't dump all Cheryl's clothes and open makeup in her suitcase, did you?" Brian said.

"So you finally believe me?" Danielle asked with a grin.

"I didn't mean to ruin her clothes," Walt said. "I just wanted to help and get the room cleaned for the open house."

"She didn't need her clothes anyway," Heather snarked.

"Not nice, Heather," Danielle good-naturedly reprimanded her. Heather countered with a shrug and leaned back against the inside of the right passenger door while she lounged on the bench seat, her feet up.

"I will confess," Brian said, "after I got to know you better, that suitcase thing kept bugging me. It seemed out of character, but I couldn't imagine who else had done it."

"So, tell us, Danielle, what lie have you worked out to explain our rescue?" Heather asked cheerfully. She looked to Brian and said, "Danielle has a natural gift for coming up with creative lies to explain the unexplainable. Except for suitcases, of course. Obviously, she never came up with a believable story for that one."

"You all managed to get free from the ropes and eventually

found your way down to the highway. Someone was driving by, going in the opposite direction from Frederickport. They stopped, agreed to call me, and we picked you up," Danielle explained.

"Who were these people?" Brian asked.

"I don't know. They wouldn't tell you their name. They were teenagers who had taken their parents' car for a joy ride. They had to get home before they got caught," Danielle explained.

Brian laughed.

"That was pretty nice of them to at least stop," Danielle said.

"What does the chief know about all this?" Brian asked.

"Unofficially, he knows everything. Officially, he didn't know about the phone call from our nonexistent teenagers until we picked you up this morning. I was afraid it might be a hoax, so I didn't want to tell him until I knew you were safe," Danielle explained.

"Did you really call him?" Brian asked.

"Yes. Just after we saw you along the highway," Danielle said.

"Wouldn't I have insisted they call the chief instead of you?" Brian asked.

Danielle considered the question a moment. "Hmm…actually, you wanted them to, but they were afraid the police department would trace their call, and then their parents might find out what they had done. Since you just wanted to get rescued, you didn't push it."

Brian laughed. "Okay. That story works for me."

"What kind of car did the teenagers drive?" Heather asked.

"I don't know. You saw them. I didn't," Danielle said.

"You might want to figure out what kind of car it was," Chris said as he pulled off the highway onto the road leading to Frederickport. "We'll be at the police station soon."

"Can't you take me home first?" Heather asked. "I so need a shower."

"Sorry, we promised the chief we'd take you directly to the station. He wants to interview all of you, and until they arrest the Parkers, he doesn't want you wandering about," Chris explained.

"I'm not going to wander; I'm going to shower," Heather grumbled.

"IT'S GOOD TO SEE YOU," Joe Morelli told Brian while he gave him a hearty handshake, which quickly turned into a hug. The others had gone into the interrogation room with the chief, where there was more room for everyone to sit down comfortably.

"While I wanted to be part of the arrest, I suppose you already have someone bringing them in," Brian said.

"You still might do that," Joe said. "Of course, not sure the chief will let you."

"What do you mean? I figured they would have been in custody by now. I know Danielle called the chief after she picked us up, told him they were the ones who drugged and kidnapped us."

"We don't know where they are," Joe said. "We've been staking out their house since this morning."

"Great," Brian groaned.

"The chief said they drugged you and then just left you there. I can't imagine what you went through. Thank God you're okay."

"The worst was coming to and finding myself tied to a tree and not knowing what was going on. But once we got loose, it wasn't so bad," Brian said.

"Yeah, but I can't imagine spending two nights out there with someone like Heather Donovan," Joe said, giving an exaggerated shudder.

Brian shrugged. "Heather's not so bad."

"She's out there."

"I have to give her credit. She didn't fall apart. As my grandfather would say, she was a trooper."

"What about Marlow? How did he fare out there in the middle of the forest? He never struck me as the nature type. A city boy. You must have had your hands full, taking care of both of them."

Brian chuckled. "Marlow would surprise you. I think he was probably a Boy Scout in his last life."

"You mean before his amnesia?" Joe asked.

"Um…yeah. Sure."

The next minute, the chief opened the door to the interrogation room and poked his head out. "We're waiting for you, Brian."

"I BET you're glad to get Walt back," Joe told Danielle when they passed each other in the hallway of the police station a few minutes later.

"Relieved they're all okay," Danielle said. "I just wish the Parkers would show up so they can arrest them, and Walt can go home."

"For the time being, it's best if the Parkers don't know they're safe," Joe said. "I would assume if word got out they were rescued, the Parkers would skip town altogether."

Danielle let out a sigh. "Yeah, I get it."

"So where are you going?"

"Running home to feed Hunny, Max and Bella. But I'm coming right back."

Joe was about to make a comment about Chris staying at Marlow House, but he caught himself. He knew it was none of his business, but he would never understand their relationship. Not hers with Chris—not hers with Walt. Not even Walt's with Chris.

"See you later. Take care of them," Danielle said before heading toward the lobby.

THE MOMENT DANIELLE climbed into the driver's side of her Flex, she noticed glitter falling from the ceiling. Shutting the door and buckling her seatbelt, she glanced over to the passenger seat and said, "What, no snow today?"

The next moment Eva appeared in the passenger seat and the glitter vanished. "I felt glitter more festive for the occasion. I considered the fireworks again, but they might be too much for inside a car."

Danielle chuckled and then slipped the key in the ignition.

"Where are you going?" Eva asked.

"Home to feed Hunny and the cats. Where is Marie?" Danielle asked, pulling out of the parking lot.

"We both popped in the station to make sure everyone arrived safely. Then she went to see what Adam is up to."

"After I feed the animals, I'll be coming back to the station. You want to go with me or stay here?" Danielle drove the car down the street, heading toward home.

Eva leaned back in her seat. "I think I'll go along with you. I imagine Hunny, Max and Bella are anxious to hear if Walt and Heather are all right. I can update them while you fill their food bowls."

"Good idea," Danielle said, turning down another street. "I imagine Sadie would like to know what's going on too."

Feeling relieved and lighthearted, in spite of the fact the Parkers were still on the loose, Danielle failed to see the woman standing on the side of the road until she jumped in front of the car. Even Eva let out a squeal in surprise when the woman appeared, and Danielle slammed on the brakes.

It was the woman Danielle had called a hippy—the one who had found the necklace—the one who had told her where the Bairds had gone. And she was now standing in front of Danielle's windshield—inches from it—the lower part of her body disappearing in the car's hood. She wasn't a hippy. She was a ghost.

Hands clinging to the steering wheel, Danielle stared at the apparition. Never looking away from it, she asked Eva, "Do you know her?"

"I've never seen her before," Eva said. "But I believe she wants to talk to you. Perhaps you should pull the car over to the side of the road."

As if she heard Eva's suggestion, the ghost stepped back from the car and pointed to the side of the road. Reluctantly, Danielle drove her car along the sidewalk and parked. A moment later, she and Eva got out of the car.

"Please help me," the woman begged.

"Help you how?" Danielle asked.

"I know you can see spirits," the woman said.

"How do you know that?" Danielle asked.

The woman laughed. "You're talking to me, aren't you?"

Eva chuckled. "She has a point, Danielle."

The woman looked at Eva and cocked her head. "Are you like her, or another spirit?"

"I'm like you. If you already understand you aren't alive, why do you need Danielle?" Eva asked.

"Because someone is about to do something they will regret. And since they can't see or hear me, I can't stop them. Please come with me." She turned and started down the street.

Danielle glanced at Eva. "What should I do?"

"Would it hurt? Might as well see what the problem is. Probably some child getting ready to play with matches or something," Eva suggested.

"Fine. But stay with me, just in case you need to call for help," Danielle said, reluctantly following the ghost.

To Danielle's surprise, the woman turned down the next corner and started walking up the Bairds' driveway. "Is something happening with Finola and her sisters?" Danielle asked, still following the spirit.

When she reached the front door, the ghost said, "Don't knock, just walk in. Please. And hurry."

Reluctantly she did as the spirit requested, and to her surprise came face-to-face with Davina Parker, who held a gun in her hand, now pointed at Danielle's head.

"Oh crap," Danielle muttered.

"I'll get help," Eva said, disappearing the next moment.

"What are you doing here?" Davina shrieked and then motioned for Danielle to move farther into the house. It took Danielle a moment for her eyes to adjust to the dimly lit living room. When she did, she saw what appeared to be Finola Baird tied up to a chair in the middle of the room, encircled by flickering candles, while the other two Parker sisters stood by her side, looking in surprise at Danielle.

"What are you doing here?" Bridget demanded.

"I really don't know," Danielle muttered, wondering how long she could stall them before one of the crazy witches used the gun on her.

"Tell them Gavenia sent you," the spirit said.

Danielle frowned at the spirit.

"Why are you here?" Bridget demanded again, this time her voice louder. She marched to Davina and grabbed the gun from her hand, and then pointed it at Danielle, her aim more purposeful.

"Go on, tell them," the spirit urged.

"Gavenia sent me," Danielle said.

All the women went motionless. Finally, Bridget asked, "What did you say?"

"Tell them you are speaking for the White Hawk," the spirit said.

Licking her lips nervously, Danielle said. "Gavenia sent me, and I'm speaking for the White Hawk."

"What do you know of Gavenia…of the White Hawk?" Aileana demanded.

"I do not understand who Gavenia or the White Hawk is, but there is some hippy ghost here telling me what to say to you." Danielle then paused and looked at Finola. "Wait a minute…I do know…"

THIRTY-SEVEN

Danielle stared at Finola a moment and then said, "You told me about her. Gavenia, that was your ancestor they burned as a witch in Scotland. Her name meant White Hawk."

"Yes. Gavenia Tolmach," Finola said, still tied to the chair.

"What is all this nonsense about some hippy ghost?" Bridget demanded.

Danielle looked to the spirit and nodded. "She is standing right here. You obviously can't see her." She then asked the spirit, "What do you know about Gavenia Tolmach?"

"Who are you talking to?" Bridget demanded, no longer shaking the gun in Danielle's direction, instead holding it at her side.

The spirit stood next to a floor lamp, facing Danielle. "I am Gavenia Tolmach."

Danielle frowned at the spirit, ignoring the four women staring incredulously at her, each thinking how crazy she looked, apparently talking to a lamp. "You can't be Gavenia. You don't have an accent."

The spirit laughed. "I have been far from Scotland for more centuries than I was there. But if you want an accent." The next moment the spirit said something in her native tongue.

Danielle arched her brows and said, "I have absolutely no clue what you just said."

THE GHOST AND THE WITCHES' COVEN

"Stop talking to that lamp!" Bridget shouted. "And stop talking about Gavenia like that. You have no right!"

Danielle turned to Bridget and said, "Please stop waving that gun around. You might shoot someone. And you don't want to kill me, because if you do that, you won't know what Gavenia Tolmach is trying to tell you."

"Are you claiming to be the White Hawk?" Davina asked, "because that is not possible. I've studied our family tree, and nowhere are you related to us."

"Are you saying you're a descendant of Gavenia's? Do you seriously have one of your relatives tied up to a chair?" Danielle asked Davina.

"None of your business. And you didn't answer my question," Davina snapped. "Are you claiming to be the White Hawk?"

"Of course not. I'm obviously not Gavenia," Danielle said.

"That's not what she means," Finola said. "In our family, the White Hawk is the chosen one."

Danielle frowned. "I thought you told me that Gavenia meant white hawk, which is why her husband carved that necklace."

"It is," Finola said calmly. "But before they arrested Gavenia for witchcraft, she gave her only daughter the necklace."

"And they couldn't kill Gavenia," Davina said proudly. "Not even when they burned her at the stake. She returned to her daughter, Blair. But Blair was the only one who could see her. Gavenia stayed with Blair and taught her the secrets of the craft."

"So why did you call me a White Hawk?" Danielle asked.

"I didn't. I said you weren't a White Hawk!" Davina said.

"A White Hawk is one who wears the hawk necklace and can see Gavenia," Aileana explained. "Blair gave the necklace to her oldest daughter. At the time she was the only one who could see Gavenia."

"It has been a tradition in our family to pass the necklace down to the eldest daughter, searching for the White Hawk to bring Gavenia back. But then Leona stole it!" Bridget hissed.

"My great-great-grandmother Leona did not steal it!" Finola snapped. "Her sister, Helena, ran away as a teenager and didn't return until after their mother died."

"By then Leona had stolen the necklace!" Bridget shouted. "And Leona was no White Hawk!"

"Neither was Helena. My grandmother said Helena never claimed to see Gavenia!" Finola countered.

223

"Says Leona," Bridget hissed.

"There have been no White Hawks since Leona's mother," Davina said. "The legacy of White Hawks has been cursed since they stole the necklace from its rightful owner."

No longer paying attention to Danielle, the sisters and Finola argued back and forth, bickering about the White Hawk. Danielle looked to Gavenia's spirit and asked, "Do you know what they're talking about?"

"I'm afraid it has been a great misunderstanding. Getting worse with each generation since Leona and Helena's mother died," Gavenia said.

"Was she the last one who saw you?" Danielle asked.

Gavenia nodded while her descendants continued to bicker.

"Were you a witch?" Danielle asked.

"I was a healer," Gavenia said. "And a midwife."

"What did you teach your daughter?" Danielle asked.

"I taught her about my herbs and potions that helped cure people."

"Over there!" Bridget ordered, interrupting Danielle's private conversation with the spirit.

Danielle looked up to find Bridget once again pointing the gun at her while the others watched.

"Unfortunately for you, you will be collateral damage like your husband and that police officer." Bridget motioned to the sofa. "Sit down."

"What do you mean by that?" Danielle asked uneasily as she reluctantly took a seat on the sofa. After she did, Davina ordered Danielle to hold up her wrists, which she promptly tied.

"When this spell is complete, it will take you away, like it did with your husband and the others," Bridget said smugly, watching her sister tighten the ropes around Danielle's wrists. She then showed Danielle the ruby ring, clutching it in one hand while holding the gun in the other.

"With this I won't need to shoot the gun in order to make you disappear," Bridget said.

Danielle looked at the ruby ring and arched her brows. "I assume that's the ring Kathy Stewart stole from her mother?"

Bridget quickly closed her hand around the ring, concealing it. She frowned at Danielle. "Did Kathy Stewart tell you that?"

"No. Kathy's mother told the police chief when she reported it stolen. They know you have it," Danielle said.

"It doesn't matter. Not when we're finished here," Bridget said.

"Oh, and about Walt and Brian and Heather, they all made it out of the forest. They're fine, currently filing charges against you for kidnapping and leaving them each tied up to a tree."

"You are lying!" Bridget shouted.

"So far, they won't charge you with murder. But if you kill Finola or me, you will face the death penalty," Danielle warned.

"They also have Finola's sisters tied up in their bedrooms," Gavenia told her. "But they are unharmed."

"Oh, and Gavenia just told me you have Finola's sisters tied up in their bedrooms. I was getting a little worried about them, if you want to know the truth. I thought maybe you had already killed them. But if they are okay, and if Finola and I stay alive, then you can avoid the death penalty."

"No!" Davina cried. "This can't be true!" She snatched the ruby ring from Bridget's hand and looked at it. "Are you saying the ruby hasn't absorbed Heather's magic?"

"About Heather. She isn't a witch. Sorry." Danielle shrugged.

"What are you talking about? We saw her flying on a broom!" Bridget said, grabbing the ring back from her sister.

"Ahh…those cameras. We wondered if you put them in Heather's house." Danielle smiled. She wondered how long she could keep them talking before Eva returned with the cavalry. "That was a little trick. Heck, I've even done it. But I can't really fly on a broom, and neither can Heather."

"I don't know where they got these notions about a ruby and witches' magic," Gavenia said.

Danielle looked to her. "Really? Nothing about magic rubies passed down in your family?"

Gavenia shook her head. "I can help cure a case of gout, and I've a wonderful salve for poison ivy—uses a pinch of eye of newt—but no rubies."

"Eye of newt?" Danielle asked. "There really is such a thing?"

Gavenia shrugged. "It's just mustard seed."

"Who are you talking to?" the Parker sisters all screeched at once.

Danielle let out a sigh and looked to them. "I was talking to

Gavenia's spirit—or ghost. And I suspect that she was in fact killed when they burned her at the stake…"

"No," Gavenia interrupted.

Danielle turned to Gavenia. "Are you saying they didn't kill you?"

"Yes, they killed me. But by hanging. Then they burned my body."

Danielle looked back to the others. "I stand corrected. You were right, they didn't kill her when they burned her at the stake. She was already dead, hanged. And then they burned her body. She wasn't still alive when she went to her daughter. It was her spirit that went to Blair, not her mother reborn. I suspect Blair was like me—a medium."

"Medium?" Finola asked.

"Yes. Medium. I can see spirits. I imagine, over the years others in your family had the gift, and they could see Gavenia, like me. It had nothing to do with some special powers of a White Hawk. Sounds to me like it's been a few generations since there was a medium in your family able to communicate with Gavenia, so those stories passed down in your family veered off into the fantasy realm."

"And seeing ghosts is not in the fantasy realm?" Finola asked.

"It's simply part of my reality," Danielle said.

"I don't believe any of this!" Bridget yelled.

"But you believe a ruby can suck out Heather's imaginary powers and make her disappear?" Danielle asked. "By the way, Heather is a medium, not a witch. And I'm happy to say, she is very much alive."

"Tell her I can prove who I am," Gavenia said.

Danielle glanced from Gavenia to the others. "Gavenia wants to prove she is really here, and I'm talking for her."

"How do you expect to do that?" Bridget asked.

Danielle shrugged. "I have no idea."

"Tell them I know why Bridget, Davina and Aileana are here."

"Gavenia said she knows why the Parkers are here," Danielle said.

"I would like to know that myself," Finola said.

"They want the Leabar," Gavenia said.

"What's a Leabar?" Danielle asked with a frown.

"What do you know about the Leabar?" Davina asked.

"I don't even know what it is," Danielle said. "But according to Gavenia, that's why you're here."

"I knew you wanted it, but that can't be the only reason you're here!" Finola said incredulously.

"Isn't that enough reason?" Bridget asked.

"You have stalked us for years. And what's with those knockoff White Hawk necklaces?" Finola asked.

"We found an artist who made necklaces similar to Gavenia's, so we showed him a picture of the one you wear," Bridget explained.

"How did you get a picture of it?" Finola demanded.

"It wasn't so hard for me to get a good one with my telephoto lens," Aileana said.

"He agreed to replicate it if we agreed to carry his necklaces in our shop. We needed you to come to us willingly for the spell to work," Bridget said.

"You needed us to come to you willingly for the spell to work?" Finola seethed. "Does it look like I came to you willingly? If you haven't noticed, you're in my house uninvited!"

"That was before this," Bridget said, hysterically waving the ruby ring in Finola's face.

"But it didn't work!" Davina cried out.

"Stop saying that." Bridget pointed at Danielle and said, "She lied. She is lying about all of it! I know it worked. Walt Marlow is gone. Heather Donovan is gone. Brian Henderson is gone! Gavenia is not talking to Danielle Marlow! She is lying. Can't you see that? She just wants it to be true because we've taken her husband from her. But soon she'll see him again!"

The next moment Bridget's last words proved true. Yet it was not what she expected. Danielle saw Walt again, the very next minute, when he and Brian Henderson walked into the house, following Eva.

THIRTY-EIGHT

Danielle saw Eva first, when she had walked through the wall and looked around, noting where everyone stood and who currently held the gun. She had disappeared back through the front wall, and a moment later walked in when the door opened. She led Walt and Brian into the house.

Later they would speculate: what had surprised Bridget more? The fact the gun in her hand flew into the air and landed in Brian Henderson's hand, or the fact Walt Marlow and Brian Henderson had somehow magically appeared.

Chaos ensued when Davina and Aileana took off running toward the rear exit while Bridget stood waving the ruby ring while loudly chanting a string of nonsensical words. It didn't sound like a foreign language, more like she was making it up as she went along —which she wasn't.

Danielle immediately got up from the sofa, her wrists still bound, yet she didn't ask Walt or Brian to untie her. They were busy. She watched as Walt's energy pulled the escaping Parker sisters towards the sofa, dropping them there, and then adding Bridget to the mix. He held the three to the sofa while Brian unloaded the gun and placed it on a top shelf and then untied Finola, who looked far more uncomfortable in her bindings than did Danielle.

The minute Brian untied her, she thanked him and then raced

THE GHOST AND THE WITCHES' COVEN

to check on her sisters. Brian went along with her while Walt continued to focus his energy, keeping the three women restrained.

Danielle stood by Eva and Gavenia, a distance from the sofa. She glanced down at her bound wrists. "Brian could have untied me first."

"Sorry, I can't help," Eva said.

"I think I'll see how Finola and her sisters are doing," Gavenia said before disappearing.

"I sort of thought you would come back with Marie as the cavalry," Danielle said.

"I tried Marie first. But Adam was not at his office, and he wasn't at home. I considered checking some local restaurants, assuming she was tagging along with him. But I was afraid that would take too much time, so I went straight to the police station from Adam's house," Eva explained.

"What is going on?" Davina sobbed. She tried to stand up from the sofa, but each time she did, an invisible hand threw her back on the cushion.

Bridget continued to chant while clutching the ruby ring. Next to her sat Aileana, and on the other side of Aileana, a sobbing Davina.

"Shut up, Bridget!" Aileana snapped. The next moment she grabbed the ruby ring out of her sister's grasp and flung it across the room. Bridget tried to stand up to retrieve it, but Walt's energy pushed her back down again. She began to sob.

A few minutes later Brian returned from the bedrooms with the Baird sisters. Danielle assumed he must have told them to restrain their anger, for while they each glared at the Parkers, the three huddled together by the door leading to the kitchen, waiting for the police to arrive and take the Parkers away.

Brian walked over to Danielle and began untying her wrists.

"I think you should know there is another ghost in this room with us," Danielle whispered as she watched Brian work to free a knot.

"Yes, I know. Eva. She came into the station, told Walt what was going on. Walt told the chief, insisting he had to leave to rescue you. He didn't want the police to show up with their sirens blaring. The chief agreed, but wanted me to come along too," Brian explained as he finally undid the stubborn knot.

"No, I'm not talking about Eva. I mean Gavenia Tolmach," Danielle said.

"Who is Gavenia Tolmach?" Brian asked with a frown.

"Someone burned as a witch about four hundred years ago, in Scotland."

Brian stared at Danielle for a moment and then shook his head. "Just another day in Frederickport?"

"You know, you might start a support group with the chief," Danielle teased. She rubbed her now free wrists.

"Support group?"

"Yeah, for non-mediums in our circle. I'm sure Ian would join," Danielle said.

"What about Lily? She's not a medium," Brian reminded her.

Danielle shrugged. "Lily is different. She had that out-of-body experience. So, in a way, she has visited the other side. You know, personal experience with the spirit world."

"What out-of-body experience?" Brian frowned.

"When her body was being held by Stoddard, and he was telling everyone she was his niece? Sheesh, how do you think I knew that wasn't Isabella? Lily told me, silly."

Brian groaned and shook his head. She chuckled as he left her side to retrieve the gun. He then walked to the sofa to address the Parkers, telling them they were all under arrest. Eva now stood by Walt's side as he continued to keep the Parkers restrained.

"It's all my fault," Gavenia said, now standing by Danielle.

"What do you mean?" Danielle asked in a whisper.

"They are my grandchildren too, every bit as much as Finola and her sisters." Gavenia nodded toward the Parkers.

"Well, I wouldn't say grandchildren per se. More like great-great-great-great—however many greats—grandchildren."

"I still think of them as my grandchildren. And if I had never stayed, perhaps none of this would have happened."

Together Danielle and Gavenia stood in the far corner of the living room while the Bairds huddled together on the opposite side of the room, and the Parkers remained on the sofa, Walt, Eva and Brian standing over them, waiting for the police to arrive.

"Why did you stay?" Danielle asked.

"At first, it was because Blair was so young. Too young to be alone."

"That was your daughter?" Danielle asked.

"Yes. I couldn't believe she could see me—hear me. I stayed with her, taught her. And when she had children, her oldest daughter could see me too."

"So you stayed?" Danielle asked.

"Yes."

"Why do your—" Danielle paused a moment and looked over to the Parkers and then the Bairds. "Why do your granddaughters believe you're a witch?"

Gavenia considered the question for a moment and then said, "In the beginning, I never thought of myself as a witch. I never believed I had some inherent powers different from other women. But I had faith in nature and its gifts of healing. I understood herbs and their healing powers."

"But the Parkers and Bairds both claim you were a witch," Danielle reminded her.

Gavenia let out a sigh and said, "Over time, and I can't even recall which century, I began calling myself a witch. But not meaning I possessed some supernatural powers or worshiped anything other than nature. In some way it was said out of respect —and defiance—for those other women like me, who were unjustly accused and brutally murdered."

Police cars pulling up to the front of the house interrupted their conversation. Danielle drew open the front curtain, peeked out the window, and spied Joe Morelli getting out of one car.

"Brian, this might be a good time to come up with your cover story," Danielle called out as she let the curtain fall back into place.

"What are you talking about?" Brian asked from across the room.

DANIELLE STOOD with Walt on the sidewalk, watching as the police put the Parker sisters in the back of a police car. The Baird sisters stood on the front porch, watching. They had promised to come down to the station to make statements, but first they wanted to get dressed and have something to eat. It had been a long morning. Inside, several officers took photographs of the crime scene.

Eva and Gavenia stood together some distance away, chatting. Danielle wondered what the two ghosts discussed.

"Here come Brian and Joe," Danielle whispered to Walt when the pair approached.

"You're going back to the station with Danielle?" Brian asked Walt when they reached them.

"He is." Danielle spoke up. "But we have to stop at Marlow House first and feed the animals."

"That's what I don't understand," Joe said. He looked to Brian and asked, "Why did you bring Walt here? I thought the chief said you were taking Walt home to change his clothes. How did you end up here?"

Danielle smiled and leaned toward Brian. In his ear she whispered, "Told you so. Cover story time." She pulled back from him and flashed a grin at Joe, who hadn't heard what she had whispered yet looked confused.

"And why were you here?" Joe asked Danielle.

Brian looked to Danielle and cocked his brow.

"Oh, I just stopped by to tell the Baird sisters that Walt was safe," Danielle explained.

"Why would you do that?" Joe asked.

"I always felt the Parkers had something to do with the disappearance. And when I heard about the Bairds being arrested for breaking into Pagan Oils right after Walt and the others went missing, I hoped they might have seen something—something they failed to tell the police, maybe because they didn't feel comfortable saying anything, so I went to talk to them. They were very nice, and while they saw nothing, they told me they thought the Parkers could be involved—which they were. I just thought, since the Bairds were open with me and seemed sincerely concerned, that I would let them know Walt was okay."

Joe stared at Danielle a moment and then asked, "But why did you park your car around the corner?"

Danielle met Joe's gaze and then shrugged. "I wanted to walk?"

On the front porch, the Baird sisters moved to one side as the officers who had been taking photographs stepped outside. One officer called out to Joe.

When Joe stepped away to talk to the officer, Brian looked to Danielle and said, "You are good at this. Coming up with a believable story."

Danielle shrugged. "The key is to keep as close to the truth as possible. Much of what I said was true. I just left out the part about

THE GHOST AND THE WITCHES' COVEN

the ghost of a woman burned at the stake over four hundred years ago jumping in front of my car and me running her over."

Brian chuckled and shook his head.

"I have a feeling Joe is going to ask you that question again," Walt said as he watched Joe, who stood out of earshot near the front porch, talking to the two officers who had just come outside.

"Yeah, he's going to want to know why you brought Walt here," Danielle said, her eyes still on Joe.

"What should I say?" Brian asked.

Danielle looked at him and grinned. "Ahh, with this new knowledge comes responsibility. You'll think of something."

Walt laughed and then said, "Come on, help him out, Danielle."

Danielle let out a sigh and said, "You guys were on the way to Marlow House, spotted my car on the side of the road, and assumed I had car trouble. When you drove around the corner looking for me, Walt noticed the Baird house and remembered how I told him, after we picked you up today, how I went to them for help, and he wondered if I stopped by their house to use their phone. You should probably say you tried calling me on my cell, but I didn't answer, so you figured I forgot to charge it."

Brian smiled at Danielle. "You are good at this."

"Consider that your freebie cover story," Danielle said. "The next one, you're on your own."

"You think there will be a next time?" Brian asked.

Walt laughed and then said, "Undoubtably."

THIRTY-NINE

The police cars drove away with the Parker sisters, while the tow truck took their van that they had parked in the garage. Before leaving, Danielle and Walt asked Finola if they could speak to her and her sisters. Finola agreed, inviting them inside. Unbeknownst to the Baird sisters, the spirits of Eva and Gavenia followed the Marlows into the living room. Walt and Danielle sat down on the love seat next to the sofa, while the spirits stood behind them.

The Baird sisters sat down on the sofa. Finola spoke first. "I don't know how to thank you. You saved our lives."

"I'm not really sure they would have killed you," Danielle said.

"How can you say that?" Ina asked. "I heard they left your husband and friends in the mountains to die." She glanced to Walt.

"Yes. But it is one thing to wave around what you think is a magic ruby, believing it will make everything you want gone disappear, including any consequences, and quite another to shoot someone and have to get rid of the body—without getting caught," Danielle said.

Finola looked at Danielle and Walt. "What I don't understand, how did that gun fly out of Bridget's hand like that?"

"What are you talking about?" Kenzy asked. Finola then told her and Ina what had happened from the time Danielle walked in the house to when she untied them.

When Finola finished, Danielle said, "I already discussed this with Brian, the police officer who untied you, and we would appreciate it if you say Bridget dropped the gun after being surprised when Walt and Brian came into the house, and Brian got to it before her."

Finola frowned. "I don't understand…"

"No, I don't imagine you do. And if you repeat what you saw, that will be difficult for the police officers Brian works with to understand," Danielle said.

"What really happened?" Kenzy asked.

"Have you ever heard of telekinesis?" Danielle asked.

"Yes. The ability to move objects with one's mind," Ina said. "I've read about it."

"Walt has that ability, but it is something we would rather not broadcast," Danielle explained.

The Baird sisters frowned at Danielle in disbelief—all except Finola, who had witnessed the gun flying from Bridget's hand to Brian's. Danielle glanced at Walt and said, "Move something, please."

The next moment the Baird sisters gasped when a magazine floated up off the coffee table and then fell in Ina's lap.

"Uh…okay…" Ina muttered, gingerly picking up the magazine by one corner and tossing it back to the coffee table as if it had a major case of cooties.

"Earlier you claimed Gavenia was here, that you could see her," Finola said.

"Yes. Another thing about Walt, he is a psychic medium. So am I. Which means we can see spirits," Danielle said. "The reason I'm here, Gavenia's spirit—or ghost—jumped in front of my car when I was driving from the police station to Marlow House. She knew I could see her, because she was the one who saw you drop the necklace the day we first met. She couldn't return it to you, because you can't see or hear her."

"I don't understand," Kenzy said.

"The story about Gavenia's daughter seeing her mother after her death. It wasn't because Gavenia was a witch and had somehow cheated death. It was because her daughter was like Walt and me, mediums, who could see her mother's ghost. Instead of moving on, as most spirits do, Gavenia stayed with her daughter."

"But others saw her too," Finola said.

"True. It seems mediums run in your family, but apparently it has skipped a couple of generations, because I know the Parkers can't see ghosts, and neither can you, considering there are two sitting in the room with us," Danielle said.

"Two?" the sisters chimed in unison.

Walt glanced to Danielle and shook his head. "No reason to complicate matters and mention Eva."

"What? I'm a complication now?" Eva asked with a faux pout.

Danielle shrugged, and Kenzy asked, "Who's Eva?"

"That's not really important," Danielle said. "I have a few questions I'd like to ask."

"Considering I believe you saved our lives, ask whatever you want," Finola said.

"Have you always known the Parkers are distant cousins?" Danielle asked.

"No. Not until this morning," Finola said. "Our grandmother told us about her great-aunt Helena. She was the oldest daughter, and by tradition would have been the one to get the White Hawk necklace and be the keeper of the Leabar. But she ran away with a boy her parents didn't approve of and didn't return until years later. By that time both her parents had died."

"What is the Leabar?" Danielle asked.

The sisters exchanged glances, and Gavenia said, "It simply means book."

"Book? It means book?" Danielle said.

"You speak Scottish Gaelic?" Finola asked.

"Um…no. Gavenia just said it meant book," Danielle explained. "But I assume it is more than just any old book."

Ina sat back in the sofa, crossing her arms over her chest and said coolly, "If Gavenia is really here with us, and you can talk to her, then you really don't need one of us to tell you what the Leabar is."

Danielle looked to Gavenia.

"I taught Blair all that I knew about herbs and potions so she could teach her children. But over time, I don't recall exactly when, they began writing it down. I suppose that was the first Leabar," Gavenia explained. "When Leona and Helena's mother was just a little girl, there was a house fire, and they lost everything, even the Leabar. So their mother—the last one who was able to see and hear me—she recreated it with my help."

Danielle looked to the sisters and repeated all that she had just been told.

"How did you know all that?" Kenzy asked.

"I told you, Gavenia is here. She just told me."

WHEN THEY BROUGHT the Parker sisters into the police station and marched them down the hallway while handcuffed, Heather stood near the open doorway of the chief's office, her arms crossed over her chest as she leaned back against the wall. The chief had said she could go home and take that shower now, but after hearing they were bringing the Parkers in, she didn't want to miss it.

Seeing the expression on their faces as they walked past her and saw in person she had survived made Heather feel delaying the shower well worth it. The chief had also told her she could watch the interrogation through the two-way mirror.

Brian Henderson was one of the last to walk by in the parade of people who streamed down the hallway with the Parkers. He stopped by Heather, allowing the others to continue down the hall.

"The chief tells me you want to watch the interrogation," Brian said.

"You bet I do," Heather said.

"Then come with me. I'm going to the observation room now."

She looked up into Brian's face. "Aren't you going to be part of the interrogation?"

"No, I'm sitting this one out."

ALONE WITH BRIAN in the office, Heather stepped up to the two-way mirror and looked into the interrogation room. It was empty save for a large table surrounded by chairs.

"I thought they'd already be in there," Heather said.

"They're checking them in, and they'll be interviewing them one at a time," Brian explained. "I imagine the chief is trying to delay it a little. A team is going through their house at the moment, looking for evidence. He probably would like to see what they find before he starts."

"I don't know why he needs any more evidence. He has us,"

Heather said, still staring through the glass. She felt Brian now standing at her side. When she turned to look at him, she found him standing closer than she had expected. His eyes stared into hers.

She frowned. "What are you looking at?"

"You." He smiled.

She wrinkled her nose. "Do I stink?"

He laughed and then leaned even closer, his nose taking a sniff along her neck before he pulled back again, flashing her a smile. "Not bad. You smell like the outdoors."

"Like a skunk?" Heather asked.

"I was thinking pine trees," he said.

She frowned. "Are you hitting on me?"

"I don't know. But you did kiss me," he reminded her.

"I did not! You kissed me," she insisted.

"Why would I do that? You are too young for me," he said.

"I'm older than Darlene was," she said.

"You are quirky," he said.

She laughed. "I concede to that observation."

Without a word, he leaned closer and kissed her lips. When the kiss ended, he pulled back and looked at her.

"Why did you do that?" she whispered.

"I don't know. But I have been wanting to try it again."

"And?" she asked.

He kissed her again. When the kiss ended, she asked, "Well?"

"I'm not sure," he whispered, and kissed her again. She returned the kiss, but abruptly shoved him away when snowflakes began falling from the ceiling.

"Eva is coming," she said.

Brian quickly stepped back from Heather.

"You know, we can't tell anyone about this," Heather hurriedly whispered before Eva arrived.

"Why?" he asked.

Heather rolled her eyes. "Seriously? You might as well tell Joe that Walt used to be a ghost and can talk to animals."

Eva appeared the next moment, ending their discussion.

BRIDGET SAT ALONE at the table in the interrogation room, her hands folded on the table in front of her as she looked down. She had just told Joe Morelli how she had gotten the ruby and why, contradicting the story Mrs. Stewart had given the chief. The ruby ring sat on the table, sealed in a plastic bag.

Distraught learning the spell had not worked and not understanding why, she had forfeited her right to an attorney and confessed why they wanted to vanquish the Bairds.

"You did this all because you wanted some spell book?" Joe asked.

Bridget looked up to Joe, her eyes red rimmed. "By rights, it belongs to me. Those spells are priceless; they have been handed down in our family for four centuries."

"What kind of spells? Do they involve rubies?" Joe asked.

Bridget frowned. "I don't know."

"You don't know?" Joe asked.

Bridget shook her head. "No. I've never seen the book. My sisters, mother, grandmother, none of us have ever seen the Leabar. We've only heard stories about it. About the great magic."

A knock came at the door. Joe answered it. On the other side, an officer held something in his hand. He handed it to Joe, who returned to Bridget after shutting the door. He placed the item on the table—it was a spell book.

"Like this spell book?" Joe asked.

Bridget looked at the book and shook her head. "No. Where did you get that?"

"From your house."

"I don't understand. The other spell from it worked. Why didn't the last one?" Bridget asked, speaking more to herself than Joe. She reached out; her right hand gently stroked the pentacle engraved on the book's leather cover.

EVA STOOD on the other side of the mirror with Brian and Heather. The three watched.

"What did he just put on the table?" Eva asked.

"Some book," Heather said with a shrug.

"I'm going to take a closer look," Eva said, moving through the mirror to the table in the interrogation room.

"We just lost Eva," Heather announced. "She's checking out that book."

"Must be interesting, just going wherever you want—through walls," Brian muttered.

"What the—?" Heather blurted.

Brian glanced to Heather. "What is it?"

"It's Eva."

"What about Eva?" Brian asked.

"I don't know what the deal with that book is, but Eva just got a close look at it and is now laughing like she just heard the funniest joke in the world."

FORTY

"I promise not to dump this one on you," Walt joked as he handed Brian a cold beer. Brian understood it was a reference to the beer Walt had dumped on him at Ian's bachelor party—when Walt was still a spirit. Brian didn't imagine Walt cared if anyone overheard him, considering the guest list for this evening's gathering. After handing Brian the beer, Walt headed across Marlow House's living room with a beer for Ian.

Brian's cousin Kitty had left for home that morning, and Danielle had called him that afternoon to invite him for dinner. She claimed it was a last-minute affair; they wanted to celebrate their safe return. It had been four days since the Parkers' arrest. He had expected to see Joe and Kelly here; after all, Joe was involved in the Parkers' arrest, and he lived with Ian's sister, Kelly. But Joe and Kelly were not here.

Ian and Lily were on the guest list. They were currently standing on the other side of the living room, talking to the chief while Ian held Connor. Brian wondered if the chief would have brought Evan tonight and left Eddy with his sister had they not been with their grandparents.

Chris arrived minutes after Brian and had mentioned Heather would be there shortly. They had just gotten off work, and she wanted to go home and change first. After being shown into the living room, and before being handed the beer, Danielle headed to the kitchen to get some appetizers, and Chris went with her to help.

Brian was about to take a sip of the beer when Lily showed up at his side. "So, are you processing all this?" she asked.

"I assume you mean the ghost thing?" he asked.

"Yeah." Lily glanced over to where her husband stood, still talking to the chief. "It wasn't easy for Ian. We sorta broke up over it."

"Really?"

Lily looked back to Brian and nodded. "Yep. But I understand. Ian has spent most of his professional life as an investigative reporter. He's seen his share of cons. So it took more than floating wineglasses to convince him."

"What about you? What convinced you?" he asked.

"You mean to believe that Danielle could see ghosts, and Walt haunted this house?" Lily grinned.

"Yes. What happened that made you finally believe it?" he asked.

"What happened? Danielle told me," Lily said.

"That's it?"

Lily nodded. "I know Danielle. I trust her. Plus, the idea of someone having the ability to see spirits didn't seem that crazy to me."

Brian glanced from Lily back over to the corner where Ian and the chief stood talking, with Connor now on the floor by their feet, playing with a small toy. About to take a drink of the beer, he paused mid sip, his eyes wide, and he sputtered, "Ahh…the baby…"

Lily glanced over to Connor and then smiled. She watched as her son drifted up from the floor and began floating around the room.

"Oh, that's just Marie," Lily said.

"Marie? You can see her?"

"No. I can't see ghosts any better than you," Lily said with a snort. "But I know the only spirit here able to harness her energy like that is Marie."

"Doesn't that make you nervous? Him flying around? What if he falls?" Brian asked, his eyes still on the baby.

"Nah, no more dangerous than anyone holding him—probably way safer."

"But doesn't it scare him? Just hanging in the air like that?" Brian asked.

"Oh, Connor can see Marie. He doesn't understand she's a ghost, or that other people can't see her," Lily explained. "From Connor's perspective, no different from me carrying him."

"Really?"

Lily gave a nod and let out a sigh, looking back to her son; she watched him seemingly float around the room. "Really. But it is going to be difficult once he gets older and starts talking. Not sure how we're going to explain who Marie is to Kelly."

"No kidding," Brian muttered, taking another sip of beer.

BRIAN NOW STOOD with the chief while Ian and Lily were on the other side of the room, talking to Danielle. Chris stood at the bar, talking with Walt, and Heather had not yet arrived.

"We haven't really discussed this," the chief told Brian.

"I assume you're talking about the ghost and Walt thing?" Brian asked.

The chief grinned.

"At least I understand why you didn't want to find out who had been tampering with old fingerprint cards," Brian said as he took a drink of his beer.

"Couldn't really tell you the truth, could I?"

"When did you learn about it all? Did you always know, because of Evan?" Brian asked.

The chief shook his head. "No. For the longest time, I just assumed Evan had bad dreams and an overactive imagination. Figured it had something to do with losing his mother. I learned about Danielle's gift first, after she spoke to my grandmother's ghost."

"Do you think it is a gift?" Brian asked.

"Sometimes. Sometimes a curse."

THEY GATHERED around the dining room table for dinner. Walt sat at one end of the table, with Danielle at the other end, facing him. To Walt's right sat the chief, Lily, and Ian. To Walt's left sat Chris, Heather and Brian. The first course had just been served, a green salad and rolls. They ate and discussed recent events.

"With how hectic everything has been this past week, I still don't understand. What was the deal with that spell book?" Lily asked.

"Which spell book?" Danielle asked. "There were two of them. The Leabar, the one with the recipes for herbal medicine, handed down by Gavenia, and the other spell book, the one they used to steal Heather's magic."

"Yeah, as if they could steal my magic, if I had any," Heather scoffed. She took another bite of salad.

"The second one," Lily said.

Heather glanced over to Eva, who sat nearby with Marie, floating on invisible chairs and listening in. The story was Eva's, but Heather would have to retell it, since not everyone in the room could see and hear Eva.

"The house the Parkers rented once belonged to an old friend of Eva's. I asked her about it after Chris and I drove by it, the day we saw one of the sisters in the alley behind my place," Heather explained.

"At the time, I wondered if they were triplets," Chris said.

"That house had been boarded up before they moved in," Heather explained. "And it looked like it needed major work. I wondered about its history."

"And Eva had known one of its prior owners?" Lily said.

"Yes. His name was Wallace. He was a playwright. According to Eva, not a very successful one, but he threw himself enthusiastically into the creative process. She told me about him when I asked if she knew the house's history. He was the author of that spell book," Heather explained.

"This playwright was a warlock?" Lily asked.

"No. But he was working on a play about witches, and to get into the topic, he wrote a spell book—basically he used his imagination and made all that stuff up. He must have put the book somewhere in the house, where it remained hidden for years. As best we can tell, the Parkers found it after they moved in. According to Eva, he died before he finished the play, but she remembered seeing that book when he was working on it. She recognized it when they brought it into the interrogation room."

"Why in the world would they assume any of it was real? They find some book, and they don't even know who wrote it. Why believe it in the first place?" Lily asked.

"Unfortunately, that's not as uncommon as you think," Ian said. They all turned to him for a further explanation.

"How do you mean?" Chris asked.

"Think about the internet. The crazy conspiracy theories out there. For example, one very popular conspiracy, believed by thousands, originated from some anonymous post. No one knows who really made that first post. It could be some kid playing on the computer or someone with a fertile imagination, like Eva's friend. Fact is, people believe what they want to believe. And the Parkers wanted to believe they found a powerful spell book. Gavenia's spell book had obsessed them for years. I imagine when they found Wallace's book in the house, they thought it was destiny, as if the book waited for them. They wanted to believe in it."

"Yeah, and imagine their surprise had they gotten their hands on the Leabar, only to discover the most magical thing about it were potions to get rid of things like toe fungus," Heather scoffed.

"Hey, a good toe-fungus potion is hard to come by," Chris countered.

"What happens to Gavenia now?" Brian asked. "Is she here?"

"No," Danielle said. "Gavenia has moved on. She believes many of the bad things that happened recently is because she stuck around so long. But I think it has more to do with the absence of a medium, and had Gavenia left years ago, all of this might have still happened."

"In what way?" Brian asked.

"It had been several generations since there was a medium in her family. So the stories about her were handed down, secondhand, and they changed and took on their own life. The Parkers became fixated on the notion they were from a line of powerful blood witches, and the secret to unlock their powers was in the Leabar," Danielle explained. "All because old family stories passed down from one generation to the next morphed into fantasy land."

"Sort of reminds me of that game I used to play with my class," Lily said. "You put the children in a large circle and then whisper something to one of them. They, in turn, are supposed to whisper it to the person next to them, and so on. When it gets to the very last person to hear the whisper, it's always much different from what the first person heard."

"What about the Bairds? They claimed to be blood witches," the chief asked.

"Yes, but I think they saw it a little differently. While they claimed they were not Wicca, I had the feeling their view of witchcraft wasn't really that different from Wicca," Danielle said. "But I believe the Bairds, like their distant cousins, the Parkers, didn't clearly understand who or what Gavenia was, considering they never knew anyone personally who had talked to her."

"Until you," Lily reminded her.

"Is it true what the paper said?" Lily asked the chief. "There won't be a trial?"

"Not exactly," the chief said.

"They're all at the funny farm," Heather said. "Until they're no longer nuts and can stand trial."

"Heather," Danielle scolded, "it's not nice to say it like that."

"And it was not nice to drug me and leave me out in the middle of the forest to die," Heather countered.

"She has a point," Brian said.

Heather smiled at Brian. "Thank you, Officer Henderson."

"It's just that it's not completely their fault," Danielle said. "They had to be unbalanced to believe all that nonsense."

"I don't know about that," Ian said. "If we give everyone a pass for buying into ridiculous beliefs, too many people in this country will avoid paying the consequences if they choose to act on some outrageous untruth they've chosen to believe. Critical thinking skills would be nice."

EVA AND MARIE left the dinner party first, not long after Danielle served the second course. Now that they were no longer needed, they had ghostly things to attend to. Lily and Ian left not long after dinner. Connor had been napping on the bed in the downstairs bedroom while they ate, but he had woken up during dessert. They felt it was time to get him home and ready for bed.

The chief said goodbye the same time Chris headed home, leaving only Brian and Heather, who ended up leaving at the same time.

THE GHOST AND THE WITCHES' COVEN

After all their guests departed, Danielle went to the bathroom, leaving Walt alone in the kitchen to start loading the dishes in the dishwasher. When she returned, the kitchen was clean, and the dishwasher running.

"You finished already? That was quick. I was going to help." Danielle said as Walt drew her into a hug. They stood together in the middle of the kitchen, Danielle wrapped in Walt's secure embrace while he rested his cheek against the top of her head.

"I was hoping we could get back to that little project of ours," Walt whispered.

"What project is that?" she asked, leaning into him and closing her eyes.

"Expanding our family."

Danielle chuckled. "Sounds like a good idea to me."

Walt pulled away from Danielle and said, "I have to go check the garage first. I think I left a light on. I'll meet you upstairs."

"Okay. I'm going to go jump in the shower," Danielle said.

Walt gave her a quick kiss.

CLOUDS BLOCKED the stars in a moonless sky. Walt glanced up for a moment, wondering if it might rain tonight. He continued to the garage. Before turning off the light, Walt heard something. He stepped out the back gate, into the alley, and heard it again.

Looking into the alley, he watched as the black figure stepped out from the shadows and meowed again.

"Max, what are you doing out so late? Danielle is going to be worried." Walt leaned down and opened his arms. The cat jumped into them and began to purr as Walt stood up, holding the cat and gently stroking the back of his neck.

"You were visiting Bella? But Heather keeps her inside… through the window?…Ahh…you miss having her around." Walt chuckled and turned back to the gate when he heard Max say something else.

"What do you mean Heather has a visitor?"

Walt frowned. It was rather late for a visitor. Considering the events of the past week, he hoped everything was okay. Without grilling Max, Walt turned back toward the alley and walked toward Heather's house. He walked by the rear entrance to his neighbor's,

Pearl Huckabee, and then reached Heather's property. Max was right, there was someone at Heather's.

Walt looked at the car parked behind her garage—it belonged to Brian Henderson. Walt arched his brows and gave Max's neck another stroke. "Interesting," he murmured before turning and heading back to Marlow House, with Max in his arms.

THE GHOST AND THE MOUNTAIN MAN

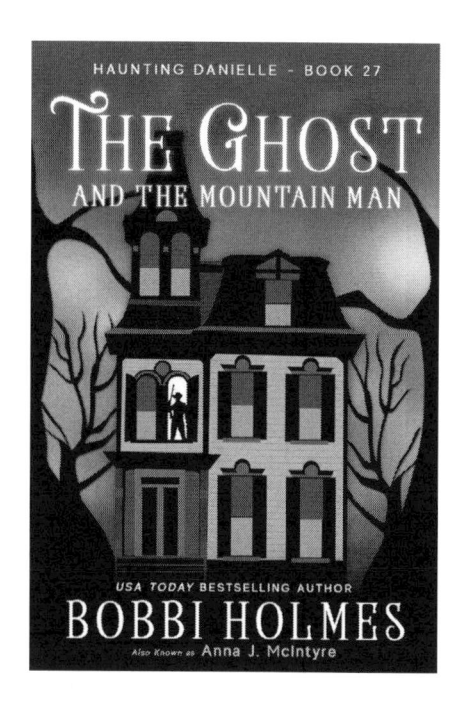

Return to Marlow House in
The Ghost and the Mountain Man
Haunting Danielle, Book 27

Life is about to change for Brian Henderson, now that he knows the secrets of Beach Drive.

Unbeknownst to Brian and the others, they have brought something else home with them after their misadventure in the forest. The spirit of a mountain man has followed them to Frederickport with a secret of his own.

NON-FICTION BY
BOBBI ANN JOHNSON HOLMES

Havasu Palms, A Hostile Takeover
Where the Road Ends, Recipes & Remembrances
Motherhood, a book of poetry
The Story of the Christmas Village

BOOKS BY ANNA J. MCINTYRE

COULSON FAMILY SAGA

Coulson's Wife
Coulson's Crucible
Coulson's Lessons
Coulson's Secret
Coulson's Reckoning
Now available in Audiobook Format

UNLOCKED HEARTS

Sundered Hearts
After Sundown
While Snowbound
Sugar Rush

Printed in Great Britain
by Amazon